A Certain Slant

A Certain Slant

The Maggie Barnes Trilogy

Mary VanderGoot

RESOURCE *Publications* · Eugene, Oregon

A CERTAIN SLANT
The Maggie Barnes Trilogy

A Certain Slant and *The Maggie Barnes Trilogy* are works of fiction. Names, places, characters, events, and institutions as they appear in these stories are products of the author's invention. Used as they are in a fictional narrative, they are not to be taken as either real or referring to real persons, places, or events. Any resemblances are coincidental.

Quoted works in the order that they appear:

Marcel Proust. *À la recherche du temps perdu*; (*In Search of Lost Times*, earlier rendered as *Remembrance of Things Past*). First published by Éditions Gallimard. In the public domain as of January 1, 2019.

Victor Hugo. *Les Misérables*. First published in 1862 by La Croix, Verboeckhoven & Cie. Under license from Project Gutenberg EBook #135 at www.gutenberg.org.

George Eliot. *The Mill on the Floss*, first published in 1860 by William Blackwood and Sons. Under license from Project Gutenberg EBook #6688 at www.gutenberg.org.

Kahlil Gibran. *The Prophet*. First published in 1932 by Alfred A. Knopf. In the public domain as of January 1, 2019.

Ben Johnson. *Discoveries Made Upon Man and Matter and Some Poems*, first published in 1892 by Cassell & Company. Under license from Project Gutenberg Ebook #5134 at www.gutenberg.org.

Pablo Neruda. "Towards the Splendid City." Nobel Lecture, December 13, 1971. Wed. 24 Jun 2020. <https://www.nobelprize.org/prizes/literature/1971/neruda/lecture/>

Resource Publications
An Imprint of Wipf and Stock Publishers
199 W. 8th Ave., Suite 3
Eugene, OR 97401

www.wipfandstock.com

PAPERBACK ISBN: 978-1-7252-8944-4
HARDCOVER ISBN: 978-1-7252-8945-1
EBOOK ISBN: 978-1-7252-8946-8

02/05/21

For Sara and Jana

My Story is Your Story

Contents

Preface

BROKEN GLASS, THE FIRST volume of the Maggie Barnes Trilogy, is a candid family saga that weaves together conflict and redemption. Maggie is a widow, and her four adult children are navigating their own complicated lives. In the unexpected company of a nurse hired to help her while she is recovering from an accident, Maggie encounters a young person who is unlike her children in many respects. Disarmed by the acceptance of her young companion, Maggie sorts through the shards of her memories and brings to light secrets she has kept from her children because she feared their judgment and rejection. Looking into the mirror of her past, Maggie faces her own ghosts. She musters courage to mend family relationships where she can and makes room in her heart to accept her family as it is.

A Certain Slant is Maggie Barnes' story assembled by others after her death. She has left her journals to her son, Rowland, but he is puzzled by gaps in her accounts, and he turns to his mother's dear friend, Alethea, for help. Rowland reviews memories he shaped as a naïve boy, and in the process is forced to admit that he was clueless about much of what was happening around him. Alethea tries to answer Rowland's questions about his mother, but as she does, she realizes that she cannot tell Maggie's story without telling her own. The hidden stories Rowland and Alethea resurrect and share with each other change them, and in the process their hearts are opened to a connection that bridges the generations.

Volume Two of the *Maggie Barnes Trilogy* recounts Maggie's story with *A Certain Slant*. It is told in five parts:

Part I

When the Journals Are Opened

Remembrance of things past is not necessarily
the remembrance of things as they were.

—*Marcel Proust*

One

MY PHONE VIBRATED IN my pocket while I was in a committee meeting. I slipped it out and held it under the edge of the table to check if the message was from the woman I'd invited to dinner on Friday night. It was a text message from my sister Laura. "ROWLAND CALL ASAP!!!" I got up from the conference table and whispered "family emergency" to the guy next to me. I said it loud enough so everyone could hear me, but not loud enough to interrupt the woman who was giving a report. Out in the corridor I called Laura back.

"I found Mom's teeth," Laura blurted.

"She had all her teeth. They were buried with her. You didn't drop the urn, did you?" I had to ask. We still have the urn with her ashes in the closet of her condo, and we're planning to inter it in the columbarium when the whole family gets together at Thanksgiving. I assume the teeth, whatever is left of them, are in there with her ashes. I don't know what happens to teeth during cremation, but I have an image of a set of teeth buried in a pile of ashes, the way it might look if old dentures were thrown into the bottom of the fireplace before the ashes are cleaned out.

"No! Of course I didn't drop the urn. It's in the closet. Besides the urn's unbreakable." Laura is the expert on details like that. She's probably read the package inserts that came with the urn. "I was going through Mom's dresser and found a plaster cast of her teeth," she whined. "One's missing. Remember she cracked off that tooth and had to have an implant? You must remember. She made a big deal of how expensive it was."

I do remember. Not how much the tooth cost, but Mom's jokes about managing without the tooth and using the money to take her friends on a cruise instead. "At my age," she said, "I'll never get enough use out of that tooth to justify the cost of it, and a cruise would be fun."

I spared Laura the content of my mental detour about the cruise and got back to the teeth. It was bizarre that we were talking about Mom's teeth and that I was thinking of her as a pile of ashes. It felt only slightly better to shift back to talking about a plaster cast of teeth made by the dentist, but at least they weren't Mom's homegrown ones. In any case I wanted to get out of this crazy conversation. "C'mon, Laura, I'm in a meeting. I don't have time right now to talk about Mom's implant and whether it was expensive. What's the problem? What do you need?"

"I don't know what to do with all the stuff Mom left here in her condo. We have to clean it out before we turn it over to the realtor, don't we? I can't just toss Mom's teeth in the trash, and I don't want to carry them around in my purse or take them home with me to Denver and stick them in a drawer somewhere in my house. That'd be way too weird." Then her voice shifted from whining mode to executive mode. "I'm going to send some things to you."

"Don't do that," I said as fast as I could. Laura's a bulldozer when she settles on a plan, and I had to break the momentum of her decision. "You *can* put those teeth in the trash. Mom'll never *know.*"

The silence on the other end of the phone told me Laura was wondering if that was true or not. Would Mom know or wouldn't she? I heard a deep inhale and then "Row, going through Mom's stuff is . . . well it's awful . . . I mean . . . like . . . it reminds me of her . . . like she's here and she's gone. I feel guilty . . . sometimes I wasn't very nice to her." Laura's voice was getting thick again, the way it does when she's winding up to cry.

I asked Laura, "What do you need from me right now?" I was thinking *what do you need from me right now so I can go back into my meeting,* but I didn't say it to her that way. A kinder tone was more likely to shorten the conversation.

"Uh, well, there's more. Dad's monogrammed handkerchiefs. Ratty old ties. Why did Mom keep that stuff? What was she thinking? I don't want to haul it home and have it hanging around in my house so my kids have to sort through it when I die. You know what I mean?"

Laura was missing Mom. I think that's what she meant. Laura was getting tangled up in her "Laura-bundle." That's what we called it when she got overwhelmed with details that look trivial to the rest of us. She was tidy and regularly purged her house, which was a model of perfect order. Laura planned her life twenty-five years ahead. In this case she was thinking about her kids cleaning up after her when she dies. Suddenly it occurred to me that Laura wasn't asking what I thought we should do with Mom's stuff; she was telling me what she had already decided to do with it. She was assigning it to me.

"Okay. Pack the stuff in a box. Don't send it! Leave it in the condo! I'll be out of school in a few weeks, and I'm coming to Chicago. I'll take care of that stuff when I get there." I'd rescued my sister by doing what she wanted me to do all along.

"Thanks. You're a sweetheart," Laura said. "I knew you'd figure out what to do. Better get back to your meeting." I closed my eyes for a second and could see Laura checking an item off her to-do list as she spoke. I'd been had.

Sometimes Laura is cool-headed and has everything under control, but Laura is sensitive too. The problem is, she never admits the sensitive part calmly. Instead she falls apart the moment she has to deal with feelings any weightier than a butterfly's wing. She's good at housecleaning. Great at organizing an estate sale. But she hasn't been good at burying Mom. I still say it that way because I can't bear to say that neither Laura nor the rest of us have been good at burning Mom. Euphemisms for cremation haven't been refined yet, and an urn filled with ashes stored in the corner of a closet is not a convincing image of final rest.

Laura wasn't the only one struggling with Mom's departure. A few days after we came home from Mom's funeral my daughter Meredith said, "Dad, I'm feeling weird about something." She turns to me now and then when her conscience bothers her about lying to a teacher when she skips school or gossiping about a friend. Meredith is a tender soul, and when she starts with "Dad, I'm feeling weird about something . . . ," she wants me to untangle the knots in her conscience.

"It's about Gramma Maggie," Meredith said. "I feel terrible. I never sent her a thank you note for my birthday gift."

"Honey, your birthday was six months ago. What do you mean?"

"I was mad at her, Dad. She sent me a gift card for my birthday, but I was mad at her, so I ignored it. Now I don't know what to do with the gift card."

It began when our families were together for Memorial Day. Cousin Melanie had a new haircut. Longer on one side than the other and part of it dyed purple. When asked what she thought of it, Gramma Maggie said it was cute and that it's a good idea to try out things like that before you're old enough to apply for a job. She should've stopped there, but she added, "What I don't understand is kids who buy jeans with holes. It's bad enough to be poor and have worn out clothes. Why would anyone buy them that way?" Gramma had committed a faux pas; cousin Melanie wears jeans with holes and so does Meredith.

Gramma Maggie normally knew better than to criticize kids, especially her grandchildren. She raised five children of her own and knew the wisdom of the adage "This isn't a hill to die on." She was lovingly silent when Jocelyn got a nose ring, and she pretended not to notice when Zach got a dragon tattoo on his calf.

For Meredith's birthday Grandma Maggie sent a gift card with a note that said, "Please use this to pick out some clothes you like. I hope you can find something without holes." The comment about the clothes with holes was the rub for Meredith.

"Gramma meant it in humor," I told Meredith. "Take it as a compliment that Gramma felt comfortable enough with you to write something like that. If it had been a text message, she would've added hearts and a smiley face."

"LOL," said Meredith, making air quotes and looking at me carefully to make sure I got what she meant. "Mom says it was judgmental of Gramma Maggie to write that." So it was Andrea who poisoned the gift card. Since our divorce, Andrea hasn't wanted Meredith to feel good about anyone even loosely associated with me, including my mother. Furthermore, Andrea knows how sixteen-year-olds feel about someone being judgmental, unless they're the ones judging. Now months have passed, Meredith hasn't used the gift card or sent a thank you note, and Gramma is dead. There's no rolling back time to give Meredith a chance to offer a tardy thank you, but I knew I had to push back against Andrea's attempt to tarnish the reputation of my mother.

"Gramma Maggie is probably in heaven right now laughing about kids with holes in their jeans," I told Meredith. "She's swapping stories about grandkids with her friend Estelle, because when they were alive they loved entertaining each other with tall tales about the grandkids they adored." Meredith was listening with wide-open watery eyes. "Gramma Maggie wouldn't want you feeling bad about a gift card. She'd much rather you remember how much she loved you."

"I knew I'd feel better if I talked to you." Meredith gave me a quick hug.

"Go buy something," I advised her. "Use the gift card. It'll feel good." I saw I'd won when Meredith smiled. Purchasing something with the gift card was going to trump Andrea's efforts to poison the memory of Gramma Maggie. I smiled back.

My mother, Maggie Barnes, was a well-behaved middle class woman who valued good manners, including thank you notes. More important than manners, however, was loving her "grands," all nine of them. The way she loved them was simple, similar to the way kids love puppies. What I'd said to Meredith about Gramma Maggie was absolutely true, and the ease with which Meredith took my advice confirmed she believed me.

I WASN'T AS CONFIDENT dealing with my mother's absence myself. In the months after Mom passed away my sisters, my brother, and I were wrapping up details. It wasn't easy, but it wasn't Mom's fault. Although she tried for years to get us ready for the day when she would be gone, we didn't take her seriously. She'd start a sentence with "after I'm gone it would be nice if . . . " and we'd toss a shitty little grin her way and tune her out. To each other we'd complain that Mom was starting "to do too much of that waiting for the last bus thing," by which we meant she was too comfortable discussing her own demise. Maybe she was okay thinking about her own death, but we weren't ready to hear about it from her.

I have premonitions of the time when my own kids will stop taking me seriously. They already give me the brush-off about matters less serious than death. They head out the door, and I say, "don't stay out too late," but they know I'm thinking, "*don't drink and drive!*" They ignore me and figure that whatever it is I'm fretting about, they've got it handled. That's how I treated Mom. I wasn't mean. Just indifferent. Then she died.

After I figured out with Laura what to do with Mom's teeth, I put my phone back in my pocket and went back into the conference room. Mentally I tried to put the conversation with Laura on hold, but for the rest of the meeting I was thinking about Dad's moth-eaten ties and wondering what other relics were tucked away in Mom's condo. I had done the thing Andrea nagged me about when we were married. "What's wrong with you Barones?" she'd ask. "All you kids do the same thing. You solve problems by making bigger ones. What's wrong with saying what you really mean?" Then if Andrea saw me take a breath or clear my throat as if I were about to speak, she'd say, "Hold it! Don't answer! I know perfectly well why you kids, the whole lot of you, are so screwed up. You never dared to say 'No!' to your mother."

That familiar stream of words, to which I was subjected more times than I can count, was like diarrhea running down the leg of a man with cholera. All I could do is stand there with a sick feeling and watch it happen, powerless to stop it.

It took me twenty years and a divorce from Andrea to figure out she was right about one thing. I had solved problems by making bigger ones. I married her because I didn't have the guts to break up with her once I purchased the over-priced diamond she picked out. I had a child and then another to ease the pain of being married to her. And then I stayed because I didn't want the children to grow up like nomads moving between one feeding ground in a house with a shrew and another feeding ground in a house with a man who was scared of that shrew.

If I go through that whole sequence in reverse order, it tumbles backward to a completely different conclusion. I can't imagine a life without Zach and Meredith, and I wouldn't have these exact kids if I hadn't married Andrea. She wouldn't have married me if the diamond hadn't been big enough. Was it fate or a series of accidents? I still don't know which order of the story to stick with, because I never learned to do for myself what I did for Meredith when she told me she was feeling weird about Gramma Maggie. I never learned to do for myself what I'd done for Laura when she called about the teeth. I'd never learned how to make a decision and be done with it.

After I divorced Andrea I could see that my problem wasn't a failure to say "no." That was only half of the problem. I also couldn't say "yes" without getting anxious about how Andrea would sabotage me. That insight blew the fuse and put out the lights of our marriage. I knew our marriage was over the day I was sitting in my therapist's office talking about Andrea and how miserable I was, and my therapist said, "Even if you divorce Andrea you'll still have to sort through your uneasiness every time it occurs to you that your mother loved you more than Andrea did, and that possibly your mother loved you more than you deserve."

"Well, what should I do first?" I asked her. "Should I feel guilty because my mother loved me more than I deserved, or should I feel stupid because I married a woman who loved me less than my mother did?"

"That question is yours to answer," my therapist replied. It infuriated me that I was paying top dollar to a respected therapist and she didn't have the decency to give me an answer to a question about which she is supposed to be an expert.

I pounced on her verbally, "It would help if you'd do the part of the work I'm paying you for." The moment the words were out of my mouth I regretted it. "Just kidding," I added quickly. "But really, is the bigger problem Andrea or my mother?"

My therapist gazed at me like an owl, the calm gaze of someone who is looking at you head-on without blinking, and you know you can't escape. "I don't think you're kidding," she said. "You're angry with me for not solving problems for you, so you don't have to solve them for yourself. Let's leave that as it is for now." She paused long enough to let me get uneasy about what was coming next. "There's no use blaming your mother. If you think it through you'll see it won't help to blame Andrea either. It's your problem, Rowland."

My neck felt hot. "So that's it?" I said. "I thought that's where I started. Isn't that why I began therapy with you in the first place? Because I'm messed up, and I blame myself for being confused about both my mother and Andrea?"

"You blame both of them, that's true," said my therapist. "Behind that little bit of emotional legerdemain you feel sorry for yourself. You've got that right as well."

Sometimes I can close out what I don't want to hear by purposely letting myself be distracted. As I heard my therapist's words, I tried to think about whether she uses a word like "legerdemain" with all her clients or whether I should be flattered that she was using it with me because she thinks I'm intelligent enough to know what it means. It didn't help. I couldn't keep out the sound of her voice.

"You feel guilty for everything that goes wrong," my therapist continued. "You feel guilty for marrying Andrea before you considered the cost of living with a woman who is harsh and critical. You put a ring on her finger and marched down the aisle because that's what you thought everyone expected you to do. I find it interesting that you don't wear a wedding ring, and you tell me you never did. Not wearing a ring was your way of pretending you hadn't made a full commitment. Ring or no ring, it didn't take long for you to discover that you were stuck anyway. Now your marriage is a dilapidated little hut on which you've been paying a mortgage, and all those payments make you feel obligated to reside there and treat it like home."

Her accusations made me angry. I considered pointing out to my therapist that she was using mixed metaphors, but instead I winced at her words and took her advice. My therapist says that she only facilitated the process and that the decision to divorce Andrea was entirely mine. That's what they always say. In any case, before I walked out of my therapist's office that day, I knew my marriage was over, but I didn't know how hard it would be to pack up and move out. What's more, I never could have predicted the terrible loneliness that flooded in to fill the space that once had been occupied by Andrea. I hate to admit that sometimes I miss the misery.

The conversation with Laura about what to do with Mom's teeth got me started. When my meeting was over and I headed for home, all this other stuff was tumbling out of my mind like trash cascading off the back of a garbage truck at a landfill. I was thinking about it as I got into my car and pulled out of the parking ramp. When I merged onto I-94 I was rehashing the lesson I'd learned from Andrea, one of the only useful things I got in the settlement of our divorce. I heard myself saying out loud, alone there in the bubble of my car, as I dodged in and out of lanes on the expressway, "I'm entitled to say 'yes' if I want to, and I'm entitled to change my mind if I need to."

I laughed. It felt like I laughed for five minutes straight, although it was probably more like ten seconds. I laughed about the thousands of dollars I'd spent to learn something so simple. And I laughed because I imagined, just above the billowy clouds, in a blue sky on a fresh Minnesota day, Mom was up there laughing with me.

For once I didn't feel I was solving a problem by making a bigger one. I felt like Meredith buying something with the gift card Gramma Maggie sent for her birthday. I gave myself permission to remember that Mom always loved me. I felt misty when I considered that she probably still loves me, and she doesn't need my sloppy confessions about what a shit I can be. She doesn't need me to fuss about her teeth or Dad's old ties either. And I don't have to explain to her or anyone else why I divorced Andrea.

I tapped the button on my dashboard, and my car filled with the sound of twangy guitar chords and then John Lennon's voice singing "Across the Universe." I smiled at "images drifting through my opened mind." As the song ended I punched the button on the dashboard again and reached for my cell phone, redialed Laura, and put her on speakerphone. As soon as I heard her voice, without saying anything else, I launched into a plan. "I've made a decision, Laura. As soon as the semester's done I'm coming to Chicago. I have the next semester off to finish my research project, which means I'm free until January, so there's no reason I can't stay in Chicago for the entire summer. I'll live in Mom's condo. Don't change anything. Keep all the furniture for the time being. Leave all the other stuff the way it is. I'll deal with it from here on, and you're off the hook. Lock the door, get on a plane, and go home to Denver. Go home to your family."

When I got off the phone with Laura, I cruised along, imagining breakfast at Mom's little kitchen table and sitting in her chair by the window to read. At my short-term-lease apartment, I flipped the deadbolt lock and opened the door to unpacked boxes and pictures I'd never gotten around to hanging on the wall. It didn't feel like the dingy little apartment was mine anymore. It hadn't ever felt like my home, but it had felt like my problem. It was a warehouse in which I was being stored, along with the ugly furniture that Andrea discarded by sending it along with me when I moved out of the house I'd once tried to share with her.

By the time I walked across the room and put my keys on the kitchen counter, I knew what I had to do. I'll call my landlord to end my lease, then I'll call Goodwill to pick up the furniture I'm done with, and I'll stow the things I want to keep in a rented storage unit. As soon as school is done I'll head for Chicago. I've never lived in Mom's condo before, because she moved there after I married Andrea and had children of my own. Even though Mom isn't there anymore, and I've never lived there with her, it's the only place I can think of that still feels like home. When I think of Mom, I think of her there.

I know this way of thinking about someone who is dead doesn't make sense, but I'm not the only one trying to figure out where to locate Mom. My sister Jenna called me last week. She was on the expressway near O'Hare airport, and above her in the blue sky on a clear day she saw vapor trails from jets flying over. "That's sort of what it's like with Mom," Jenna told me. "She's left vapor trails or something like spirit trails. They're gradually fading away, but sometimes I catch sight of one, and it feels like she's still around." Jenna cried, and we were quiet for a minute. Then I said,

"Mom would probably understand that you see her in the sky, and I agree with you that she's still lingering around. We'll get through this, baby sister. We'll get through this together."

"I hope so," she said. "Anyway, I knew I'd feel better if I talked to you."

I still think of Mom having breakfast at the little table in the kitchen of her condo or sitting in her reading chair near the windows that look out over the park. It's like thinking of her in the next room. The door's closed, but she's there. Then the hard part hits me. I'll never see Mom come through the door again with a sparkle in her eye. I'll never again feel the hug that assured me she was glad to have a son like me, even if . . . and that's as far as I can go with it for now.

Two

IN MOM'S CONDO THERE are reminders of her everywhere. Her energy is in the walls. Being in her space puts me inside her head. Inside her memory. I don't really have the right word for what it puts me inside of, surrounded here by the relics of her life. The first morning I took a shower I wondered if the soap in the dish was a bar she used before she died. I wondered if I was using her towels or a guest towel. The evidences of her everywhere are reminders that she isn't coming back.

My mother moved from our family home on Woodward Street to her condo in Oak Park after Dad died. Prior to the move, Laura labeled the things Mom wanted to take with her, and word went out to the children and grandchildren that, from what was left, we were welcome to take anything we wanted. Jewelry, family heirlooms, and the best pieces of furniture went to my brother and sisters.

I didn't claim any of Mom's stuff for myself because her preparations for the big exit were off-putting for me. Dad had died, and I didn't want to think about Mom dying too. I also didn't want to appear indifferent, so I told Mom that sometime in the future I would like to have her pictures and old family papers, but there was no hurry. I figured it would be a long time before I'd have to step up and make good on my offer.

There were practical reasons I didn't take anything from the old house on Woodward Street. I couldn't imagine Mom's end tables in my living room or her art on my walls, because I knew if I even hinted at the possibility, Andrea would make a stinking fuss about it. In all the places I'd lived together with Andrea, I'd been a visitor passing through: Rowland bunking in at Andrea's house. Even after we had children and bought a four-bedroom house to which my paycheck was committed, it never felt like *my home*. If I'd made a claim to any of Mom's possessions, I would have gotten tangled up in negotiations about having Mom's stuff in Andrea's house.

The leftovers I took to my bachelor apartment when Andrea and I split up were the things she didn't want. I ended up with a white leather couch I hated. Andrea bought it during her Florida-style decorating phase. That couch and pastel pillows might have been fine in a beach house in a sunny climate, but sun-bleached colors and sea-shell themes never felt right in our Minnesota house in the dead of winter. The couch was cold, and the afghans we put on it to warm it up didn't like the couch any more than I did; they always slipped off onto the floor. When Andrea redecorated again, because our house was a scene of perpetual redecorating, the white couch ended up in my small office in the basement. We called it an office because it had a desk, but actually it was the room to which I retreated to watch movies by myself. My artsy tastes didn't match the tastes of my family. I liked films that won awards at Cannes; they liked movies that got rave reviews from high school kids who gathered at our house to raid the refrigerator and watch action flicks with high-speed chases and guns.

When I moved out, the couch followed me to my new apartment, like a mongrel dog no one else would take. In my small bachelor pad it didn't fit. On the few occasions I brought a guest home with me, I was quick to say the couch would be the first thing to go when I got around to decorating. I was concerned that someone I was trying to impress would think my taste was gauche. There was a nice woman who taught in the Music Department, and I invited her out for dinner a few times. One evening after dinner I invited her back to my apartment for a drink. When I mentioned that I was planning to redecorate, she told me that at least I had one good piece to build around. She meant that lousy couch. Little did she know that liking the couch was a deal-breaker. I never asked her out again.

Of all the women I dated, Polly was the only one I kept calling. The first time she came to my apartment I tried the couch apology routine, and she said, "Rowland, I don't know what your problem is with that couch, but if you think I choose men to date because of their taste in couches, you've got me completely wrong." She sees through my pretensions, and from the very beginning she's had the courage to tell me so.

Not wanting Mom's stuff had another sub-text. I didn't want my brother or sisters to think I had sentimental attachment to anything that belonged to Mom. The problem was not Mom; it was my fear that the others would think I was too glued to her. Laura used to call me a "mama's boy." My twin brother Will once told me, "Cut the apron strings, buddy, and you'll save a lot of that money you're wasting on therapy." My younger sister Jenna was kinder than the other two, but when I asked her if she thought I was abnormally attached to Mom, she said, "Oh, Row, don't worry about it. We all need someone to cling to."

Jenna's feedback tripped me up. I'm a slightly eccentric college professor, but I'm normal. Jenna's suggestion that I'm clingy bothered me because she's without guile. If Laura had said that, I would have assumed the insult was intended. If Will had said it, I would have known it was meant to one-up me. But Jenna? I have to listen to Jenna because she's one of those soft people like my daughter Meredith. They're honest and without malice.

My family's opinions played into my reasons for telling Mom that instead of taking anything from the house on Woodward Street, I would like to have her family papers. I figured I could leave them with her for the time being, and if later she insisted that I take them, I could box them up and store them somewhere.

I was glad to take Mom's photos because I like old photos. I collect them. I especially like old black and whites printed on cottony paper or the ones with lacy edges that come in yellow-gold packets held together with a metal clip. Like a boy who goes through an old box of postage stamps hoping to find one with an upside-down airplane, I sort through a box of old photos and negatives hoping to find a treasure. As it is, even if what I find are only pictures of people I never knew, at a picnic in a park I've never visited, I find old photos nostalgic. I know what my sisters would say if they knew this. They'd say I'm a social misfit who's capable of enjoying pictures of a picnic more than the picnic itself.

I didn't have a plan for what I would do with Mom's family papers, although initially I pictured myself on some future evening in the dead of winter, sitting in a den with a fire in the fireplace, sorting through a cardboard box of yellowed documents to see if there was anything interesting. Most of it I'd toss into the fireplace, one leaf at a time. Maybe there would be a letter or two I'd want to keep. Maybe tucked in among the papers I'd find a few photos I'd never seen before. For the rest it would be "poof," up in flames, and I'd be done with it. With minimal effort I could fulfill my promise to Mom and preserve my status as a dutiful son.

Now Mom's gone, and I feel guilty about my indifference. I admitted to my therapist that I'd created a blind spot for Mom. My therapist had a Freudian-sounding explanation. "Rowland," she said, "we bury parents twice. The first time is when we start ignoring them because we think we've surpassed them and don't need them anymore. The second time is when we return them to the earth."

I hadn't intended to get that deep into it with my therapist. What I wanted to say is that I didn't mean to insult Mom. She was my mom, and I thought I had her figured out. Is that such a crime? My advice to Meredith about the gift card for her birthday is coming full circle now. I want to believe Mom is up above those billowy clouds smiling at me, even if sometimes I'm obnoxious.

ONCE SETTLED INTO MOM'S condo, I opened the carton containing her papers. There was a note that makes me wonder what will happen to my own letters and journals if something happens to me. Unlike Mom, who often thought about dying, I've never thought about who will clean up after me if one night I fall asleep at the wheel and drive off the road, or get too confident on the ski slopes and hit a tree. Her note said:

Row,

I'm leaving my journals with you. I should discard these papers, but I can't bring myself to give up the memories. It gets harder as my friends pass on, and memories are all I have left. If I don't get around to taking care of the things in this box, you'll have to decide how to dispose of them.

Love, Mom

After reading what Mom had written, I knew I'd joined the generation at the head of the march. There's no one left in our family from an older generation. There's no one to whom I can go to say I feel weird about something I haven't handled right.

When Mom moved out of our large family home on Woodward Street, she moved into a condo in the building where her friend Alethea lives in Oak Park, and that's where Mom lived until she died. I'd already been at Mom's condo for two weeks when I went out one noon to get a sandwich and coffee. As I returned, some distance ahead of me, I saw an older woman pause at the outer doors of the apartment building. She rested her cane against the building while she searched in her purse for something. I figured she was looking for her key. It was Alethea, and I hurried to catch up with her.

"I didn't recognize you at first," she said. "Dressed like that, you look like a fellow out to make trouble." It hadn't occurred to me that anyone could think I was menacing, dressed in jeans, a hoodie, and the black tuque I use for ice fishing in Minnesota. I tried to explain myself, "I'm on a quick back and forth to pick up a sandwich and some coffee. I didn't want to interrupt my work, but a hungry man's got to eat."

"You should make your own sandwiches at home. Coffee's easy too," said Alethea. "Your mother has a very nice espresso machine. I'm sure there are instructions for it somewhere."

Alethea already knew that I'd offered to clear the rest of Mom's belongings out of the condo during my summer vacation. She also knew about Mom's teeth and the phone call with Laura. After the conversation about the teeth, Laura called Jenna, and Jenna called Alethea to put out the word that I'd be arriving. The news cycle of women is a mystery to me. I grew up with two sisters who keep track of each other's business, but the amount of trivia that includes never ceases to amaze me.

As we went up in the elevator, Alethea explained why she walks with a cane. "I hate being a fretful old women," she said, "but if you look old, there are people who think you're an easy mark. I don't need this cane for walking, but if I had to, I could whack somebody with it. I could do damage." She nodded as she spoke, as if she were trying to convince herself.

I walked Alethea to her door, and as she was fitting the key into the lock I said, "I'd like to come to see you, if you'll have me. I'm reading Mom's journals, and I have some questions."

"Tea would be fine," Alethea said. "Tomorrow afternoon." As I turned to walk down the hall Alethea added, "Row, if you want to get along in this neighborhood and with the folks who live in this building, you might give some attention to your wardrobe."

Alethea reminded me of Polly, the woman I've been dating off and on. They don't look alike, and they don't know each other, but in some odd way Alethea and Polly are the same type. My mother would have said, "they're cut from the same cloth." An old-fashioned figure of speech, charming even if judgmental. There is a point to it though. Alethea and Polly aren't afraid to say what they think, but they're not like Andrea, who has to take a pound of flesh in order to prove beyond a doubt that she's right.

When I have thoughts and no one to share them with, I think of Polly. I imagine going out with her for an evening, then going home to her cozy apartment, getting sweet with her and staying over, waking up next to her and quietly getting up to start the coffee. Polly is the kind of woman I can enjoy breakfast with, and by the end of breakfast we can have a plan for how to spend a Saturday together. I was thinking of Polly again as I rode up the elevator to Alethea's condo for my first visit. I'd been spending too much time alone.

BY THE TIME I knocked on Alethea's door for our afternoon visit, I'd had my hair trimmed at the Quick Cuts, pulled a shirt with a button down collar out of my suitcase and pressed it, and picked up a new pair of khaki pants at Target. The beginning of our visit was somewhat formal, or maybe it's more accurate to say it was old-fashioned. She offered me tea and put a plate with slices of pound cake on the table between us. As soon as the tea was poured, she nodded to me to let me know I should help myself to the treats on the plate.

"Alethea," I said, "you haven't changed at all. I hope you aren't saying the same about me, because you've known me since I was a kid, when I was insufferable."

Alethea put her hand out with the palm toward me like a stop sign. "Do you really want me to say you were and possibly still are insufferable?" Her fingers were gnarly and didn't line up quite right, but they delivered a firm message. "For some time now most of what I've known about you is what I got secondhand from your mother. Do you have any idea how much she adored you? I don't know if you are or aren't insufferable, because she hardly qualified as an objective judge. The rest of what I know about you I get from your sisters. And, Row, some of the time they don't know what to make of you."

"You're right," I said. "My remark was awkward."

With Alethea there was no pretending; she'd set me straight if I needed it, but I also knew that her affection for me was a reflection of Mom's affection for me. She was like an aunt.

I told Alethea I was going through Mom's papers and needed help. "Truth be told," she said, "I was perplexed when I heard that Maggie left her papers with you. I would have thought she'd leave them with your sisters. Maybe not Laura, but I would think she'd trust Jenna with them." I must have grinned as Alethea spoke. She squinted a little and said, "Do you find that comical?"

"Not funny exactly. It's just that I don't often hear someone use that expression. 'Truth be told.' People don't say that anymore. It's code for the way people used to think. Frankly it sounds like Mom. She could've said something like that. That's why I grinned."

"Your mom likely did use that expression. When she promised the truth, you got the truth." Alethea watched me as she spoke. "She had character, and I don't apologize for sounding like her.

Furthermore I don't mind being old-fashioned. Your mom would understand that too."

"If you're like Mom, then I'm in good company," I said. "Let's at least agree about that."

Alethea pushed her teacup away. She had set a small notepad on the side of the table, and she pulled it toward herself as she picked up her pen. "I have a concern," Alethea said. "Your sister told me that you are working on the journals, but it's all a game to you. She doesn't think you can be trusted with your mother's reputation. I hope to heaven that's not true."

I knew what Alethea was referring to because one night after a few too many refills on the scotch I was sipping, I called Jenna and read a passage of the journal to her. I also told her I could make Mom's writing more interesting by adding a little x-rated material where she had left it out. I never guessed Jenna would report that to Alethea. What ever happened to keeping conversations private?

To Alethea I said, "Let's put Jenna's comments aside and get down to business. We can start on neutral territory. I found a story tucked in with Mom's papers. It's a rough draft, composed on an old typewriter. It's about Mom's friend Estelle. If we start with it, you and Jenna can set aside your concerns about protecting Mom's reputation." I had my own reasons for being interested in Mom's friend Estelle, but I didn't tell Alethea why I was curious.

Alethea didn't object, and I continued. "I assume you can answer questions about Mom's friends; you knew them too, right? The writing in her journals isn't particularly good. There's a feminine type that emerges, a trope. It's the good-housekeeping woman of the 1950s. The kind that was in Betty Crocker ads. There's also a Darwinian tinge to the story, in the sense that Mom and her friends were struggling to survive the oppression of an era before feminism."

"Rowland, slow down! You may know some things about literature, and you may know some things about your mom, but what do you know about your mom's friends? Who are you to judge that we were all the same type? We're people, Rowland, not pages. And you're just Maggie's boy. 'Trope.' 'Darwinism.' Really now! What's happened to you?"

Alethea put her fingers on her forehead and closed her eyes, like she was channeling someone. I found the gesture comical, but I determined not to grin. When she opened her eyes again she said, "What basis do you have for judgment? You owe it to your mother to be careful. What you do with her papers says something about the kind of man you are." She was talking to me as if I were a boy caught doing something of which Mom wouldn't approve.

"Facts or truth. Truth or facts. Come on, Alethea. Mom's journals aren't exactly Pandora's box. What do you think is going to come flying out? You're being too hard on me. If we get stuck on points like this, we'll never get around to reading the journals."

Alethea wasn't done. "Your mother was my loyal friend, and I intend to be careful. The question is whether you intend to be careless."

"Okay," I said. "I get the point."

"We'll see," said Alethea.

"I'd like to suggest a way we can move forward," I told her. "Let's take a story and both read it. Then let's sit down again together and talk about it. Would that work? I'd like to get back to the story about Mom's friend Estelle."

". . . Yes." The answer was so slow coming, she could as easily have said "No."

Before giving her a chance to change her mind, I said, "Okay. I'll run off a copy of the story about Estelle and drop it off to you."

Alethea tipped her head very slowly once to the left and then to the right. It was a perfectly ambiguous gesture. I guessed that she wanted me to understand she wasn't all in. I was going to have to prove myself to her, but I didn't know what I was trying to prove.

I walked toward the door, but before stepping out into the hall I turned back and said, "Hey Alethea, do you do email? I could take the story about Estelle to the service counter at the library and have it scanned. That way I can email it to you." I saw the shadow of disapproval cross her face. "Should I make a photocopy? Would you prefer to work with a hard copy?"

"Yes, a hard copy," said Alethea. "I like something solid I can hold in my hand, and I still have great respect for ink on paper."

Three

I DIDN'T TELL ALETHEA at our first visit that I had been in for some surprises when I opened the box of things Mom left for me. I expected to find her diaries and papers, but an additional item immediately caught my attention. It was a large envelope in which Mom had tucked all sorts of things that might have gone into a scrapbook: baptism announcements, wedding programs for her children, a newspaper picture of her own wedding, and the obituary for Dad. One item stopped me dead in my tracks. It was a postcard from Spain, and Mom had sent it home to herself. The message was one sentence: "I now know the meaning of AWE." The image was the endless sequence of arches and pillars in the Mezquita in Cordoba.

I made that trip with Mom not long after Dad died. I was scheduled to go to a conference in Madrid, and on a whim I invited Mom to come with me because I wanted to do something nice for her. During the day, while I was at my meetings, she explored the Plaza Mayor, visited museums, or sat on a park bench and watched people strolling through the Parque del Retiro. In the evening we had dinner together.

The places and sites on Mom's list of things to do in Madrid were touristy things, but Mom loved being a tourist. She loved heading out with good walking shoes on her feet and a travel bag over her shoulder, packed with a city guide, camera, collapsible sun hat, compact umbrella, bottle of water, and two energy bars. Even though she had the map, to find her way she'd ask strangers for directions. If she couldn't understand the first stranger, she'd act as if she did, and then she'd flag down another stranger a block later and ask again. It worked for her. She got where she wanted to go.

It wasn't like Mom to demand much for herself, but as we were preparing for our trip she did make one request. "I've always dreamed of visiting Cordoba," she told me. "Is it possible that I could go there for a day trip while you are at your meetings? I could take the train, or I could go on a bus tour." I didn't ask her what it was that drew her to Cordoba. There were other cities equally old and equally interesting. She could have visited Toledo or Salamanca, Seville or Granada, but she had her heart set on Cordoba. Why Cordoba?

I checked it out online and discovered it would be quite simple to work a side trip to Cordoba into our travel plans. Trains depart back and forth between Madrid and Cordoba multiple times in both directions every day, and the trip is less than two hours through the beautiful countryside region of Andalusia. "I'll go with you," I told her. "And let's not just dash back and forth. Let's stay over for at least one night. We'll add it to the end of our trip." Mom was delighted.

Cordoba is an impressive city, and by the time we got there Mom had gone to the library and done her research. As we walked around the old city I let her lead the way. We went to the 14th century Sinagoga, and in the Plaza de los Capuchinos we had coffee. She especially loved the gardens at Alcazar. Here and there she'd stop at a postcard kiosk to pick up the pictures she wanted to send home to her friends. But clearly what Mom looked forward to most was exploring the Mezquita. It was the height of her visit.

Twelve centuries ago someone built a mosque on this spot near the river, and over the centuries it became more lavish. Inside the walls there is an orange grove, and the minaret towers over the city. When the fortunes of the city changed, the new regime claimed the space and built a chapel inside the mosque. Later a grand cathedral was added to the complex. Clearly this was no ordinary mosque. Mom was most impressed by the endless hall whose eight hundred columns leave an indelible impression, and that was the image on the postcard she sent home to herself.

There are two memories of Cordoba that stick with me. Maybe it would be more accurate to say they stay with me like a scar. Finding the postcard among Mom's papers was a jarring reminder. The one memory is from the Mezquita, and the postcard could be a photo of a spot at which we stood. We strolled through the columns, and once we were at what seemed like the middle, Mom stopped and slowly turned around in a complete circle, very slowly as if she were trying to absorb the sight in every direction.

"Row, can you imagine how many prayers have gone up from this city over a thousand years?" she asked. "From this mosque and cathedral? And from the synagogue too? Like the sand on the seashore or the stars in the sky. More than anyone can count. What I love most about this place is the light. I feel surrounded by it." Her eyes were slightly watery and her lip trembled a little, but she was completely in control of herself. She was taking it all in, and she was deeply moved.

I don't know what the devil got into me, but what I did next still makes me squirm. I did not consider with her how many prayers had gone up from this city over the centuries. It would have been like me to up the ante and remind her that there are cathedrals, mosques, synagogues, and temples all over the world from which prayers have gone up. It wouldn't even have been out of character for me to question, in a calm and confident voice, how much all these prayers have accomplished, observing that they haven't stopped wars or death. That's the way I often think about religious sites over-run with tourists. I think of the negatives, and I think of myself as above being impressed.

On that day in the Mezquita I outdid my own past failures of empathy. I turned to Mom and said, "You know what I think when I stand here and look around?" She looked at me expectantly, and then I spit it out. "I think of how damned annoying it is to be in a herd of tourists with clicking cameras. This is like Las Vegas or Disney World. Whatever is being preserved here, they long ago ruined it. These tourists milling around for a few minutes before they get back on their tour busses have no idea what they are seeing. They'll take pictures to look at later, but probably they won't be able to remember the name of the building in the picture. They'll send postcards home, but in the end they're just bored people collecting souvenirs to show their equally bored friends that they went somewhere on vacation where their friends have never been."

I don't know what got into me. Maybe spiritual jealousy or resentment that Mom could be so confident about something. Maybe it annoyed me that, given her comments were about religion, she wasn't being more modest and tentative. Whatever it was, it pissed me off.

Mom didn't say anything. She didn't argue. She didn't walk away. She just very slowly turned herself around in a complete circle again to refresh the impression she'd taken in before. Soon after we walked toward the entrance and left. As we walked along the street, she wove her hand through my arm. It wasn't typical of her to do that.

"The street's uneven, isn't it?" I said. "Are you afraid of tripping?"

"No. These shoes are good. No problem," she said. She was tethering me, staying connected to me in the simplest way she knew how. Refusing to give in to what I had said, she wasn't going to let her arrogant prick of a son ruin this trip together. Mom never mentioned it again. Not my arrogant and thoughtless statement or her impression of the light in the Mezquita. I did hear her telling others after our return about the trip we took to Spain together, and she was always enthusiastic and grateful. But in my presence she never again spoke of Cordoba.

We stayed a second evening in Cordoba before catching the morning train. Mom was tired from all the walking, and after we went back to the hotel following an early dinner, she decided to rest a little, write her postcards, and then go to sleep early. I wasn't ready for that, and I decided to go out for a walk. I told Mom not to worry if I was gone for a while because I'd probably stop off at a bar to chat up some locals. She laughed.

I went through the security routine I always follow before going out to the bar in an unfamiliar city. I emptied my pockets of valuables: credit card, passport, and most of my money. Instead of putting my valuables in the hotel safe, I left them on the dresser in the room with Mom. They felt safe there; I knew she wouldn't be going anywhere. Into my pocket I tucked my phone, my hotel key, and a bundle of small euro bills: two 50s, two 20s, and two 10s. I also had a few loose coins for tips.

The streets were still busy. I walked through a narrow lane with whitewashed buildings and colorful geranium planters on the walls and found my way to an avenue with little eateries and bars. I wasn't hungry, but I took a seat at a place that looked friendly, and I ordered beer and tapas as an excuse to sit for a while.

A young woman seated alone caught my eye. When I looked her way again she smiled. We tossed a few more glances back and forth, and then she came over to my table and asked, "Do you speak English?" I told her I did, and she let me know that she likes to practice her English with visitors because she is studying to become a tour guide. Her English echoed standard phrases in language programs for the hospitality industry; my stumbling sentences in Spanish were resurrected from my college foreign language class. She was especially quick with translating things that tourists need: band-aids, haircuts, shoe repair, and sunscreen. She also helped me translate the names for the fish and food on the menu. I invited her to order some for herself.

After we had covered the basics of the restaurant and the menu she asked me what kind of work I do, and I told her I am a teacher. She knew that already, she said, because I look very intelligent. "Muy inteligente?" I asked with an exaggerated accent. We both laughed. I knew she was flattering me, but I took it as well-intended.

The conversation tumbled on. Yes, I had been in Madrid, and, yes, I liked it. Yes, the Spanish people are friendly, and, yes, I like her country. She bragged a little about the food in Andalusia, and then asked if I have ever been to New York. Of course I have, I told her. She told me she has not been to New York but her cousin lives there, and she would like to see it. Also she would like to go to Hollywood.

Finally I asked her name. "Isa," she said. "I am the big queen Isabela of Alcazar. Very rich. Muy cruel." It occurred to me that this young woman might be smarter than I'd estimated. Was she politely referring to the Inquisition? On the other hand, why wouldn't she know the name of a queen whose castle was in the center of her own hometown.

"Do you know about Christopher Colombus?" I asked her.

"Of course," she said. "Cristobal Colon."

We were running out of things she knew to say in English or I knew to say in Spanish. "If we walk I can show you some nice things," she said. I paid my bill and hers, and we walked toward the river. From the old Roman bridge the city looked enchanted in night light. "It is very old," she said repeatedly.

"It's Roman," I said. "Two thousand years old."

"Very expensive," she said as she pointed to a neighborhood in the distance.

We turned then to walk back into the city, and as we passed shops she pointed out the ones with good prices and the ones with bad products. We passed a park. "We shall rest?" she asked, taking my hand and leading me toward a quiet corner. I knew we were heading into new territory, but I let her lead me. On the far side of the park we sat down on a bench. She leaned against me and wove her arm through my arm. "I can give, you know, for 30 euro," she said and clarified with a gesture what was included in the offer.

"Isa, I'm not that kind," I said.

"I am a student," she said. "I don't have money. Sorry, sorry. No money then. I like you. I like to practice English."

It was awkward. Neither she nor I said anything more about the failed bargain. She was still leaning against me, and then after a very long pause, she said, "It's very nice, do you think?" She assumed I would agree that whatever it was she had in mind, whether the city or the park or the weather or the company, I too would think it was very nice.

"Si," I said in a whisper. I needed to say something. I didn't want to be rude.

Gradually Isa became more familiar, resting her hand on my leg, taking my hand and examining it closely, commenting that American men are tall and she likes that. At last she suggested, "If you come with me I can show you some things very nice to remember from Cordoba." I knew by then she didn't mean a tourist

T-shirt. She must have sensed my reservations. "Do not think money," she said. "You are friend. I like you." She giggled softly.

I wondered what she was thinking of a man who would accept her offer if it was free but was too cheap to give a working woman the money she needed. What I thought was an effort of regard for her honor, she probably thought was stinginess. I put my face against her hair and said, "You smell good."

We left the park and walked through the streets. She walked close to me, and rather than bumping against her it seemed easier to put my arm around her. She put her arm around me too, and now and then she stroked my backside. It wasn't overdone, but it wasn't innocent either. We were drifting into an unfamiliar part of the city. At last we turned into a narrow street where in the middle of the block we came to a large wooden doorway between a nail salon on one side and a motor repair shop on the other. She paused there. "This is my casa," she said. "You are welcome. I like to make you comfortable."

Now I realize that was my last chance to say, "It's getting late. I'll be on my way, but thank you for a nice evening." That's the way I am thinking now, but that isn't the way I was thinking then. I was in a strange town an ocean away from home. I was a single man on my way to divorce, and she was pretty. She was willing too; it wasn't as if I was taking advantage of an innocent girl. I took note of the fact that she was older than my students. All the things that should have made me cautious seemed to fade away.

She took out her key and worked it into the lock on the heavy wooden door. She was familiar with the door, but the lock was cumbersome and she couldn't get it to open. "I will ring my friend," she said. "No problem, no problem," and she pressed one of the buttons next to the door on what appeared to be buzzers for the apartments above street level. We waited. "She's coming," Isa said, "no problem, no problem."

We waited a little longer, and the door swung open. A young woman greeted Isa and smiled at me. She stepped aside to let us into a poorly lit entryway that looked shabby and smelled bad. Stairs went up on one side and there were two bicycles and a trash container against the wall on the other. "Students," I thought. Why do I remember that detail?

Suddenly everything speeded up. Like the seconds before a car crash when everything outside the moment fades away and all the attention is hostage to what is happening. The two girls slipped out through the door and into the street, slamming the door behind them. I was left standing in that shadowy entry at the bottom of the stairway. From out of the shadows along the side of the stairs, a man slipped between me and the door. His arm came over my shoulder and around my neck. In his hand was a knife. He stunk of sweat and cigarettes. Out of that same dark space a young boy stepped forward. With lightening speed he riffled through my pockets. First my money clip with the bills, then the mobile phone I'd purchased at the airport. In my pants pocket there was a handkerchief, which he threw onto the floor. The man behind me laughed. When the boy took out my hotel key, he looked at it and put it back into my pocket, a gesture about which I still wonder.

As suddenly as it began it ended. The man behind me opened the door and shoved me out into the street, like a drunk being bounced from a bar. My knee went down on the ground, and I caught my fall with my hand. Before he slammed the door shut again, the guy waved the knife one more time and said, "Stupid American! You pay the lady. You not get laid."

I walked away quickly in the direction of the well-lit corner from which we had come. Cars were passing, and bars were still open. My heart was pounding. There was a spot of blood on my pant leg where it was torn, and the palm of my hand burned where it was scraped, but I wasn't hurt badly. I walked aimlessly, trying to drain off the tension while orienting myself to the Torre del Alminar, the minaret of the Mezquita. I knew if I found my way back to the mosque complex, from there I would be able to navigate my way back to our hotel.

As my fear shrank, my rage and humiliation grew. I'd been mugged. More than that I'd been duped. I can't say what shamed me more, the wiles of a pretty woman or the knife in a vulgar man's hand.

I'd like to say I've never thought about it again, but that isn't true. From time to time I think about that visit to Cordoba, and I feel uneasy all over again. I've never told anyone about my harsh words toward Mom when we visited the Mezquita, and I've never told about being lured into a trap by Isa and her thuggish friends. I've always known, though, that one day some evidence of them would pop back into sight when I least expect it. And this was the time. The day I found a postcard with Mom's written message, "I now know the meaning of AWE," it was like a message from the grave. There it was, tucked in with what Mom had left for me in a box with a note asking that, after she was gone, I dispose of the contents as I see fit.

Part II

The Seal on Old Stories Is Broken

Those who do not weep do not see.
—*Victor Hugo, Les Misérables*

Four

ROWLAND SLID A COPY of the story about Estelle under the door of Alethea's condo. He put a sticky note on it that said, "Let me know when you've had a chance to read this." Estelle was a neighbor who'd lived around the corner from where Rowland's family had lived on Woodward Street when he was a kid. She was his mom's friend. Children in the neighborhood played together, and Rowland knew Estelle's children better than he knew her. While most of the dads were strict, and none of them was easy-going, Estelle's husband was several degrees more severe than the rest of them. When he showed up, kids slinked away around a corner.

Rowland chuckled at the recollection of being a boy who'd creep away to avoid a cranky adult, but then it occurred to him that Estelle's husband had disappeared too. At first he was around, but about the time Estelle and her children moved out of their house on Woodward Street and into an apartment above a restaurant, he dropped out of the picture. Estelle still visited with Rowland's mom, and Rowland knew her children from school, but her husband was gone.

Kids don't consider what it means that parents have friends. Rowland remembered moms and dads having drinks on each other's porches or occasionally having dinner together at each other's houses. So what? It wasn't unusual, but it wasn't interesting either. Rowland saw dads leave for work in the morning. His dad did that too. In the afternoon he saw the same cars come back down the street again. The dads were home from work, and it was dinnertime. A young boy playing in the backyards or riding around the neighborhood on his bike didn't concern himself with what grown-ups were busy with all day. Leaving for and returning from work, mowing lawns and washing cars, grilling in the back yard, relaxing in their easy chairs, watching baseball on TV, or reading the newspaper on the porch. That's what dads did, and that's as far as Rowland's interest in them went.

Moms were different. They were around more. Rowland could recognize their voices on the phone, and he could identify their laughs when he heard their voices across the backyard fence. He knew who was generous with cookies and who was strict with manners. He knew in which houses there were babies sleeping in the afternoon and where you had to take your shoes off before coming in. As far as the boy on his bike was concerned, adults had always been adults, and it never crossed his mind that once upon a time they too had been as young as he was.

Why had his mom kept a story about Estelle and put it in the carton of papers she left for Rowland? Had she intended it for him? Was there something she didn't want him to forget? Or had she only wanted to keep it for herself a little longer? There are always loose ends, and his mother had tied up more loose ends than most. Was this story of Estelle one of those loose ends that had slipped by her? Had death caught up with his mom before she finished her final house cleaning?

This little story tucked in between pages of his mother's journal was as good a starting place as any for a conversation with Alethea. It was a step removed from his mother, and Alethea wouldn't have to fret about whether Rowland was protecting his mother's reputation. Furthermore, Rowland had his own reasons for being curious about Estelle. Her family had left sharp burrs in his memory.

Reading the story of a girl who grew up in England, married an American soldier, and eventually moved to a suburb of Chicago stretched Rowland's imagination. It took effort to cobble that story together with his own memories of Estelle, a grown woman who was one of the mothers in their neighborhood and his mom's good friend. There were huge gaps in his memory of Estelle and her family, and, scattered through the same story that had gaps, there were memories so shameful they made Rowland squirm.

❖ ESTELLE'S STORY ❖

Estelle's father was a workingman who ended each day at the pub. Sometimes he stayed until closing time, and other nights he left when the barkeep told him he'd had enough. Estelle was always in bed before her father got home, tucked in tight, with lights out, but she didn't sleep. Instead she lay awake, listening for the front door, for the squeak of her father's footsteps on the treads. As soon as she heard him she turned to face the wall and pulled her nightgown down as far as possible, wrapping it tight around her legs. Even in summer she wore flannel.

Sometimes Estelle heard the door of her room open and footsteps come to the side of her bed. She felt the blankets pull back and cool air against her neck and feet. She heard him breathing heavily, while she tried to breathe lightly as if she were not there. Finally she felt the blankets fall back over her again, heard the five steps to the door, and then the click of it closing. Only then could she let herself breathe normally again.

Years later, after Estelle and her husband, JR, moved in around the corner from where Maggie and Ross lived on Woodward Street, Estelle told Maggie about those nights. She hadn't meant to tell anyone ever, but with years and an ocean between her and that narrow little bed on the second floor of her parents' house, it didn't seem necessary to keep the secret anymore, and Maggie listened.

The nighttime visits began when Estelle had barely started school, although there was a brief reprieve the summer her father went to Manchester to work in a factory. Estelle was glad he was away. When he returned he brought a doll with long golden curls and eyes that opened and closed. "It's a beauty," he said, "but not as pretty as my little beauty." His words made Estelle feel strange.

Estelle knew she was pretty because people complimented her mother about Estelle's curls and striking blue eyes. Her mother was pretty too. Mr. Riggins, the handyman who came by one afternoon to repair a light in the parlor, chatted as he worked. "In all the years this town never produced another one like your Mum. At school she turned every head. The girls in envy and the boys wishing they could have a dance with her."

Estelle complained to her mother about her father's night visits, but her mother brushed it away with the excuse that he was only checking to see if Estelle was covered and warm. That was the excuse in winter. In summer the excuse was that he was checking to see if the window was open and the room had air. "Don't bring it up with him," her mother cautioned. "He doesn't like to be questioned."

Estelle could tell that her mother said nothing to her father because his nighttime visits continued. When Estelle was old enough to go next door to Lucy's house in the evening to watch television, she was tempted to complain to Lucy or to tell Lucy's mother. She envied them because there was no one to be afraid of at their house. Lucy's dad didn't live with them.

Estelle complained again to her mother after her Uncle Brian visited. At half past nine her father announced the men were going to the pub. On the way out he ordered Estelle not to stay up late because she needed her beauty rest. As he spoke he turned to his brother and said, "She's a dazzler, don't you think? I've got to make sure she doesn't spoil those looks." Estelle's skin crawled when her father talked that way. It was a certain tone of voice similar to the one he used when he gave her advice about not letting boys get fresh with her. After the door closed and she knew her dad and uncle were gone, Estelle pleaded with her mother, "I need you to tell him. I don't want him to come into my room anymore. Please, Mum, do something."

"In a few years you'll be old enough to be out on your own," her mother said. "Don't set him off. It won't turn out well." There was a mix of impatience and fear in her mother's voice, but Estelle wasn't sure whether the frustration was with her father or with her for complaining.

Estelle was desperate, and when her brother Randolph came home for his school vacation she begged him to help her. He was three years older than Estelle, sturdy and strong, and loyal to his little sister. She'd felt safer when Randolph was still living at home, before he went to live at school, and she was relieved when he returned for the summer break, but she knew he would be gone again when the vacation was over.

Randolph promised to watch out for her. She didn't know precisely what he meant by that, but hearing him say it already felt better. The next time their father went down the hall toward Estelle's room, Randolph was ready. He stepped into the hall, watched through the small gap of Estelle's door, long enough to give their dad time to step up to the side of Estelle's bed, long enough to pull back the covers, long enough to be caught red-handed. That's when Randolph went after his father with a cricket bat.

Randolph didn't strike his father on the head because he knew a cricket bat could be a lethal weapon. Instead he caught him flat across the back and knocked the wind out of him. As his father bent over gasping, Randolph saw the open zipper. This time he aimed for his head, and this time his father put up a hand to protect himself, but Randolph caught the guilty hand square with the edge of the bat.

In the days that followed their father sat sunken into his chair in the lounge room. When his children passed through the room, he gazed down at his cast arm, sometimes poking at it with his other hand, as if he were checking the details of the gauze and plaster. Randolph glared at him, but Estelle tried not to look in her father's direction. Their mother bustled about as if nothing had happened, as if the dark and silent man occupying the chair in the corner were only an apparition.

WHEN IT WAS TIME for Randolph to return to school, Estelle and Randolph packed their belongings and took the train to Randolph's student flat near Bristol. No one asked why Randolph's sister was staying with him in his small room. One of his roommates had kept his sister for a few weeks after she went off with her boyfriend on Guy Fawkes Night and didn't come home until afternoon the next day. Her father bruised up her face to teach her what he thought of girls with bad reputations. "I'll not have a slag in my house," he said. "Get out and don't come back." She found refuge with her brother in his student quarters, and his roommates asked no questions. This time it was Estelle's sanctuary.

With Randolph and Estelle gone, their mother took work as a housekeeper at the funeral parlor. Each week she wrote them a letter that arrived on Tuesday in a neat envelope with tidy handwriting. Estelle noticed that her mother's return address was from Delores St. George and not Mrs. Peyton St. George, the way her mother used to write it on letters. Estelle imagined her mother writing at the dining table in the evening when her father was at the pub. She didn't want to think that her father was there when her mother was writing. She tried not to think about her father at all.

The letters reported local news. Mrs. Willis fell and broke a hip. Loretta Sims is engaged, and the wedding will be in summer. There was a car crash at the roundabout. Tucked inside the letter was a bit of spending money with an apology for not being able to send more, and as always, Estelle's mother mentioned how much she liked her work at the funeral parlor.

The letters had motherly advice for each child. For Estelle it was encouragement to find a job and warnings about not spending money carelessly. The advice for Randolph sounded like quotes from *A Manual for Manliness*. "Breakfast is the foundation meal of the day," her mother reminded Randolph in one letter. "The condition of a man's shoes is a statement of his character," she wrote in another. Randolph didn't write to their mother, and Estelle was glad to write for both of them.

When Estelle found her mother's letter in the post box she had a wave of homesickness, although it wasn't that she wanted to be home. She missed the comforts of Sunday dinner, or feeling tended to on laundry day when she found her clothes washed, ironed, and neatly folded on the chair in her bedroom. Away from home in a place where she didn't fit, no one noticed when she was hungry, and Estelle washed out her own laundry in the lavatory sink of Randolph's apartment.

By the time Estelle reached the end of her mother's letters, by the time she had read the news of the neighborhood and noticed the glaring absence of any news about her father, Estelle knew she didn't have a home anymore. A mother? Yes. A home? No. That was the feeling that lasted until she saw another letter in the box the following Tuesday.

Estelle found a job in a tearoom. She began work early enough to serve "elevenses" and stayed through the busy hours for late afternoon tea. Patrons liked Estelle. Now and then from over her shoulder she'd hear someone at a table comment, "She's a lovely young lady, isn't she? Such good manners." She tried to remember the regular customer's names, and some of them remembered hers. That felt good.

With the modest pay from the tearoom Estelle was able to move into Mrs. Gladstone's rooming house. Two other girls also had rooms there, but their company was no substitute for the safe feeling she'd had at night when she slept on Randolph's student cot, and he took a bedroll on the floor. The only place for him to put it was in front of the door, and during the night when Estelle woke up and saw Randolph there, she felt protected. At Mrs. Gladstone's boarding house Estelle was on her own.

Walking to the tearoom, Estelle met JR. Only later would she learn that his full name was John Robert, but he had been called JR from the time he was a little boy and still preferred his nickname. He took breakfast and coffee at the sandwich shop that Estelle passed on her way to work, and when the weather was good he sat at a table outdoors. JR was clean-cut and handsome, and as she walked by he smiled and greeted her. The first time this happened she wondered if he was a school pal of Randolph's, but she didn't greet him back because she didn't know him. When Estelle mentioned the stranger to the other girls at work, they guessed he was an American employed by a company connected to the defense program at Fairford. They had a reputation for saying "hi" to girls who passed by, whether they knew them or not.

Estelle walked past JR a half dozen times before he got up from the table and fell in stride beside her. "Thought I'd walk with you," he said. That's how Estelle met JR, and it wasn't long before he told her that from the first time he saw her he knew she was a girl for him. It didn't seem to concern him that he knew nothing about her, and she wondered how he could be so sure.

Estelle had been trained to do as she was told, so when JR told her he was picking her up to go to the cinema, she made sure she was ready on time. And when he told her that some day she'd be going to America with him, she didn't say "no" or that she needed time to think it over. She said nothing, and JR went right on talking as if with her silence she had agreed.

Estelle went back home to visit her mother twice. The first time was when her mother had surgery on the veins in her leg. She was homebound and needed to keep her leg elevated. Estelle stayed with Lucy, who still lived next door, but during the day while Estelle's father was at work she visited with her mother and tidied up around the house. They drank tea, and her mother entertained with stories about the funeral home.

Estelle's mother prepared clothes for dead people, whom she called "the deceased" and whose relatives she called "the loved ones." When families brought garments that were too large she pinned them together in the back to make a good fit. If they were too small, she slit the fabric at exactly the right places in the back so they didn't pull across the front. The families never knew the difference. "If it's the last glimpse the loved ones are ever going to get, you want the deceased looking proper," Estelle's mother explained. "You don't want anyone to remember that there was a smudge on the shirt and a button missing, or that the garment was ill-fitting."

Mr. Tollman, the funeral director, trained Estelle's mother to style the women's hair after the body was prepared. She described the "preparation room" as if it were a holy place into which only the initiated were admitted. The sign on the door said "Staff Only," and the picture over her workstation said, "We Create Eternal Memories." It was a poster Mr. Tollman brought home from a convention for morticians. To Estelle her mother's work seemed ghoulish, but it was obvious her mother was proud that she'd found a niche where she was appreciated.

Estelle did not see her father until the second visit. On a Monday afternoon at the beginning of an ordinary week, Estelle was bringing orders out to tables at the tearoom and chatting with her favorite guests. Her boss came out of the office at the back and instructed her to come with him. Judging by the pinched look on his face, Estelle thought she was about to be fired and wondered what she'd done wrong.

In the office the boss handed the phone receiver to Estelle, and coming through it she heard her mother's voice. Her father was in hospital; he'd had a heart attack. Estelle was barely off the phone when Randolph came into the shop. Their mother had called him first to let him know that he and Estelle should come as soon as possible. When Estelle called JR to tell him she would be away, he offered to drive Randolph and Estelle.

At the hospital Randolph and Estelle were greeted by their mother and the news that their father had passed away. Her mother seemed shaken, but not sad. Estelle said the only thing she knew to say, which was "Oh, Mum, I'm so sorry." Randolph said nothing. He took Estelle in his arms and held her for an unusually long time, surrounding her as if he had rescued her from a sinking ship and freezing waters. JR stood by and watched. Later, in unkind moments, he was known to say, "It was like three icebergs bobbing in the sea. I've never seen a family with less feeling." That was not what Estelle remembered of that day. Held against Randolph's chest, she felt him shudder. He was crying the way men do, without tears or sound, because he had to be brave for his little sister.

The funeral was difficult as funerals always are. At the visitation, neighbors and coworkers stopped by and said the usual things. Grown men told Randolph, "Well lad, you're the man in the family now," as if they were authorized to assign him a new role. Estelle couldn't count the number of times she was told, "Having fine children like you and Randolph will be a great comfort to your mother."

Estelle peered at her father in the coffin. His broken hand with bones that didn't line up was the one on top. It had the brittle and discolored nails of a workingman. The left hand underneath, in which he held his cigarette, looked waxy where the undertaker had applied makeup to cover the stain. The patch of scaly skin on the side of his neck was not as red and irritated as usual. Estelle noticed the large vein that used to stand out on his forehead had gone flat. His lips were thin as if they had not smiled for a long time.

Estelle wondered about the perfectly laundered shirt. Had her mother prepared it at home or at the mortuary workshop? Her father's tie was new, but the suit was the one that had hung in the closet for as long as Estelle could remember. She wondered if it was slit or pinned in the back. She tried to guess if he had shoes on or socks. She remembered his purple feet with thick toenails and hoped they were covered. She knew he had a tattoo with an anchor on his bicep and tried to remember which one. She could ask Randolph if she really needed to know, but instead she turned away. She didn't want to imagine any more details, and she made it a point not to look at him again.

Estelle's mother was chipper, especially before and after visitors arrived, when she helped Mr. Tollman straighten the room and check the flowers. She was at home in the funeral parlor, moving around as if it were her own living room. During the visitation, Mr. Tollman busied himself, as funeral directors do, with small courtesies that allowed him to be there without interfering. Twice he came to Estelle's mother and asked, "Is there anything you're needing, Mrs. St. George?" The second time, Estelle saw Randolph bristle, and she heard him mutter under his breath, "Why doesn't that clown find something to do in the back room so he can stay out of our way?"

"Randolph," whispered Estelle, "don't be like that! It's rude. He's trying to be helpful."

"Too helpful, Essie."

"What do you mean?"

"He's buzzing around Mum like a fly hovering over dung."

"Randolph, you shouldn't say things like that. He means well."

"That depends on your definition of meaning well. It's a fact of life, Essie; once everyone figured out what a wretch Dad was, it was open season on Mum. She's too good to waste, and Mr. Tollman is going to make sure that doesn't happen."

Estelle noticed that some of the neighbors, who came to the visitation and said kind things to her mother, were women who'd been friends in the past. They faded away after her father's hand got broken and her mother went out to work. There was no news of them in her mother's letters. Did a woman in open season have friends?

Some visitors said they hadn't been aware her dad had heart trouble. When there was a pause between visitors, Randolph whispered, "I can't stand all this nonsense about Pop's heart trouble. The poor sap was drinking himself to death all along, and they're probably thinking it's lucky for Mum he finally keeled over."

The day after the funeral, Randolph and Estelle braved their way through a farewell with their mother, while JR waited at the curb in the car. Their mother pressed a box of sandwiches into Randolph's hands. "It'll save you expense on your way," she said. To Estelle she handed a baker's box tied up with string. "These are left from yesterday. They're your favorites. Empire biscuits and fruit slices, the ones made with currants."

As JR put the car in gear, their mother turned to walk into the house, then paused to watch as her children drove away. Estelle waved, and her mother waved back. What would happen to her mother now, she wondered, and she choked back tears because she was determined not to cry. Once they were out on the highway Estelle peeked into the box of goodies and realized that her mother's job no longer allowed her to call Estelle's favorite sweet treat "Fly's Cemetery." So much had changed.

At Mrs. Gladstone's house Randolph got out of the car with Estelle and told JR, "I'll see Essie in. I want to speak with Mrs. Gladstone." As the taillights of the car disappeared around the corner, they were still standing in front of the house, and Randolph suggested they walk. He apologized for the rude remarks he'd made about his mother, but he didn't apologize for what he'd said about their father. They walked on in silence for a while, and then like a bolt out of nowhere Randolph said, "Essie, I'm going to leave botany."

"Wait! What are you talking about? You're joking. You're good at science. I mean you *are* good at science, aren't you? Is there a problem at school?"

"I'm okay in science, but I want to study something else."

"Like what?"

"Something bigger. Philosophy maybe, or theology."

"Oh, no! Not a parson!" The thought of the mumbling vicar who'd done her father's burial made Estelle giggle. "I hope you're joking. You'd look odd in vestments." She preferred to think of Randolph in cricket flannels.

"I'm not joking. I'm serious, Essie. I don't know if I'm cut out to be clergy, but there's nothing wrong with that, just because Dad thought vicars were fools. I want to study. Deep things. I don't want to dabble in plant communities, or rare species, or hydrology. Leave that to someone else, someone who already has peace of mind. "

"Randolph, of course you don't have peace of mind. We just buried our father."

"I've been thinking about this for a while," he replied, "but this week has shown me that I need to make up my mind."

They walked on.

Finally Randolph asked, "What about you Essie? What's going to happen to you? You can't serve in a tearoom for the rest of your life."

"I know. I'll find my way."

"Essie, we need to stick together. We're all we have now."

"What about Mum? Do you think I should move home and live with her?" Estelle felt she ought to offer.

"No, Essie. Absolutely not."

"Don't you think she needs someone around?" Guilt was pushing Estelle. The words were coming from the same awkward place that people foraged for things to say at visitations in funeral parlors.

"Mum's relieved that Dad's gone, and we're not around. She can do what she wants now."

"What's that?" Estelle asked.

"She can live in a little apartment and capitalize on being a widow instead of a pathetic wife. She can have her job at the funeral parlor and carry on with Mr. Tollman."

"That's disgusting. Besides, how would you know? You're making that up." Her brother's confidence irritated Estelle. "That's the thing about you, Randolph. You think you have everything figured out."

"I told you the truth, and now you're mad."

"What if you're wrong? Why would Mum do that?"

"Mr. Tollman will take care of her. You're the one who two minutes ago was talking about going home to be with her, because she can't make it on her own. Why should she think she can make it on her own, if we don't think she can?"

"What about his wife?" Mrs. Tollman had a large mole on her cheek, and she always wore very large earrings, as if she could hide her mole by drawing attention away from it. She wasn't particularly attractive, but she was nice. "Why would Mrs. Tollman put up with that?"

"Mum's employment is a good cover-up all the way around," said Randolph. "Mrs. Tollman doesn't have to endure being left in a lurch, penniless, with kids and a load of shame in a neighborhood where people talk behind their hands. She doesn't have to worry when she's in the shops that she'll hear someone whispering about her, saying that what's happened to her is such a pity. Mum's established herself as an employee, fair and square. It's the perfect pretext, and Mrs. Tollman can still pretend that everything is plum. I suspect both Mrs. Tollman and Mum put up with the arrangement for the same reason."

"What reason?" Randolph couldn't mean sex. Estelle's mind flipped to Mr. Tollman. Bald with dry hands and pale eyes. It made her sick. She thought about Mrs. Tollman and her mother. She thought of them naked. On her mother's image, like on a woman posing on a velvet chaise lounge in a bordello, she painted a flirtatious smile. She wanted to wipe the image from her mind, but it wouldn't go away. "Really, what reason?" she asked Randolph again.

"The pension's good," said Randolph

"You think Mum does it for money? That's a lowdown thing to say about your own mother. And you're thinking of becoming a vicar?"

"She does it because she's weak. She needs a man to make her feel she's worth something." Randolph paused to let what he'd said sink in before he continued. "By the way, I'm a man too, you know, and vicars don't have to be blind. Our mother is attractive. When she was young she could turn heads, and now even with a few years on she's pretty. What about being truthful? Can we please agree on that?"

That was the night Randolph apologized for not stepping up sooner to protect Estelle from her father. He begged Estelle to forgive him. Said he should have known what his father was doing. Accused himself of being a coward. His dad had pushed him to "be a man," but it was the kind of man his dad admired and not the kind of man Randolph wanted to be. His father slipped girlie magazines under the door of Randolph's room. One night his father took him to the pub, and when they were walking home he wanted to buy the girl who loitered along the dark side of the train station. "You've got to start somewhere," his father told Randolph, "and this one's as good as any. She's been around the course a few times, so she'll know what to do. Just do what she tells you. It's time we make a man of you."

When Randolph refused, his father laughed at him derisively and accused him of being a coward. Not a real man. "You'd better start using that thing before it shrivels up and falls off," he said.

The insult gave Randolph a surge of courage, and he told his father the magazines and buying the girl were an insult to Estelle and his mother. He said his mother was a good woman, and his father should treat her better. That is what Randolph was saying as they took the short-cut through the croft next to the bakery, where his father grabbed him by his jacket and put him up against the wall. He raised his knee and pressed it into Randolph until he winced. "Don't you insult me," his father said. "Try that again and I'll turn you into a choir boy. What did I ever do to deserve a worthless nob like you?" That's the way Randolph recounted it to Estelle, but later when she thought about it she was sure her father's remark had been more vulgar than that.

Randolph knew his father was drunk. His face was red and he was unsteady, but he was strong. Randolph had always admired his father's strength, but it changed that day. In place of the longing for approval from this big and powerful man, Randolph carried a nugget of hate. It was like a knot of lead carried in his chest close to his heart, a knot that became molten when Randolph was unsure of himself. Sometimes he wished his father were dead. Even years later after his father was dead, Randolph sometimes played out in his imagination what would have happened if he'd landed the blow with the cricket bat to his father's head. He imagined the sound of a bat on a skull.

Estelle listened. Shocked. But Randolph wasn't done. "I want to go back to what I said before. It's been ugly, but we've got each other, and we need to stick together."

"I know, you're right," said Estelle.

"You can count on me. You know that, don't you?" Randolph wanted her to answer.

"I do," said Estelle. "I wish I could say that you can count on me."

"I do count on you, Essie."

"Oh, for sure." She swallowed hard. "For what? What can you count on me for, Randolph? You don't have to say that so I won't feel bad."

"I count on you to keep me true." Randolph's voice shifted. It was tense and hoarse. "I count on you to set me straight if I ever start to be like that man. If I become like him, I hope someone will put me out of my misery."

"You'll never be like him." It hurt Estelle that Randolph would think it.

"I've got a dark side, Essie. After all those people came to the visitation at the funeral and said that false stuff about Dad, I was so angry I thought of going to the cemetery during the night and pissing in the hole before they put him in it. I feel no sympathy for him at all, but I feel bad about myself for feeling that way."

"But you didn't. You didn't piss in his grave, did you? Tell me you didn't, Randolph!"

"No I didn't. I thought of it, and I wanted to, but I didn't have the courage. That's not much virtue, is it? So what's the difference if I thought it or I did it?"

Estelle didn't answer. She didn't feel entirely innocent herself. She'd already wondered how normal people feel when their fathers die. Her relief to be rid of him had a prickly shell of guilt around it. It had occurred to her already that when she married she would shed her father's name. She would be glad to be rid of it, and she felt a wave of pity for Randolph who was stuck with it. For the rest of the way back to Mrs. Gladstone's house they said little. Just before Estelle went inside, Randolph said, "You know now, don't you, why we have to stick together. We can't let him win."

Things returned to normal. Almost normal. Estelle wrote letters to her Mum and read the ones that arrived on Tuesday. Most Tuesday evenings Randolph came by to read the letter while they sat together in Mrs. Gladstone's parlor. After the letter they went out for a walk to have some privacy, to get away from Mrs. Gladstone, who listened from the other room. Mrs. Gladstone didn't allow the girls to entertain men in their rooms, not even brothers.

Sometimes Randolph told Estelle about his new studies, and he told her about Lillian, the girl he was dating. When he talked about Lillian, his normally serious face broke into a smile. She was sweet and kind. Always saw the best in him. Once he said that Lillian reminded him of Estelle, and then apologized because he thought saying that about his own sister was daft. Estelle thought it was dear.

On Fridays Estelle went out to the cinema with JR. Sunday afternoons they took a blanket and lounged in the park by the river, where they had a picnic of sandwiches Estelle brought and tea from a thermos. JR was not as available as he'd been when first they met, but Estelle made sure she was available whenever JR was. The spending money she could scrabble together she spent on clothes, because JR criticized the way she dressed. He liked escorting a woman other men glanced at admiringly, but if Estelle happened to notice that a handsome man was looking her way, JR told her to stop acting like a tart.

One evening on the way home from the cinema, instead of dropping her at Mrs. Gladstone's house, JR drove to his apartment. He didn't ask. He just turned to the left instead of the right at the High Road. That was the first step. The next step was after a visit at JR's apartment, when Estelle said it was getting late and she should be getting back to Mrs. Gladstone's house. JR said he would drop her off in the morning because he didn't like getting up again after he was settled in. He was annoyed that Estelle cared about what Mrs. Gladstone might think of her. He told her he didn't give a damn about fussy Mrs. Gladstone, and Estelle could walk home if she was going to let that batty old woman run her life.

After they'd been seeing each other for a year, JR didn't bother taking Estelle to the cinema anymore, and most Sundays he played touch football with the other Americans he knew from the base. Some evenings on his way home from work, after he'd stopped off at the pub for a few beers, he'd swing by to pick Estelle up "for a visit." But he didn't drive her home anymore, and Estelle got used to walking home through the empty streets at night.

Finally Estelle wound up the courage to talk to Randolph about JR. "You know I can't go after him with my cricket bat," Randolph told her. "You're going to have to take care of this yourself."

"I know I should, but it's so hard," said Estelle.

"You're too good for him. There's no use trying to work it out because he won't change. I know men like him. They are what they are. Whatever he agrees to now, it won't stick. He'll do whatever he wants without any consideration for you. It sounds like he's doing that already, and you deserve better. Tell him goodbye."

Estelle knew Randolph was right, and she decided to tell JR it was over. The problem was when to tell him. There was no right time. JR had bought her a dress for the Christmas dance at the base. He spent a lot for the right one because he wanted her looking good. After the dance she decided to wait a few more weeks because it was Christmas, and at New Year's Lillian and Randolph were celebrating their engagement. Lillian's parents were planning a party, and it seemed inconsiderate to add a dark note to Randolph and Lillian's happiness.

Then it was too late. JR was furious, and he accused Estelle of having a baby to trap him. They had a simple ceremony in the registry office, before which JR made it clear he was going through with it only so he could collect dependent's allowance. A baby meant he'd have to find family housing because he couldn't expect his roommate to put up with "a squalling kid."

In early summer Randolph and Lillian had a beautiful wedding at a country estate. Estelle realized that even if she hadn't lost out on being the bride at her own wedding by getting pregnant, she could never have had a wedding like Lillian's anyway. Some people have better luck than others, and it starts out that way from the beginning. Estelle didn't have a family like Lillian's. She'd never catch up. That's just the way it was.

By autumn Michelle was born. In November JR announced that his assignment in England would finish in March, and his company was moving him back to Chicago. Estelle had known this would happen sooner or later, but the timing was off. She wanted to stay for Randolph's ordination at Easter. She also played with the idea that, after he was ordained, Randolph could officiate at Michelle's christening. Timidly she brought this up to JR, but he wouldn't have it. He didn't see any reason to hang around so that they could watch Randolph "put on the dog."

"What does that mean?" Estelle asked JR. "What does it have to do with a dog?" It was an American expression she'd not heard before.

"It means your brother's an ostentatious toad. It'll be good to put an ocean between you and him. The last thing I need is for you to start thinking you're like his snobby wife. If Randolph St. George wants to let a woman lead him around by the nose, that's his business, but it's not happening at my house. And what's the point of having him baptize Michelle? It's superstition. If having her baptized will make you feel better, take her to the local vicar and get some water sprinkled on her, but don't make a big deal of it. Keep Randolph out of it."

On a cloudy day before Easter, JR, Estelle, and baby Michelle boarded a flight at Heathrow and flew to Chicago. They moved into a furnished apartment, and Estelle began a new life in America. From the start, JR was immersed in work, and Estelle passed her days pushing Michelle's stroller through the neighborhood of an unfamiliar city. In the afternoon Michelle napped, and Estelle busied herself preparing a dinner so it would be on the table when JR returned from work. As soon as they could pull together funds for a house, they began scouring the real estate ads for the right place in a good neighborhood. As luck would have it, the one they found was next door to where Maggie and Ross lived on Woodward Street.

❖

THE FIRST TIME ROWLAND read through Estelle's story, he wondered why his mother wrote it, and even more he wondered why she kept it. Was his mother trying to preserve a memory, or was she proud of the fact that she had written something? He understood if she didn't have the heart to throw away writing over which she'd labored. Rowland had a whole file drawer of useless writing he couldn't bear to toss. Every time he pulled open the drawer and thought of thinning it out, something stopped him. Destroying your own words is harsh. He assumed that's why his mother kept the story about Estelle.

A day after Rowland left the story about Estelle at the door of Alethea's condo there was a message from her on his phone. "Shall we meet to discuss the story? Tomorrow at 2:00 for tea works well for me. Unless I hear otherwise, I'll expect you."

Five

For his visit with Alethea, Rowland prepped like he was interviewing for a job. In the morning after showering, he shaved and put some stuff in his hair to tame it. Just before heading up to Alethea's apartment he went down the street to the Good Foods Market to find something in the floral section. He chose carefully. The cactus planter was too prickly, and the bright shades of Gerbera daisies were for sick rooms. He wanted something refined. He bought African Violets in a clay pot.

Alethea opened the door to her condo, and Rowland followed her through the entryway into the living room where she offered him coffee or tea. He declined. They moved on to her dining room table where he put down the papers he'd brought with him. It was clear that Alethea planned to work; the copy of the story he'd sent ahead was on the table, and he could see she'd read it. Tabs with arrows, like ones used for documents needing signatures, marked the pages. The margin on the first page had carefully penciled notes, which Rowland tried to read from across the table, but Alethea's handwriting was very fine, and he couldn't read it upside down.

"Well, what do you think?" Rowland asked when they both were seated.

"Let's begin with you," Alethea said. "What kind of feedback do you want from me?"

Rowland cleared his throat, sat back in his chair, and spun his pen between his thumb and forefinger, the way he often did in meetings when he was preparing to say something he thought deserved to be heard. "I've been thinking about Mom's journals in general. Why do people bother to write about themselves? They don't want to be forgotten. In a post-idea age, people read fewer books because ideas come and go so quickly, but they still like to imagine the story of their own life taking a permanent form. That's why they buy those books with blank pages."

Alethea tipped her head. Her nod didn't suggest agreement, but it did indicate she was listening. "Fortunately for us your mother's journal pages aren't blank," Alethea said, "and she didn't try to bind them into a book. Quite the contrary. She unbound them and left a carton of pages filled with words that meant something to her. Isn't that the point of reading her diary? It doesn't make sense to start with what they mean to you. Put your ego aside, Row! Start with a story that she valued enough to keep for herself to the very end."

Rowland was startled at the edge in Alethea's voice. He knew she could be direct, but this seemed surprisingly confrontational. He shifted obviously in his chair, as if he were inserting a paragraph break. "Back to the story about Estelle then," he said. He didn't like being instructed by Alethea. He was an expert in these things, a professor of literature, and he wanted to regain the advantage. "The first step is looking for an implied reader? Who did Mom think would read this story?"

Alethea was still listening. "That takes some conjecture."

"I would call her writing unconsidered," Rowland explained. "She has something she wants to record, but it has no style. No technique or craft." As he spoke Rowland nodded to indicate that he agreed with himself. "Mom's writing lacks polish. It's like a grocery list, something she puts on paper only for herself. There is nothing to suggest an ongoing conversation with a reader or any effort to engage cultural themes. That's what I mean by amateurish. I don't need to belabor this, do I?" Rowland asked because he noticed that Alethea wasn't nodding with him anymore.

Alethea closed her eyes. "I know the difference between literature and personal diaries," she said. "I'm a librarian. We put literary journals out on the shelves with other books, and we store folk diaries in the archives with other odds and ends that may never be looked at again."

Alethea looked down at her right hand. She made an odd gesture. She closed her fist very tight and rubbed her thumb very firmly against the side of her forefinger. Rowland wondered why she did this. Was this an old woman's habit that helped her concentrate? He cleared his throat again. He wanted Alethea to know he was earnest. That he was making a fresh start. "Let's begin with the story we've both been reading." He tried not to be patronizing when he smiled, and he wrinkled his brow a little to indicate that he was serious about the criticism coming next. "My other impression: this was Mom's try at writing short story." Rowland dropped the article to indicate he was commenting on genre. He was analyzing the way a professor of literature might when assessing the written work of his students. Critical but not cruel.

Alethea nodded and smiled. "It's been a long time since I read this story. It brings to mind things I haven't thought about in years."

"Do you think Mom intended to send her manuscript to *Ladies Home Journal* or *Women's Day*?" Rowland asked. "Readers could do that back then, you know."

"Yes, I know," Alethea responded.

"There was a time when Mom wasn't working at the library anymore. She had too many little kids, including me." Rowland punctuated his statement with a chuckle that was barely more than a little huff. "Maybe she flirted with becoming a writer. I don't like to think of Mom first dreaming of becoming a writer and then being thwarted. What do you think?"

Alethea caught Rowland's gaze, but she didn't hurry to answer. "I don't like to think of my dear friend Maggie that way either."

Rowland wanted to nail down the point he was making. "Why didn't Mom write her own story? I advise students to begin with the story they know best, which is their own." He said this with the confident voice of a professor who already knew the answer. "She couldn't have known all those details of Estelle's childhood. Her writing pushes narrative limits. You see, that's the lack of craft I'm talking about. It's clumsy."

"You're assuming it was Maggie telling this story. You think it's your mother's writing." Alethea spoke in a level voice. "How carefully did you read it? Do you think the writer intended to hand it to a reader who would scrutinize it with a cold eye?"

Rowland knew this was a poke at him. Momentarily he felt like a car running out of gas. Lurching forward and slowing down at the same time. Mentally he scrambled. *The story is packed in the box with other journal pages. I remember Mom tapping away on the old Underwood typewriter we had in the library on Woodward Street. She bundled up these pages and put them in file folders around which she put ribbons and rubber bands to hold them together. Why is Alethea so defensive? What have I said to offend her? I'm a professor of literary studies. We make comments about texts.* Mentally Rowland was trying to realign something that had slipped off track. Struggling to come up with a good response to Alethea's questions, he felt a flood of embarrassment, and then it dawned on him that he'd made a fool of himself. He'd not committed an offense against his dead mother; he'd insulted Alethea. He'd navigated his way up the proverbial shit creek.

"This isn't Mom's story? Is that what you're saying?" he asked weakly.

"Let's start again from the beginning," said Alethea. "Who wrote this story? Why did your mother keep it?"

Rowland could feel sweat under his collar. He flashed back to the first day they'd visited when he made the awkward comment about being insufferable. He put his pen down on the table. "Game point. You win. I give up."

Alethea sat back in her chair. "Too much drama," she said. "So you guessed wrong about this story. You jumped to a conclusion and made a mistake. Why do you try so hard to be an expert? These are just papers your mother left behind in a carton in her closet. We aren't doing research."

"Why do you keep inviting me if you think I'm insufferable?" Rowland's voice was tight.

"You, your sisters and Will, are children of my friend Maggie. You matter to me for her sake, and now that you're adults I'm interested in knowing what has become of you. I don't have children of my own; I don't have nieces and nephews, which makes my friends' children important to me. But, Row, do you have to make it so complicated?"

Rowland stifled the urge to say, "I'm sorry." He didn't want to be ingratiating.

Alethea went on. "You don't have to be a professor with me. I knew you when you were a boy. You were playful, goofy, sometimes unpredictable, but a real treasure. Who *are* you now? For heavens sake, just be real with me, Rowland."

"Can we wind the clock back a few minutes?" Rowland asked. "Can we go back to where we started this conversation?"

"Let's try," said Alethea. "Let's begin with why I wrote this story about Estelle. That's the first bit of useful information. I took an evening class called 'Writing Your Own Story.' I wrote my own story for the instructor and the other students. Our second assignment was to write about someone else. That was harder. I knew Estelle well, but there were so many details from her childhood that I didn't have. Her fiftieth birthday was coming up, and I decided to give her the story as a gift. She knew I was working on it, and once I began writing we talked a lot. She wanted a story she could leave with her children someday. No idealizing. Do you have any idea how much courage that took on her part?"

"So you were Estelle's amanuensis?"

Alethea shook her head. "No. Definitely not. I was her friend writing her story for her birthday."

"Did she like it?"

"I think she did. I think she found comfort in being known."

"Did you write my mom's story for her fiftieth?"

"No . . . no . . . no!" said Alethea. "It was around that time your brother Steven died. Someone told your parents that Steven was cooking drugs, and when they figured out what that meant, they considered turning him in to the police, but they couldn't do it. He was their boy. When he died, it turned their world upside down. Your Mom was heart-broken. We spent time together doing ordinary things. Gardening. Canning. She wanted to take up knitting, and we shopped for wool. I still have some of it. We focused on things that would take us away from agony, not deeper into it. Writing her story would have been cruel."

Both Alethea and Rowland tried to get their conversation on track, but there was too much debris. The space between them was cluttered with misunderstandings. Alethea looked at the grown man sitting across the table from her, and she tried to merge that image with her memories of little Row playing with his Lincoln Logs under the library table on Woodward Street. What had time done to that boy? She thought about Estelle too, and it hurt her that Rowland had not allowed the tragedy of Estelle's life to touch him. He'd viewed it from behind the protective shield of professorial pretense, like a scientist in protective gear putting toxic stuff into test tubes.

"Did you ever hear Edith Piaf sing 'Non Je Ne Regrette,' that tragic song about her life?" Alethea hummed the first line to jog Rowland's memory.

"I have," said Rowland, " but I like Frank Sinatra singing 'I did it my way' better. I like his voice. Hers is too tinny for my taste. Anyway, your point is? Let me guess. If you don't let the past go, it'll beat you up. Is that what you're getting at?"

His comment brought Alethea back to a day when she was with Estelle and Maggie, having tea at Maggie's house on Woodward Street. She couldn't remember if it was before or after she had written the story about Estelle, but it was close to that time. Maggie had a new recording of Edith Piaf, and she put it on. "Listen to this," she said, and the three of them sat in silence and listened to it together.

When the music finished Estelle said, "I could never move past my regrets that way. There's too much." Estelle began to cry.

Maggie was tearful too. "Regrets or no regrets, we're here for each other," she said and moved her own chair beside Estelle's. "We've all got regrets."

"Why would anybody sing a lie?" Estelle asked, and her voice turned angry. "Listen to her. She doesn't sound satisfied with her life. She sounds desperate. It's like a confession. She can't face the fact that the greatest regrets hang around forever. That's sad enough, but why would she make a public show of it?"

There was no way Alethea could explain this to Rowland, and she couldn't get past it either. Turning back to the story about

Estelle and treating it like a school assignment was more than she could stomach. "Well, that's it then," she said. "You prefer Frank Sinatra." She fixed her eye on the table, and Rowland could tell their visit was over.

When Rowland disappeared through the door and Alethea heard the familiar click of the latch, she breathed a sigh of relief. She closed her eyes and shook her head the way one might about a child's misbehavior, but in her heart she was not feeling generous with Rowland.

"What's happened to him?" she asked herself, as she walked back to the table and gathered up her papers.

As ROWLAND WALKED DOWN the corridor from Alethea's condo, he was stuffed with humble pie. In the elevator he muttered to himself, beating himself up. *I can't believe I did that. Good thing Mom doesn't know. Geez, I hope she doesn't know. She'd be embarrassed.* In the days that followed, Rowland immersed himself in the pages of his mother's journals, and he wondered what was written on the missing pages. Had she written about Steven? About his dad? Had she destroyed pages on which she'd written about him? Some entries were brief, and in many cases he couldn't place them on a timeline. He needed Alethea to fill in the story, so he emailed her.

> Hello Alethea,
>
> I'm embarrassed about my bad behavior. Will you give me another chance? I need help with Mom's journals.
>
> Warm regards,
> Rowland

> Hello Row,
>
> Sunday at 2:00? Send anything you want me to read in advance.
>
> Yours truly,
> Alethea

Six

As ROWLAND AND ALETHEA plodded their way through Maggie's journals, the tension between them showed when Alethea's index finger bobbled as she spoke and her tone of voice turned schoolmarmish. She might have been embarrassed if she'd seen a video of herself. She couldn't bear having her dear friend made over into an entirely new character by a brash young professor who felt entitled to treat memories like a manuscript in need of editing.

Rowland was courteous, but deep down he thought Alethea's view of people and the way she told stories about them was so . . . not modern. He tried to stifle an edge of sarcasm in his voice, but his sense of superiority crept out from time to time in the form of a subtle, dismissive chuckle. If he had been on campus discussing student papers with his colleagues, he might have used the four-letter word that was de rigueur among smart people. He'd dismiss Alethea's views as blankety-blank simple-minded.

Alethea didn't care that Rowland was an expert. She wanted him to be loyal to his mother. Rowland smirked when Alethea said that. "Let's begin," he said, "with the simple fact that we have random pages from a diary that belongs to neither of us. Actually all we have is text, left by an author who is no longer accessible." Rowland said this with surety, and Alethea thought he was pompous, but she said nothing.

Beneath the artifice with which Rowland discussed the content of Maggie's journals, he was hiding his real interest in her writing. The stories were about him, at least about his family, and Rowland was deeply interested in himself. He wasn't ready to admit that notes written by his mother could teach him anything significant about life, but Rowland knew the feeling of emptiness, and that feeling was stirred when he read what his mother had written. Posturing as an expert with an unbiased curiosity about texts made him less vulnerable.

Because Rowland was well educated, he was as confused about life as he was about texts. He was beleaguered. That was a word he used in reference to himself in other contexts. He knew the etymology of the word; it referred to a city under siege. Numerous times he used the word over drinks with a friend when he was bemoaning his life. "With all the work I have to finish by the end of the semester I'm absolutely beleaguered," he'd said one evening with scotch in his hand and his elbows up on the bar. That was the same evening on which he'd said, "I need to set my work aside now and then to find balance in my life." He liked the poetry of "beleaguered" when he used it as a faux expression of his own importance. When Rowland left the bar to go home, or when he woke up the next morning with someone he barely knew beside him in his bed, he was still as beleaguered as before. Having the right word for describing his predicament didn't free him from it.

Maggie's notebooks came to Rowland when he was upside down, the way the mortgage on a house is upside down when you owe more on it than you can sell it for, but you can't afford to live in it anymore, either. Flawed choices were catching up with Rowland, and he was looking for a way out of trouble that wouldn't cost him too dearly. He was depressed.

Someone looking at Rowland from the outside might not have seen how troubled he was. He was an ordinary guy, physically fit, with a profession, and nice kids. On the campus where he worked, there were plenty of other people around who, like Rowland, were divorced and having midlife crises. It wasn't unusual. In Rowland's case, however, there were additional complications. The reason he couldn't figure himself out was *definitely not* that he hadn't given it enough thought, read enough self-help books, or done enough therapy. On the contrary, Rowland had read too many books and thought about too many alternatives. He was swamped.

When Rowland was feeling most beleaguered, or upside-down, or swamped, he sometimes caught himself musing about his mother. On one occasion when he caught himself thinking about her, he questioned if it was nostalgia or depression. He looked up the terms on the Internet, and he followed a link to a site that described complicated grief reactions. The symptoms listed included depression and preoccupation with bygone events. It didn't help him much. He didn't like thinking of himself either as mentally ill or as stuck in the past.

Rowland thought back to the time before his divorce when he felt distant from his own family and in short supply of friends. That's when the word "lonely" played on the edge of his consciousness. What he was searching for was the opposite of that word. He'd asked his mother how she found the friends she called her sisters. That's what Maggie called her friends. Estelle, Lorraine, and Alethea were like family to her. "We were just lucky," Maggie said, but that answer didn't satisfy Rowland. He wanted more. What's the magic? What's the glue? Rowland couldn't get a purchase on the metaphor, but he knew what he was looking for; he wanted real friends who'd stick by him the way his mother's friends stuck by her.

Nothing about their childhoods indicated that the special "sisterhood" of his mother's friends was written in the stars. Their origins were like millions of others, ordinary girls who grew up in ordinary families, all of which were dinged and dented in all the ordinary ways. In the beginning, the way the four "sisters" found each other was pure accident, but by the time they were old, they had a match made in heaven.

Smart-assed Rowland called his mother's circle of friends "lucky elective tribalism." That is how he described it when he talked on the phone to his brother Will. Maggie and her friends just happened on to each other, and by sheer random circumstances they found some useful emotional capital in what the others had to offer. Rowland would not have dared to describe it that way to Alethea. She would've found it obnoxious. Maggie would have too. And so would Estelle and Lorraine. They didn't think it was luck. They thought it was something far more precious than that.

Snooping through his mother's journal pages Rowland found an interesting passage:

> *Row asked me how I found my friends. First we were like strands of wool loosely woven together. We were thrown together by the accidents of living in the same neighborhood, working in the same library, or having children in the same schools. Then life put us to the test. It scalded and steamed us, until we grew tight and inseparable like old-fashioned boiled wool.*

Maggie could be verbose when she wanted to make a point, just as she could use words like a smoke screen when she wanted to evade a question. Rowland knew that, but he also recognized his mother's voice in the fragments of her writing. He recalled the time he asked his mother how to make friends. He wasn't divorced yet, but he was already lonely.

"Mostly we liked each other's company," Maggie said. "Each of us went through horrible patches, and having steady sisters kept us from going stark raving mad."

"Was it that tough?" Rowland asked her. He wondered if she was being dramatic.

"We all had complications, and it was life-saving to have friends who stood by us. We had quarrels with each other too, sometimes. Mistakes that hurt, but we got through them. We loved each other."

The journals reminded Rowland of that conversation and how jittery he felt when his mother talked about love. It was a sloppy word. Who uses a word like "love" when talking about friends, except fickle people who also use the word "love" to describe their favorite yogurt or brand of shampoo? Now even more than before, having gone through a divorce and a spate of casual dating, Rowland was convinced that love is fickle. He was willing to make an exception for his children. He loved them. Of that he was certain. He was willing to go as far as saying he admired Polly, but he wouldn't let himself consider that it was love, because he was working hard to avoid getting tangled up in commitment. With other adults, especially women, what seemed like love at first glance could a few hours later leave him feeling he wanted to go home and have a shower.

That day when his mother talked about loving her friends, Rowland challenged her. "Don't you think using a word like 'love' is a little overdone when you're talking about your neighbors?"

"Maybe it is," Maggie said. "Let's say I cherish them. Is that word more comfortable for you? Less intense? I don't have a better word right now." Her retort annoyed Rowland because "cherish" is an archaic word, and he thought his mother used it to dodge his question.

You never win in a verbal duel with a smart woman. Andrea and his divorce had taught him that, and his mother's ability to deflect his questions was only further proof of it. It flashed through his mind that once he'd said something of that sort to Polly. "No use arguing with a smart woman," he'd said to her. And, she'd told him he was right, and he should get over it.

"What about the quarrels you had with your friends? What were they about?" Rowland asked his mother, but Maggie never filled him in on the quarrels. Instead, she slipped away from his question. At least in her private journals, Rowland thought, she could've been less reserved and filled in more of the backstory. That's why he thought the journals lacked art. There wasn't enough exposure. Hidden thoughts weren't laid bare. The writer didn't give herself completely. Rowland knew what he would do to make the writing more tantalizing. He'd spice it up with a little sex. Hint at something taboo. Add a little cruelty or shame. There must have been at least a touch of that in his mother's life. There was a touch of that in everyone's life. Revealing it made writing come alive. He'd figured that out in a Hollywood second.

What Rowland described as lacking art, Maggie would have attributed to privacy. She had a whole collection of expressions about privacy, left over from a time when people kept public business and personal matters separate. For example, Rowland could remember Maggie saying, "You never really know what goes on behind someone else's closed doors, and maybe you shouldn't know." In response to this, Rowland was inclined to ask, "Who says? Why not know?" He didn't understand the way privacy and dignity were forged together in his mother's value system.

In Rowland's value system privacy and discretion were both archaic. Already as a teen-ager he'd figured out that being uptight was unattractive. He'd polished that idea in therapy where he learned that kept secrets are a breeding place for shame, and shame is bad for self-esteem. His therapist encouraged him to offload judgmental messages he'd internalized as a child, and listen to his own inner voice. "It will be more validating than the lingering voices of authority figures," she'd said. Rowland tried out his therapist's advice, but he didn't find that his inner voice was helpful. Sometimes it was sharper than a scalpel, carving off chunks of him and leaving scars.

Rowland wanted to believe that it is better to be open. He thought he was open with Polly. He'd been absolutely frank about the fact that he enjoyed Polly, but wasn't ready to make a commitment to her for the future. Not letting today's commitments become tomorrow's dishonest obligations was a high priority for Rowland, and saying this straight out, without apology, made Rowland feel progressive and free. More than anything Rowland didn't want to be passé, and making commitments under the pressure of old-fashioned expectations was definitely passé.

Rowland's ideas about relational freedom fit in well with Rowland's other conviction that "everyone has the right to speak *their* own truth." This is exactly the way he said it to his own kids, even though at the very moment he heard his own voice uttering this out loud, he was judging himself for committing a grammatical error. Deep down he also knew a dogmatic protest against dogmatism didn't quite make sense, and he hoped his kids wouldn't catch the logical flaw in his advice. That's the way it always seemed to go. Damn! Never simple. The grip of authority is so hard to shed. If he couldn't get rid of his own inner critic, at least he didn't want his children to be burdened by one.

Meanwhile Rowland tried to be judgmental about the right things. He wasn't moralistic about sex, drugs, and other kinds of self-indulgence. Although he didn't dip into all of these himself, he was scrupulously tolerant of those who did. He was freer about pointing out grammatical errors or poor style because they weren't mortal sins. Noticing a grammatical error, he was quick to point out, isn't an attack on someone's self-esteem like shaming forms of moral judgment are.

Rowland, a professor of English, was fastidious about not stifling creativity with judgment. When his creative writing students shaped characters, he told them, "Reveal the character and the problem, and let the reader come to a conclusion. Leave out the judgments. Your readers don't care what you have to say about what's right, or true, or decent, or proper. They don't even care if what you write is formally correct. The reader wants to be engaged. If you snag the reader, the writing's good." Rowland was nimble at turning personal conundrums into literary rules of thumb.

The simple truth was that Rowland often used poor judgment. He wasn't discrete about what he revealed of himself to others, and he was careless repeating what others confided to him. On more than one occasion he'd entertained a new lover by recounting the awkwardness of a former lover in bed. His loose-lipped gossip was way beyond open. His poor judgment was a spin-off of loneliness. He was like those people about whom his mother was likely to say, "Trusting him with your private business is like trusting a sieve with water." By pushing the limits of discretion, Rowland created temporary bubbles of risky togetherness, but they had no staying power. As Rowland caught a glimpse of how different he was from his mother, he felt a spark of anger, but also a wave of deep sadness. What he didn't allow himself even a glimpse of was the depth of his longing. He hadn't found a word for that yet.

Seven

ALETHEA SAW ROWLAND STRUGGLE as they talked about Maggie's journals, and sometimes their "friendly" debates lingered long with Alethea. She wasn't worried about being estranged from Rowland, because she knew he would bounce back and soon again be at her door. The struggle for Alethea was that she didn't trust Rowland to honor Maggie by honoring the memory of her.

On the one hand Rowland could be immensely intuitive. Almost clairvoyant. He'd been that way as a child, able to pick things up out of the air. At other times Rowland was careless, as if he didn't understand the power of words. As a young man he'd honed his sense of humor and his appreciation for sarcasm on repeat viewings of *Monty Python's Flying Circus*. He'd learned to be sacrilegious when in doubt. Not sacrilegious in a religious or spiritual way, but in the way he could devalue what is delicate or precious.

Rowland was glib about love, careless with devotion, and sarcastic about death because he thought he could relieve his angst about these things by laughing them away. He didn't know when to be reverent. For all these reasons, when Rowland made a statement with an air of absolute conviction, Alethea didn't look away, and she didn't counter what he said, but she did wonder if Rowland believed it himself. She didn't apologize for questioning whether Rowland could be trusted.

Alethea was committed to her friends. She'd been to funerals for Estelle and Maggie, but they definitely were not closed accounts. They were still open, and Alethea was still drawing on them. She knew what her friends would think about all sorts of little things, and in Maggie's case Alethea knew she would find Rowland's way of prowling through the journals intrusive.

Reading Maggie's journals stirred memories of events Alethea hadn't thought about in years. It's not that Alethea didn't think about her friends, but she rarely thought of them as living only in the past. The major events mentioned in their obituaries weren't Alethea's connection to them. During the years she had lived alongside her friends, she had learned that life has large swaths of time when nothing dramatic is happening. Those times are precious. They were settled in her consciousness like thoughts of warm summer sun or a fresh spring day. They were primarily memories of comfort; the specific date and place were secondary. Alethea didn't just remember her friends; she *knew* them, and every day she continued to enjoy them.

In the past when Alethea's friends were gathered at one of their homes for a meal together, Lorraine was always the extra set of hands. She could walk into a kitchen and pitch in as if it were her own. There was ease and grace in Lorraine's way of helping, so that the hosts she helped enjoyed the evening as much as their guests. When Alethea thought of Lorraine, she could hear the tones of her reassuring voice. She could picture her in an apron and could feel the firm rhythm of Lorraine's footsteps as she worked in the kitchen. When Lorraine was busy, she hummed, and Alethea hummed too sometimes when she was working. Often when she did, it reminded her of Lorraine.

On those many evenings when Alethea had shared a meal with her friends around a dining room table at one of their homes, it had usually been Lorraine who orchestrated the call to the table. When all the guests had arrived and settled in, and when the last details in the kitchen were complete, Lorraine would come out from the kitchen to the living room and say, "It looks like everything's ready, folks. Come! The table's prepared for us. Come and enjoy it!" Lorraine had perfected the lyrics of welcome, even when she was in someone else's home. Precious Lorraine. Wherever she went, she carried that aura of hospitality with her.

Sometimes when Alethea sat at the teashop enjoying her morning coffee, she closed her eyes and transported herself to the table she'd shared with her friends. She could see them gathered there, each in her usual place. It warmed her heart. Observing from across the teashop, someone might have noticed Alethea's smile and thought it was approval of the scone that was on a plate in front of her. Little did they know, it was a sweet moment with Estelle, Lorraine, and Maggie all there around the table again. They were still Alethea's daily companions. Death didn't change that.

When Alethea had a scone at the tearoom, she did think of Estelle. No one could make scones as good as Estelle's. As Alethea savored the first bite of the teashop scone, she mused, "*It's good, but a little drier would lighten the texture, don't you think, Estelle? And I have to admit, on nice china a scone tastes so much better than it does on a paper plate, but of course you know that. You never served scones on paper.*" Alethea didn't *remember* Estelle. She *knew* her. She knew what Estelle would think of the scone and of the paper plate.

In the morning when Alethea stood in front of her closet deciding what to wear, Estelle was usually beside her. Alethea was perfectly capable of picking out her own clothes for the day; her tastes were simple, and her closet was full. Still, she liked to have Estelle there. Her friends called Estelle "the "accessorizer" or sometimes "the queen of taste." They teased her about it, but the truth was they respected Estelle's sense of style. She could bring an outfit to life with one small item of accent or color. She could do the same with a flower arrangement.

Alethea usually avoided the eccentric habit of old women who talk to themselves in public, but in her condo she talked out loud to Estelle. At the closet or standing by the rack where she kept scarves and costume jewelry, she'd say in a soft voice, "*Okay, Estelle, help me out here. This outfit needs something. I know, don't overdo the accents. A little is good, and too much is worse than nothing. So what do you think? Would this be a good choice for today? I think so.*"

At the visitation before Estelle's funeral Maggie had whispered to Alethea, "Leave it to Estelle to die beautiful." Estelle always said her friends were beautiful too, but it wasn't by looks or clothes that Estelle assessed beauty. She knew that people were beautiful when they felt good about themselves, and it was easy to feel good about yourself when you were with Estelle. Although she was the prettiest by far of the four friends, Estelle was not competitive. She had that golden quality that distinguishes beautiful women who want to be good friends from those other beautiful women who strive to be the queen bee.

Maggie was present too in Alethea's daily reveries. Maggie hovered over her shoulder like Tinkerbelle when Alethea read books. Together they'd catch a word, delight in a phrase, or revise a line if it was clumsy. Especially when Alethea read something that made her laugh or cry, she'd share it with Maggie. "*Oh Maggie, don't you just love this*?" she'd say. It went in the other direction too. Sometimes Alethea would turn to Maggie and say, *Well, Maggie, this is a good idea, but the two of us could write it better. Word choice. That's it, isn't it? The word choice isn't quite right. Let's see. What word would work better here?"*

Maggie had often claimed that if you met a good character in a book and bothered to get acquainted, you'd have the character like a friend. She talked about her favorite characters as if she'd been on long vacations with them, or lived next door for years. As she grew older, Maggie blurred the lines a little. She'd recall an event, and Alethea would have to remind her, "Maggie, that's in a book. You're talking about it as if you were there." That Maggie overstated things was part of her charm; it's what was so endearing about her to a friend like Alethea, who felt deeply but tended to understate things. Maggie brought drama. She wasn't hysterical. She didn't create chaos. She savored vividness. She added texture. She turned black and white into full color. That's what Maggie brought, and she knew how to invite her friends to join with her in it.

Alethea and her friends called themselves "sisters" even though they had no more DNA in common than strangers do, which is about 99% of the DNA all humans have. Sisters or friends; the term was irrelevant. When your sister dies, she doesn't stop being your sister. Sisters are permanent. That's why Alethea and her friends were sisters, and that's why death didn't cause Alethea to love them less, or even think of them less often. Alethea spent some of every day with them.

Alethea found that hard to explain to Rowland, but she knew she had to try, because Maggie had left her photos and journals in a carton with a note for Rowland. Apparently Maggie wanted Rowland to understand her, and Rowland needed help.

Part III

And the Woes of the World Fly Out

Those bitter sorrows of childhood!—
when sorrow is all new and strange,
when hope has not yet got wings to fly . . . .
—*George Eliot*

Eight

NEITHER ALETHEA NOR ROWLAND was pleased with the way their conversations were going, but both of them looked forward to their visits. It was an odd thing. They'd start off with good intentions, and then they'd get off-track. At their best moments they both could admit they'd not established "trust." Neither of them liked that word, but it was the best they had. Rowland thought the word was old-fashioned, and Alethea thought it was psychobabble. On this they could agree, however: the word was an "X" that marked the spot where they misunderstood each other.

Rowland wondered what entitled Alethea to think she owned his family's story, at least his mother's, more than he did. Alethea was getting in his way because she was proper and controlling. A son has entitlements that come with the territory, Rowland thought, and he had every intention of staking his claim. What rights does a friend have?

Alethea thought along the same lines, but from the other side. She found it arrogant of Rowland to assume that being a son gave him rights to his mother's story. Rowland was careless about the interests of others when his ego got in the way. If he wasn't willing to take responsibility for protecting his mother's dignity, didn't he forfeit his rights? Furthermore, friendship is a commitment in its own right, and Alethea intended to stick by the commitment she'd made to Maggie.

Rowland and Alethea were both strong-willed, but they were also intelligent enough to see that if they got stuck in a showdown they would both lose. It was Rowland who came up with a solution.

He found pages from Maggie's journals that referred to her father, her mother, and events in Maggie's childhood. After reading the entries carefully, and despite his best efforts to knit the story together, Rowland had run stuck. He asked Alethea if she would look over what Maggie had written so they could talk about it.

Row asks me about my father. Is it because he is named after him? Last night Row said, "Mom, why did your Dad drop off the map? When your mother died he should have tried to be around more."

Whenever I sent Daddy a letter I got a note back. He was courteous, but he didn't tell me about the Vets Home or his day-to-day life. He made himself invisible. He was like an old dog that senses the end is near and crawls off to die alone somewhere. Men in his generation were like that, especially war veterans.

Silence and courage were the same thing to Daddy. Admitting suffering was whining. He didn't talk about the battlefields and the trenches. He came home and packed it all away with his uniforms in a trunk with camphor. It stayed there in the attic, in dark and wooly silence. Were the young men of his generation imprinted by death so early they never got over the shock of it? Were they terrorized? Or is it more universal? Are most men by nature silent about fear and pain? Are they born that way?

When Mama died, Daddy changed. It's hard for me to remember what he was like before that. With Mama it was different. I still know how it felt to be curled up on her lap in the rocking chair. She smelled like soap. Sometimes when I hold my own toddlers, I try to bring that feeling back. I want to be that kind of mother for them.

Memories of my mother are tinged with guilt. I didn't like to be near her after she got sick. Looking at her through the glass partition in the visitor's room, all I could see was her sadness. I couldn't make her happy or call down from heaven a cure for her.

I tried. I truly did, but I wasn't able to save her, and my helpless-
ness hardened into guilt.

When I went to college I left my old life behind because I wanted
to build a new one. That gets me thinking. Did I build my life, or
did it get built up around me by others? In childhood my daddy
shaped my life: I lived in the house he chose for us, and I went
with him where he took us. Is my adult life any different? Is Ross
shaping my life now because I live in a cage called Marriage, or
do my children define who I am?

Ross wouldn't be interested in asking who's building his life be-
cause he thinks he is designing it. Whether that is true or not
is another matter. He caters to his boss, to the financial needs of
our family, and to holding up the honor of his father and broth-
ers (which is not an easy matter). He makes certain things pos-
sible in my life, as I make certain things possible in his. So who
builds what?

Of one thing I am sure: I muse about my life more than Ross does
about his. He looks out into the world and considers what he can
accomplish, but I look inward and try to understand what has
happened to me.

My children ask about my childhood, and I tell them I was
raised in Oklahoma, that my mother was a schoolteacher, and
my father was a country doc (of sorts). They know my mother
died, and they know my brother and sister went to live with our
Aunt Marlene. I've never told my children much about my aunt,
because there is not much worth telling. She was not a pleasant
person.

Since Daddy's shocking letter I have another reason for not going
back to review the story. I'm confused. If I went back now to tell
my children the story of my childhood, I would have to revise it.

My children ask about their grandparents, when they are trying
to find out about themselves. They want to know what they got

from whom. A nose? Intelligence? Perfect pitch? A dimple? Left-handedness? A contagious giggle? I don't mind guessing with them about those details, but I avoid the drama of revision.

What would happen if I shared the last letter from Daddy with my children? In the noisy clatter of conversation everyone would be scrambling to make sense of it. It's hard enough to make sense of it by myself. I don't want to do it in committee.

When Alethea and Rowland met on Sunday afternoon, he put the journals in the center of the table between them and suggested that both he and Alethea tell their own version of what they knew about his grandparents. Maggie's journals on the table were like a third person in the conversation, and both Rowland and Alethea wanted to do right by her. Rowland volunteered to go first. "I don't know where I got these impressions exactly," he said. "I picked up fragments here and there over the years when Mom told stories. I can't promise it'll be accurate, but I'll give it my best shot."

❖ Rowland's Tale ❖

My mother, Mary Margaret Barnes, was born in the panhandle of Oklahoma. My grandfather's name was Rowland Barnes, and I'm named after him, Rowland Barnes Barone. He was a veteran of the First World War, a medic who served in France. After the war he settled down in Oklahoma and became Doc Barnes, the country doctor.

My grandfather was a confirmed bachelor for a long time but eventually married the local schoolteacher. He was over fifty, and she was twenty-five years younger. Why did he stay single so long and then rob the cradle? Was there a shortage of eligible guys out there in the panhandle, or was Grandpa a player?

Mom was the first child in her family, and they named her Mary Margaret but called her Maggie. Her own mother was Magda Eweleen, named after her two Polish grandmothers, both born on farms in villages near Krakow. One died in the village where she was born, and the other died on a farm in rural Wisconsin. When Mom came along, her parents named her after saints instead of grandmothers because they didn't want to burden her with a foreign-sounding name, although Mom told me once that she liked having a name similar to her mother's. Maggie and Magda.

Apparently old Rowland and young Magda were still at it, because when Mom was eight, her mother had twins. When Mom was fourteen, Magda got tuberculosis and went to a sanitarium. She never came home again and died when Mom was sixteen. I don't have details about those years. The entries I'm reading now in Mom's journals give me more information than I've ever had before, and I still don't know much.

I've seen two pictures of my grandmother. Mom kept one on her bookshelf. Grandmother is standing by a cutoff pillar against a background that looks like a garden. It must be a fake backdrop used by a photographer for portraits, because I can't imagine any rural town in Wisconsin or Oklahoma had a real garden that looked like Versailles. The young woman is slender and has a sweet face. Her white linen dress has eyelet lace around the neck and finely tucked sleeves. Her shoes are pumps with small metal buckles. It's odd to call this young woman "Grandmother."

The other picture is in a black enamel locket that opens up, a mourning locket. On one side is a tiny clipping of dark hair. Was hair a bit of the body that could be preserved indefinitely, a last desperate protest against letting go completely? On the other side of the locket is a picture of a young woman in a dark dress. She has big eyes and high cheekbones. Her hair is parted in the center and pulled back. No curls in this picture. I hope my sisters didn't sell the locket in an estate sale.

I mix up this image of my grandmother with the gloomy haunting picture of Emily Dickinson that was in my high school English textbook. The picture in the book has large anxious eyes and a ribbon around her neck. It's on the same page as the poem "Because I could not stop for death." The line that caught my attention was the one about the dead person being taken away all alone in a carriage. My mother said when she was a girl in Oklahoma the hearse was horse-drawn? The picture of Emily Dickinson and the tone of the poem match the cloud of sadness that floated into place around Mom at the mention of her parents. I'm sure of that.

The same textbook that held the poem about death held that other poem that begins with the line "There is no frigate like a book . . . ." My brother Will and I referred to our English textbook as "this friggin book," when Mom was around. We did it to bait her because she would say, "Clean it up, boys!" and then we would say, "Mom, that's a quote from Emily Dickinson. It's in our English book." She had a good sense of humor, and that would make her laugh. I never mentioned the other poem about death or the picture of Emily Dickinson to my mom. I never told her that it reminded me of my grandmother.

There are a few other things I know about Doc Barnes. He had a one-room office in a parlor on the front of their house. If he got a message that someone needed him, he made house calls, like appliance repair guys. After her mother died and the twins went to live with their Aunt Marlene, Mom sometimes went with Doc Barnes on house calls in remote areas. He didn't want to leave Maggie home alone if he had to tend his patient through the night or for several days. If they stayed through the night, Mom found a corner of the house where she could put down her bedroll and pillow, and that's where she slept.

From the corner of a parlor or around the corner in a dining room, Mom listened to adult conversations. Families had dark secrets, and adults waiting for death had somber thoughts. Some was confession, and some was gossip. On one of those nights at a farmhouse where Doc Barnes was at the bedside of a dying man, Maggie heard two sisters talking in low voices in the parlor. It was about the farmer's daughter who disappeared after giving birth to a baby girl. One day she went to town and never came back. She left the baby to be raised by her mother and her sisters.

Mom played with the little girl when families had summer picnics in the park, next to the ball diamond. The farmer's family attended the Methodist Church down the block from where Mom's family attended Holy Sacrament, and when families gathered at the park on Sunday afternoon, the adults kept separate, but children played together. Mom told us numerous times about Sundays at the park and a sad little girl who didn't have a mother. I took the story to mean that Mom expected her children to play with kids other people rejected. She was always a defender of the underdog.

I was an adult before Mom filled in the rest of the story. As she listened to the hushed voices of the women in the parlor that night when she was at the farmhouse with Doc Barnes, she heard a sentence she didn't understand. "Do you suppose the poor darling will ever figure out that her father is her grandfather and her grandfather is her father?" To Maggie it was a riddle. The tone of voice she heard in reply was hostile. "That revolting bastard. Soon enough when St. Peter's looking him in the eye, he's going to have some explaining to do. I hope he gets what he deserves." Maggie couldn't make sense of that either.

From an early age Mom knew more than her fair share about the ugly side of life, but she was cautious about repeating those stories around her children. She did tell a story about a house call to deliver a baby. Doc Barnes instructed her to boil water and find a clean towel or some clean cotton clothing. It was needed for swaddling. Mom stood beside her father as he welcomed a baby, who looked like it had lard spread on its head. That detail must have impressed Mom because she always included it when she retold the story. Before tucking the newborn into the waiting arms of its mother, Doc Barnes said, "Go into life, little one, and live it well."

Mom cherished that memory of her father handing over babies. "He commissioned them," she used to say when she told the story. I loved that story about my grandfather, and repeated it to Polly once, describing for her the picture in my mind of Mom telling this story at a christening party. I heard Mom tell the story many times, but I've merged them all into one. The cork has already been popped on the champagne at the christening, and the men have already broken open a large bottle of whiskey and poured their first drinks. They head out to the porch or to the circle of chairs set out under a tree in the yard. The women are in the kitchen. One at the sink, another at the stove, and someone is getting a large pan of jello out of the refrigerator in the corner by the door. Mom is at the table visiting with the baby's grandmother, but all the women in the room are listening as they work. Mom is telling the story of her father commissioning babies. I wonder how many times I heard that story.

When I think of my grandfather and his frontier adventures, I have an image that's a cross between Davey Crockett and Charles Olsen of *Little House on the Prairie*. I've never seen a picture of my grandfather's face other than the one in which he is standing with five young guys, all dressed in what looks like brand new military uniforms. They are boys, not men. If you could Photoshop the picture and put basketball gear on them, it would look like a high school team. But they weren't headed off to a game. They were headed to war.

I have another picture of an old man in a fishing boat. I assume it's my grandfather because Mom kept it in a small frame on her desk. It could be someone else for all I know. I can't see the face. He's wearing baggy pants and what looks like a dress shirt with the sleeves rolled up. Odd clothes for fishing. He has a cane pole in his hand and is wearing a straw hat. His face is in shadow. I wish I could see it better because Mom told me that Doc Barnes had a scar along the side of his face. It was a war wound, a medal of honor earned in combat. I said that once to Mom, and she protested. "A slash on your face is not a medal of honor. It's a reminder of an awful war. Don't glorify it." I don't agree with her. I still call it a medal of honor, because he deserves some credit for getting his face slashed open while serving his country.

When Mom and Doc Barnes were driving home after a long night at a patient's bedside, they sang songs he learned when he was in the military, songs like "It's a Long Way to Tipperary." Mom told us about this when we were on long car trips. She'd get us to sing together so we wouldn't fight in the back seat. We thought singing in the car was stupid, but she promised us each a quarter if we joined in, and we figured if we put our quarters together we could buy a bag of licorice twists. Dad sang too. He had a good voice. It was deep and manly, and I tried to sing the way he did.

I have a mental picture of Maggie and Doc Barnes singing in the car, but in this case I know it's one I've created in my imagination. A man behind a very large steering wheel in an old model sedan. The wheels are large, and the headlights are small and round. He's wearing a fedora. Next to him is a girl in a white blouse and a plaid skirt. I have an actual photo like that of Mom in her school uniform. If Grandpa's voice trailed off, and he stopped singing, Mom was supposed to nudge him awake. If it got really bad, he'd pull over and stroll the margin of the road for a few minutes to walk off the drowsiness.

When I was a little guy, Mom sang songs for me if I had trouble falling asleep. So she wouldn't wake up the other kids, she put her head on the pillow next to mine and hummed the song just loud enough so that I could hear it and feel it against the side of my head. I've never forgotten the feeling of Mom next to me humming.

❖

When he finished Rowland smiled and said, "This is my raw material. It's what I know about Mom's parents, and it's the best I can do for now. Next time it's your turn. Let's set up a time to get together again soon." Alethea sensed that Rowland was trying to be authentic. He was still creative and playful, but the professorial posturing had been set aside. She could still picture little Row as a boy playing with his Lincoln Logs, assembling them on the square of carpet he claimed for himself under the library table that held the old *Webster Unabridged Dictionary*.

The "library," a small den off the living room in the house on Woodward Street, was the room where Maggie set out the tea when Alethea stopped in for a visit in the afternoon. Two comfortable chairs were set at angles on either side of a small round table. Alethea wondered if it was the room in which Maggie kept the old Underwood typewriter on which she tapped out her journals, but Alethea couldn't picture anymore where the typewriter might have been.

While Maggie and Alethea visited, Rowland played. Now and then he'd pop up and run to the window because he heard children's voices outside, and he needed to check if the neighbor kids were playing in the yard or only getting into the car to go away with their parents. He'd hear the neighbor's dog bark, and he'd go to the window to see who was walking down the sidewalk. Rowland was an alert boy. There was little he missed.

Alethea could still picture Row like this. Playing. Listening. Absorbing. Momentarily distracted, but always returning. More than his older sister Laura and his twin brother Will, Row liked to be in close proximity to his mother, tethered to her by the sound of her voice. He was the child for whom Maggie would interrupt a conversation that was straying off into material only suitable for adults, and she would say, "Be careful! Little elephants have big ears."

The similarity between Maggie listening in on adult conversations from her bedroll in the corner of a country house, where Doc Barnes was tending the dying, and Row playing with his Lincoln Logs under the library table, was striking. There was a difference, however. Rowland's generation was raised on *Charlie and the Chocolate Factory,* given to them by adults who wanted to assure children that good things happen to good people, and that even when bad things happen, more of the good is just around the corner. Maggie's childhood lacked that optimism.

Rowland was curious about the dark side, but he also was practiced in holding the reality of it at arm's length. In his conversations with Alethea he never called anything "sin," because by the time he was old enough to commit some, he had substituted words that neutralized the guilt. He preferred to use words like "mistake," "poor choice," or "careless oversight." Rowland complained to Alethea that Maggie's references to sin were quaint, a leftover from an old-fashioned religious past.

Alethea's understanding of Maggie had a different slant. She knew that Maggie respected sin because she'd seen its misery. She'd witnessed the frantic widow and orphans of a man who lost a gunfight. She'd seen poverty and hunger that didn't make people sweet. In the dustbowl of Oklahoma she'd known a woman from their town whose name later got carved into a very small stone in the public cemetery after an abortion, performed by her neighbor on the kitchen table, went wrong. Maggie didn't have a rosy view of the frontier or of sin, but she was surprisingly forgiving of people, because she understood the desperation of a hard life.

Alethea had tried to explain this to Rowland in one of their earlier conversations, but he argued that it's unfair to use a word like "sin" to blame people for misfortune. "Most of the time when people get tripped up they didn't start out with bad intentions," Rowland insisted. "People make mistakes. Shit happens." He would have preferred his mother not use the word "sin" at all, but given that she did, he was relieved to know that his mother was forgiving.

"Mostly Mom was forgiving," Rowland said, "but sometimes she was punitive. She sent Will and me to bed without supper when we unrolled the ribbon on her typewriter to see how long it was. She wasn't pleased with the stripe of ink left on the upholstery of her reading chair, and she fumed as she worked the ink out of the carpeting. Okay, we probably should have known better on that one, but there was another incident when I was barely old enough to go to school. I lost my mittens for a second time, and she made me pay for new ones with my allowance, out of respect for Oklahoma kids who knew the value of mittens. No pie for kittens that lost their mittens at our house." Rowland laughed.

Rowland judged that his mother's reaction to the carelessness of a child was "excessive." He had to scramble to find the right word. The mix of his normally kind mother and the calculus of sinfully losing a mitten in a freezing winter was a far stretch for Rowland. "Let's write it off as Mom having a bad day," he advised. "Everybody's entitled to a bad day now and then. Even my Mom is." That was Rowland's version of sin and forgiveness. As he spoke, Rowland was thinking of a few instances of his own more recent "poor choices." He was glad his mother didn't know about them, because he didn't like to think of her calling them "sin."

There were things about his mother that Rowland couldn't understand, but Alethea could. Alethea had understood when Maggie told her that, when hearing about someone's "sin," Maggie had felt guilty for overhearing what was not meant for children's ears. It was an adult world, and she was a little girl who was supposed to know her place. Maggie didn't ask her father to explain the riddle about the girl whose father and grandfather were the same man. She knew instinctively that it shouldn't be mentioned again. She also knew that if she admitted to having overheard it, she'd be reprimanded for eavesdropping.

Maggie was born in Oklahoma, and Alethea was born in Philadelphia, but they both knew that adults hid bad behavior, with a hope and a prayer that it would stay hidden, so life could go on "normally." In small towns and ethnic neighborhoods that lacked the buffers of anonymity, the loss of "normalcy" was a threat to both the guilty and their victims. Alethea's mother kept a small figurine on the coffee table in their living room. It was three monkeys, one with eyes covered, one with ears covered, and one with its mouth covered. It sat there on the table like a religious icon. Alethea's mother knew too well what it was like to be the object of gossip.

For a girl like Maggie, listening from around the corner, the guilt of hearing outweighed the curiosity of not understanding a strange sentence whispered at a deathbed. Alethea had felt that same guilt when, as a young girl, she wondered about things that had happened in her family. When Alethea thought back to the way secrets used to be handled, she felt relieved that times had changed. At least they had changed somewhat.

Alethea doubted that she could explain to Rowland that it was not only the handling of secrets that had changed but also the definition of normal that had been revised. That little inner scale that tipped to advise both children and adults what was and what was not acceptable had been rebalanced. What once seemed so normal now seemed cruel, and what once seemed so abnormal had become acceptable. Alethea had lived on both sides of the revision, but Rowland had not.

The day Rowland overheard Maggie telling about the farmer's family and the shameful secret she'd heard in the night, he didn't have the same reserve that Maggie and Alethea had when they were children. From over in the corner where he was playing under the library table, Rowland broke in with "What does that mean, Mom?" And Maggie had replied "Oh, buddy, that's a story we'll leave for when you're older." Rowland accepted Maggie's decision, but felt no guilt for having asked.

Rowland must have remembered what he'd heard, and somewhere along the way he'd been given the details, because he repeated the story without hesitation. The farmer's behavior was still taboo, but repeating the story was acceptable now. Alethea, on the other hand, had an uneasy feeling hearing it spoken out loud. She'd never forgotten the tragic story of the dying farmer, his angry sisters, and a little girl who silently carried her family's shame. These memories mixed with her own gave Alethea courage to tell her version of the story of Maggie's parents. Rowland was still waiting.

❖ ALETHEA'S TALE ❖

DOC BARNES SERVED IN the First World War, and after the war he moved to Oklahoma. Townspeople called him "Doc Barnes," even though he was a battlefield medic and not a real doctor. The sick folk, to whose homes Doc Barnes went with his black bag, looked to him for hope. They didn't concern themselves with his diplomas; he was all they had. They trusted him for comfort, and Maggie used to say about her father, "Even though he wasn't a real doctor, steady people can do a lot of good."

Doc Barnes was over fifty when the new teacher came to town. She made visits to the office at the front of his house, because she needed a salve for the skin irritation that was breaking out on her hands. She had "nervous eczema," and it had gotten worse since she started teaching. Like everyone else, she was at ease with Doc Barnes.

At the end of her first year of teaching, Miss Zeller went back to Wisconsin to spend the summer vacation with her family. When she returned at the end of summer to begin teaching again, she was not feeling well, and she consulted Doc Barnes about her weariness and upset stomach. It took Doc Barnes only a few obvious questions to conclude that she was pregnant. Being a gentleman, Doc Barnes offered to marry her.

In the circle of her close friends, Maggie talked easily about the surprise of her birth. She would laugh and say that her parents pulled off a double feature. They gave their neighbors a May and December romance to gossip about, and then sprang a shotgun wedding on them for good measure. Even though they were strict Catholics, Maggie's parents never hid the details of her birth from her. "My birth was one of the few times in my life I've been that early for anything," Maggie would say.

When talking about her Oklahoma childhood, Maggie was more likely to talk about her mother than her father. She made visits to the sanitarium where her mother was being treated for tuberculosis, and the visits were guilt-ridden. Maggie was bright enough to know she hadn't caused her mother's illness, but the guilt would churn up when her father said to her, "Come, Maggie, we're going to visit your Mama. Seeing you will make her happy. The twins are too young to understand what's going on, but set a good example for them. If you're cheerful, they'll be cheerful, and your faces will be your Mama's sunshine."

Doc Barnes meant well, but the suggestion that Maggie had the power to make the twins cheerful and her mother happy was too much for a young girl. When finally they were at the sanitarium, and Maggie could see her mother through the glass window that separated them, the scene was anything but cheerful. Her mother would sob, and Maggie would do everything she could to choke back her own tears. She would beg her mother to come home, and her mother would sigh and say, "Only time will tell, honey." Maggie understood that to mean her mother wouldn't be coming home again. If happiness was the elixir that could heal her mother, Maggie couldn't deliver it.

Later talking with friends she could trust, Maggie would relive those sad years. "I loved my mother," she told them. "I needed her, but I dreaded going to see her. I couldn't fix her. I couldn't keep her alive." As her circle of sisters listened, each one of them nodded at different points in the story. They knew what she meant. They too had shouldered burdens too big for children, burdens placed on them by adults who loved them but didn't seem to understand that the woes of the world could weigh them down. No one ever took them aside and said, "This isn't your fault."

"From the very beginning," Maggie observed, "our brothers were spared those assignments. They were taught to fix doorknobs and shovel snow off the walks; we were taught that it was our job to fix broken hearts. As adults we repeat the cycle. Men defend families from bankruptcy and burglars; we make sure no hearts are broken and everyone's happy. It's not fair, and by the time we see what's wrong with this arrangement, we can't stop ourselves anymore."

Estelle challenged Maggie. An ocean between Estelle and her mother was a deep buffer, and she'd not had to face the death of her mother at an early age. "It used to be that way," said Estelle, "but now it's different. We grew up thinking we had to keep our parents happy, and now we think we have to keep our kids happy. Something got turned upside down just as we were getting ready to cash in. I knew from the start that I'd never be an ideal mother, but I didn't bargain for the fact that when something goes wrong and my kids are unhappy, it's automatically my fault." Estelle said it in half humor, because it was not like her to be bitter, but she meant what she was saying. As she spoke, the others nodded in agreement. Each of them could think of instances in which a world turned upside meant that everyone else's needs came before their own.

There wasn't much more Alethea could add to the story of Maggie's childhood. "I'm sorry, I got off track," she told Rowland, "but that's about it. I don't know more details. When I try to put the story together, it takes me back to the times we talked about it with our friends. I remember their reactions to Maggie's story better than I remember the story itself. What all four of us had in common was the awareness that childhood used to be harder on children. When we were young, the adults weren't concerned with our feelings, possibly because they had other things on their minds, and life wasn't easy on adults either. Anyway, that's what I know about Maggie's childhood."

❖

AFTER ALETHEA FINISHED TELLING what she knew about Maggie's childhood, Rowland confronted her about knowing more than she was saying. "Our conversations remind me of the ones I used to have with Mom," he said. "She tied herself in knots to be discrete, censoring everything and talking to me like I was a boy even after I was an adult. My grandfather was still living when Mom had kids of her own, but what happened to him? He disappeared, and we never got to know him. We heard stories about him, but Mom never made an effort to introduce us to him. Alethea, you must know why. Did he get arrested for practicing medicine without a license, or was he a drunk? Did he take up with a scandalous woman or become a grifter? Something went wrong. People don't disappear for no reason. Tell me the truth. I can handle it."

Alethea had to decide whether to leave the story of Rowland's grandfather intact. The image of Doc Barnes that Rowland had already assembled for himself was good. It was the portrait of an honorable man, a source of pride for a grandson. But Alethea knew another version of the story, and in the thick of their conversation about it, she couldn't sort her ambivalence quickly enough to decide what to say about it to Rowland. Instinctively she sidestepped his questions.

"It's remarkable how much you've pieced together," she said. "I can't add much to it. Your mother left you with what she could. What you have . . . well that's what you have." Alethea shrugged a little to suggest that she didn't have anything more to say, but the silence was awkward, so she added, "The past is like that, you know. So much of it is beyond our reach. If I think about my own family . . . well . . . what I don't know far outweighs what I do know. We just have to settle for that." She could tell as she was speaking that Rowland didn't believe her.

Nine

ALETHEA KNEW WHAT HAPPENED to Doc Barnes after his children went to live elsewhere and he went to live in a Veteran's Home in Iowa. Maggie wrote notes to him but heard little back. At most she'd receive a picture post card with a sentence or two about the season or the weather. Maggie had not been able to keep up contact with her younger brother and sister either. After their mother died, they went to live with their Aunt Marlene, a single woman with no children of her own. She adopted them, changed their last names, and did what she could to disconnect them from the "sadness of their past." Maggie never understood why her father allowed this.

The loss of her father and her siblings was a thread of grief that wove through the fabric of Maggie's life. Birthdays reminded her of them, and holidays never seemed complete without them. "I'm a holiday orphan, and so are you," Maggie would say to Alethea. When Rowland brought her another set of pages from Maggie's diary she was reminded of those sad times again.

> This morning I watched Ross and the boys load the car. Will put the grass-trimmer in the trunk, Row got the old tin watering can down from the hook where it hangs in the garage, and Ross gathered the other garden tools into the canvas carrying bag. Before leaving Ross came back into the house and asked me for old newspapers. He will put them down on the floor of our station wagon when they stop at the garden shop for plants to put at the Barone family gravesite. The boys move proudly when they work beside their Dad.

After they pulled out of the driveway I began to think about two graves somewhere else. Daddy's grave is in Iowa in the veterans' section of a cemetery. I wonder if this week they mowed the grass for the first time this season? Did someone put small US flags in the brass holders at each grave to honor the veterans? Maybe while some families were tidying the graves of their own loved ones, they checked around Daddy's grave too, and pulled the dandelions out by their roots or clipped back the errant crab grass that tends to overgrow the flat brass markers.

I have been thinking of my mother's grave. It is up on the rise in the little cemetery behind Holy Sacrament Church. I went to it on Memorial Day with Daddy after Mama died. One year Daddy went back home to get a bucket and a scrub brush, because birds had perched on her stone and left droppings. He said it was disrespectful to leave it that way.

The birds didn't mean any offense, but those messy dribbles down the side of the stone hurt Daddy's feelings. The stone has her full name, Magda Eweleen Zellers Barnes. Was Daddy thinking that someday he'd be in the empty space beside her? Was he wondering who would clean the bird poop off his stone? Do people begin to think that way as they age?

My first memory of Mama's gravesite is before the stone was in place. We stood around a deep hole whose sides were draped to keep the clumps of dirt from tumbling back in. The coffin was carried from the church by men in black suits. I don't know who they were, but they were carrying my mother away.

The priest, walking ahead of them, was carrying an open book and glanced at it as he walked, as if it had a map to tell him where we were going. On that day as we were walking behind the box that carried what little was left of my mother, I tried with all my might to believe that the box was empty. I was desperate to believe that if I prayed hard enough, I could call her back, either from out of that box or from heaven.

After we left the cemetery, I still had fading hopes that we would go home and she would be there at the kitchen sink or standing by the stove. I wished it with all my heart. I prayed so hard my chest hurt, but when we turned into the drive, the curtains were still drawn and the front door was not open. It didn't make any sense to imagine her in the sanitarium any more either, although I would have gone eagerly to visit her there again. The hollow space she left inside me began filling in with guilt. What if she wasn't with us anymore because I hadn't prayed hard enough or believed it possible? With all my might I had begged God to cure her, but had I believed he would? Did believing it make all the difference?

I must have looked sad while I was caught up in my dark ruminations because my darling Jenna came and gave me a hug. "Mommy are you sad?" she asked. I tried to explain to her that this is a day when we remember the people we love who are not here anymore, and that I was thinking of my Mommy and Daddy. She hugged me again and said, "You have us, Mommy. We'll take care of you."

How differently we train our sons and our daughters. Our sons are tending to the honor of the family today by pulling weeds and planting flowers. Our daughters are learning to be the companions of sadness. Steven is too young to go with the boys this year, but I can predict that Ross will find a task for him and draft him for the team in another year or so. Is Ross training his sons to take care of our graves, his grave and mine? That's a sobering thought.

Jenna keys into something about this day. She picks up hints. It brings to mind the way lilies and gardenias always remind me of funerals. Those small hints that fill the air with sadness. Can a child as young as Jenna already recognize grief? She is delicate, and I must be careful not to weigh her down with my own dark feelings.

How will I teach Laura about sadness? I suppose I should leave it to her. If I were to guess, before the end of the day she will get out paper and the colored pencils she keeps carefully lined up in their box, and she will make a sign reminding everyone about Memorial Day. She will decorate it with flags and flowers and maybe even a bright sunshine in one upper corner. In one of the lower corners she will proudly sign it "Laura Anne Barone," and she'll put it on the refrigerator with the magnets that are waiting there.

No one would describe Maggie as a woman inclined to depression. On the contrary, Maggie was lively and bright. She took hold of happy events in life with a full embrace, but that didn't mean that she forgot what had been lost. Alethea mused about how private grief had been in the past. Those who carried sorrows deep enough to last a lifetime also kept those sorrows from public view. Alethea thought about her father's silent sorrow when he lost a son. He was admired for the way he pulled himself together and went on with life. Alethea thought about her mother too, a disappointed woman who never missed an opportunity to put her grief on display. Alethea overheard the critical remarks about her mother's unending self-pity.

Something had changed. Grief had gone public. The expectations were different now. "Each person has a unique way of working through loss," people were prone to say, "and no one should judge it." Letting sorrow be visible was a right. Not spoken, but implied, was the notion that those who hid grief were unenlightened, and those who expected them to hide it were cruel. Alethea wondered if those stalwart people in the past were less kind. She doubted it, just as she doubted that those more open about their losses were less weighed-down in the long run. Grief couldn't be purged. Visible or not visible, the losses were permanent, and the memories didn't fade. Times had changed. Alethea was sure of that, but she wasn't sure to which time she belonged.

These thoughts carried Alethea back to the day Maggie came to her house with the letter she'd received from her father. As Alethea read the letter out loud, Maggie was sighing, as if no matter how deep she breathed, she still felt as if she were drowning. Here and there she'd break out with a comment that would have fit anywhere in the letter. "Can you believe it" she'd say, or "This is impossible?" When Alethea got to the end of the letter and folded it back into the envelope Maggie said, "I feel like I've overdosed on some really bad drug, and I don't know what's real anymore."

My Dearest Maggie,

I must share difficult news with you. I have become ill with a condition called Huntington's chorea. It is an incurable disease of the brain that begins with moodiness and poor coordination and leads to death. My father also had this condition, and it runs in families.

Soon after my father became ill I enlisted to serve our country in the The Great War. I was a Quaker, so in keeping with my family's pacifist beliefs about war, I requested an exemption from combat and served at the front in the Friends Ambulance Unit. We medics worked in the trenches to treat rat bites, feet rotting in wet boots, ailments that came from bad food and polluted water, and much more. After attacks we went into the battle areas to gather wounded or comfort those who, though too far gone to survive, had not yet breathed their last breath. This is the world into which I fled to escape the agony of my family and fear for my own future.

I returned to the United States after the war and went to the Oklahoma panhandle because there was a shortage of doctors there. I was still a medic, but people began to call me Doc Barnes, and I did my best to live up to their trust. I dispensed extra kindness when I knew my training was limited, and I never lied about my lack of diplomas.

For nearly twenty years I lived alone, treating the sick the best I could, and I was known in town as the bachelor doctor. I was not indifferent to pretty ladies who were friendly to me, but I kept my promise not to marry and have children. I only needed to think of a fine young lady consigned to childlessness and bound to the uncertain future of my family's disease, and my interest in her quickly waned.

When I was well into my forties, your mother was hired as the teacher in our small school. She caught the eyes of the single men. I noticed her too, but I kept my distance so as not to feed my fantasy that, if it were not for the curse I bore, I could live my life beside someone as lovely as Magda.

During the school year your mother lived with a local family. She came to me for treatment of an eczema she had on her hands, and in addition to picking up the medicinal cream, she would linger for a visit. During the first summer vacation she went home to be with her family in Wisconsin, and when she was gone I missed her visits. Although normally she was shy in groups, she was talkative during her visits with me. She told me that, unlike conversations with young men who showed interest in courting her, our visits were different. This both pleased and confused me.

When your mother came back from the summer vacation she was not feeling well and came to consult me. She complained of nausea and said she was tired, but I noticed that she was rounder in body and didn't look like a sick person. She was shattered by the news that she was going to be a mother because she knew that the town would not accept a single schoolteacher with an illegitimate child, and she did not want to go back to her family in Wisconsin or the man who was the father of her child. The reasons were complex, and I will not burden you with them.

I told Magda that I would marry her. I apologized for my age, told her about the burden of my family's illness, and was clear with her that I would understand if she turned down my offer. It was clear from the start that we would have no more children.

Magda was concerned about causing harm to my reputation, but I insisted I was too old to care about things like that. Furthermore the prospect of living in the orbit of her kindness more than offset any fear I had of local gossips. I knew from my experience with families in these circumstances, that when it comes to gossip about surprise births, people get over it. There is always new material, and old stories fade.

At mid-year the new schoolteacher started, and by early spring you were born. Although it didn't matter much to me, it concerned your mother that I was a Quaker and she Catholic. I agreed you should be christened in the Catholic Church, and by the time you were school age there was a Catholic elementary school in town, which you attended.

I was always pleased that you were my daughter and that your mother was my precious wife. After my years alone I received this as a gift that I did not question. It is only now that I need to explain the oddities of this arrangement in order to reassure you that you do not carry my family's illness. If ever I had a moment of desire that you could have been the issue of my body, it was nothing close to the comfort I had from knowing that you would not be the bearer of this dreadful disease.

There is another question that no doubt is raised by this letter. You may be wondering about Nate and Rita. It might appear that by the time they were born, I had either weakened in my resolve not to have children or failed in my efforts to prevent that. This I must explain to you.

You may remember the school vacation when you were eight years old, and we went to serve in a lumber camp. There was already a doctor with a diploma in town by then, but there was no one to do any first aid or medicine at the camp. I agreed to go, and your mother and you came with me.

Toward the end of summer a couple stopped at the camp compound in their car. They were traveling to California and the young woman was expecting a child. She claimed it was early and that she planned to be in California by the time the little one arrived, but she had lost her water. When the little one was born, much to the surprise of the mother and the father, there was a second baby as well. That there were twins may account for their early arrival.

The husband was a rugged fellow and shamelessly rude to his wife. He wanted to get to California, and the babies had interrupted his plan. The young wife was fragile in the face of his brashness. As sometimes happens with stressed first-time mothers, her milk did not begin. I advised them that without this means of feeding the infants, and given their small size, they should wait to continue on to California. The husband would not hear of it and insisted he would go on alone. The young wife was terrified of staying behind alone in a lumber camp, and she begged him not to leave her. He refused to adjust his plan.

On the morning of the father's planned departure the mother came and asked if she could leave the infants behind. There were some half-hearted words about the couple coming back for them sometime, but we knew it was not likely. Your Mother took in the twins with all the love she had always shown for you. She thrived even more with three children than she had with one. Before the onset of winter we decided it would be best for us to return to town. When we arrived back with three children our neighbors and friends congratulated us on the birth of the twins during our absence, and we did not correct their assumptions.

I have only one regret from those years before your mother became ill. I need to relieve my conscience. We were sitting outside watching our three children play, and I said to her, "I must have done something right because today I am the luckiest man in the world." She got a frightened look on her face. When I asked her what it was she replied, "Be careful what you say and don't taunt divine justice. Not all of this has come about as it should have."

I realized then that your mother still harbored guilt for your birth. I could not accept this and was stern with her. I said, "Our Maggie is not a mistake. She was given to us to heal our hurts. It's wrong for you to deny that." I accused her of clinging to a dark Catholic view of punishment. I did not say it in a kindly way, and she began to cry. You were there and you noticed. You asked if I was being mean to your mother. If this event has stayed with you, then I want to say I am sorry. It has bothered me because I know it hurt my dear Magda, and I have worried that it also hurt you.

I still think I was right, but I realized only too late how unkind it was to say it to her that way. It is one of the only regrets I have about our short life together. I only hope that she did not believe a wrong was being punished when she was stricken with TB. I have wondered if that is why her mood became so dark during her illness, or was it because she was missing her children and our family life? Sadly you know the rest of the story.

Perhaps now you can understand why I came to the conclusion that I could no longer be a father to my children. I was relieved when you married Ross, as I believe him to be an honest and dependable husband for you. I also was relieved when Magda's sister Marlene agreed to adopt the twins.

I have struggled about whether I should explain this to you. You might hear of it from another source, and unless you have a clear explanation you may worry unnecessarily. It is for that reason I write this letter with the help of my physician. I have dictated it to him, and his secretary has agreed to type it because I can no longer hold a pen firmly enough to write. I hope with all my heart that reading this will not cause you grief or worry.

Your mother's death was the low point in my life, but I still had you. A father could never have wished for a more loving daughter. I send you this with all my love and with great gratitude.

Your Daddy

Maggie's children had never seen this letter. Although Maggie left her journals for Rowland, she had given the letter from her father to Alethea. She sealed the letter and gave very specific instructions for what was to be done with it. Laura had started a genealogy project and asked Maggie how she could find birth and death records for her grandparents. She wanted to know where they had lived and where they had died. Maggie speculated that if Laura obtained a death record, she might also discover the cause of Doc Barnes death.

"Put this away for me," Maggie told Alethea. "You don't have kids who might prowl through a drawer and find it accidentally. In my house I can't think of anywhere safe enough to keep it. If Laura ever digs up family history and sets loose a crisis, then maybe it will be time to share this letter with my children. Until then, let sleeping dogs lie."

Alethea wanted to honor a decision Maggie had made long ago, but she also knew that times had changed. What would Maggie do if she were still living? Families didn't have to hide these things anymore. At last Alethea sat down at her dining room table with Rowland, and they read the letter together. It was a flashback to the day she had done the same with Maggie.

Rowland was stunned. "Why did Mom keep secrets from us?" he asked. "We could have handled it."

Alethea tried to explain that Maggie grew up in an era when people hid illnesses that ran in families. Before the discovery of DNA, genetic guesswork wasn't much help, and families lived with ticking time bombs. They suffered from gossip about "fits," or "madness" or "lameness" or "feeble-mindedness." In addition to the burdens of illness, these families lived under a cloud of shame.

After Maggie married Ross, she was hurt by her father's distance, but after she received her father's letter her disappointment took a new form. She cried when she spoke of her father and her mother. "It's hard having parents who were victims, and the secrets make it worse." Added to her tangled feelings about her parents was the hurt that stemmed from Ross's pragmatic advice that she put loss behind her and move on.

"Did my dad read this letter?" Rowland asked. "Did he know what happened to Doc Barnes?"

"It's never occurred to me before that he didn't know," Alethea replied, "but now that you ask . . . it's possible that your mom kept this letter from your dad. She sometimes hid her feelings about other things from him. So why not this?" Alethea remembered Maggie's complaints about Ross. She was a passionate person, and he liked calm. He wanted their household to run smoothly, and if she got upset about something, he'd chide her for being overwrought. Any time she showed emotion he would remind her that she owed it to her children to be strong. "Don't brood," he'd say. "You should be counting all the good things in your life."

Maggie couldn't face sharing the tragedy of her father with her children when they were young, and once they reached adulthood she was afraid they would be angry with her for not telling them sooner. She kept putting it off, and, as it turned out, Maggie had guessed right. Rowland didn't accept the revelation about Doc Barnes graciously.

"I liked it better when my grandfather was a hero," Rowland protested. He had enjoyed picturing Doc Barnes like Johnny Appleseed, a tough guy who knew how to survive on the frontier, a lady's man in buckskin with a few day's growth on his jowls and piercing eyes that had a twinkle if the right young lady caught his attention. Rowland imagined a handsome man with a scar on his face, the proof that he was a hero, and Rowland had been proud to be named after him. All of that was in question now.

"You're not being fair," Alethea objected. She wanted to rein Rowland in so he wouldn't dump blame on his mother. "The fictions we construct are fragile," she said. "I know. I've done it myself. I wasn't happy with the family I was given. They let me down, but it was the only family I had. No one comes from a perfect family, Rowland. Be careful!"

"I hate lies," Rowland snapped back at Alethea. "Why can't you understand that? They're lies, aren't they? You can't deny that. Mom withheld the truth from me because she didn't think I was man enough to handle it. So what if she told lies for good reasons? Lies are still lies."

Alethea wasn't keeping count, but she was aware that Rowland was protesting again that he was man enough to handle something. *He protests too much*, she thought silently to herself. *He doesn't believe anyone trusts him.* The pain was written on his face.

"One more thing," he said. "My grandfather's letter is pompous. He sounds like a stuffed shirt. Where's the heart? I mean, who drops a shitload of bad news in a letter and then signs off with 'I send you this with all my love and great gratitude.' How out of touch is that?"

"Oh, Rowland," said Alethea. "For heaven sakes, don't analyze the text! Doc Barnes was a sick man dictating a last letter to his doctor. It was a long letter. The pen was in his doctor's hand, and likely some of the words came from his doctor too. Do you have any idea the effort it took a dying man to send this letter? He was doing the best he could with his last chance."

Rowland was roiling, like a man caught in a riptide. He cracked his knuckles. His mouth was dry. Alethea reached over and rested a calming hand on his back, but he shrugged it off. "Damn!" he said. "Where does this stop? What can I trust? I don't know who my grandfather was, the mystery man I don't even have a name for. And I don't know who my stand-in grandfather was except a guy who couldn't tell the truth. Doesn't that make him an imposter? I don't know who my grandmother was either because obviously she was running away from something she was ashamed of and trying to keep hidden. It makes me wonder if I even know who Mom was. Did she know who she was? Does anyone ever tell the truth straight? Is it always told slant? With something missing? Something hidden?"

Alethea let Rowland catch his breath, but she was determined to defend the undefended. "Your grandfather wasn't out of touch. He was an old-fashioned gentleman, a man of his generation.

When they were suffering, they held themselves to a high standard of courtesy. No blame. No pity. No excuses for drawing others into their suffering. My own father was like that too. Millions of men in their generation were like that. They believed they were being silent in the service of love."

"Love? You're kidding. How about pride?" Rowland rubbed the back of his head.

"I can't say if it was love or pride," said Alethea, "but neither can you. They're gone now, so we can't ask them."

Rowland took a deep breath. "One thing's clear," he said. "It's not over when the undertaker cashes the check. They stick around for a while more to make us miserable. It looks like Doc Barnes is getting the last word."

"That's the last word? I doubt it." Alethea objected. "Your grandfather told the story the best he could. Your mother did too. Each with a certain slant. And also your telling of it will have a certain slant, if you bother to repeat it. That's what will happen until the stories are forgotten."

"With falsehood layered on deceit?" Rowland shot back.

"No, it goes on that way until eventually we aren't remembered by anyone anymore, and the last glimmer of evidence that we lived once upon a time gutters out like a candle. No one living knows us by name, or when we lived, or who we were. If we've not left a book, or a scroll, or a drawing on a cave wall, then what? You still have your grandfather. He left you a slightly off-kilter story and a test of character, although he probably didn't do that intentionally. The memory of him is yours now, and you have to decide how you want to tell his story."

"You're older than I am," Rowland said. "I mean that respectfully, but are you still trying to figure this out?"

"Lives are messy," Alethea admitted. "Mine, your mom's, yours, everyone's. Do we ever have the final version?" Alethea paused, took a breath, and then continued. "The story depends on who tells it. We can only see part of it, and each time it has a certain slant. Why wouldn't it? That's also true of our own stories. I've made mistakes, and I have regrets. I have scars too and resentments. Still I have no desire to roll back time and live it over again as if I could make a better second run and produce a better story. My future? It won't be long, because I've already had most of my birthdays. Whatever the future holds, I accept it already, but the story is hard to tell because it isn't finished."

As Alethea spoke Rowland searched her face. It was a face he'd known since he was a boy. There was not much new about it. A few wrinkles maybe, and some places where gravity was winning out under the eyes, around her mouth, and under her chin. But it was still the same face. And the voice too. It hadn't changed. He could remember it from long ago when he was a little boy sitting under the library table, surrounded by the safe duet of Alethea's voice and his mother's.

"I can say this for certain," Alethea was saying. "For all the mish-mash it's been, I'm glad I lived. I wouldn't have missed it for the world." Rowland looked at her and saw she was smiling. She looked at Rowland, and she could tell he believed her.

Ten

TALKING WITH ROWLAND ABOUT his grandfather had softened Alethea. Often after they had tea together, she'd find herself musing about Maggie, and about Rowland, and about the things they discussed. That's when she was most likely to have inner conversations with Maggie, conversations that were a little like prayers, messages from her heart directed toward someone she believed was listening. Sometimes it was easy to believe Maggie was listening. Other times doubt crept in. The conversations were most real when Alethea needed Maggie.

After telling Rowland about his grandfather, Alethea turned to Maggie for support. *Once you start telling the truth it's hard to stop, Maggie. I know you understand this. You were always more outspoken than I was. I learned early to be guarded, to barricade my feelings from hurt. It's different now. I'm an old woman, and I shouldn't have to be so careful anymore. Is it time to loosen my grip on all the proud and untrusting reasons I've had for holding back from Rowland? He's sweeter than I realized, and he's searching. Is it too much to say he's searching for a mother? He still needs one, and he misses you so much. I hope you're with me on this. You're going to have to trust me, Mags.* As Alethea's thoughts meandered, she was waiting for a sense that she'd caught up with Maggie, and that Maggie was there in step with her.

The next time Rowland came for tea, Alethea got right to the point. "I told you I wrote stories for a class I took. Do you remember?"

"Of course I remember," he replied. "I've been curious what happened to your story, but I didn't want to ask."

"Would you like to read it? It would help you understand why it meant so much to me to have a friend like your mom."

Rowland was learning that sometimes in conversations with Alethea fewer words were better than too many. He was also learning that courtesy went a long way. "I'd be honored," he said, using an expression that sounded like his mother.

"It was my first try at writing," Alethea went on. "No literary criticism please."

"It's a deal," he said, and his smile was boyish.

❖ ALETHEA'S STORY ❖

UNTIL I POURED OUT my heart to Maggie, I carried my past around like a shameful tattoo, trying to keep it hidden. Maggie was the first person to whom I confided the bleak years when I was Alethea Constantinides growing up in Philadelphia. I'll never forget the day I sobbed out my story and admitted to Maggie that I felt like an orphan. She listened and assured me, "Thea, I get it. I get it completely. I know why you feel like an orphan, and that makes two of us."

My poor dad was a factory worker, and my mother a depressed young woman. She never enjoyed us, because for her each of her kids was another load of work. I remember the day Papa brought home cotton candy for Teddie Junior and me. He'd picked it up from a stand just outside the factory gate, and like the other guys trailing out of the factory after the whistle that afternoon, he bought a paper cone of pink fluff as a surprise for us kids.

We were delighted with the cotton candy, but it was one more thing for my mother to grouse about. As soon as she saw the cotton candy, she let my dad know what she thought of it. "Ted, do you ever think past your damn Greek nose? That sticky crap will end up in their hair, on their clothes, and all over the furniture. And I'll be the one cleaning it up."

"Aw, honey, just let 'em eat it outdoors," Papa said. "Little kids need a sweet treat once in a while. I'll sit out there with them and make sure we don't get it in our hair." He winked at me because he knew I was listening. He knew I'd catch that he was going to have a few pulls of the cotton candy himself.

That didn't convince my mother. She was always sure she was right and didn't hesitate to make Papa look stupid. She took the precious puffy candy from his hand, walked over to the wastebasket, and stuffed it down into the garbage, making it clear there was no use trying to retrieve it from the onion peels and coffee grounds. Maybe she was mad because Papa didn't bring home something for her if he had money to spend on frivolous things. Or maybe she was mad because that is how she started out every day, and that was where she still was by the end of it.

When I was eight I got tangled into the web of my mother's rancor and never got free from it again until after I left home. It was a summer day that started out like any other. My dad went to work at the plant, and as soon as Teddie Junior and I finished our Wheaties, my mother gave the order, "Out to play kids. I've got work to do. Alethea, you keep an eye on Junior."

That's the way our summer days went. We played hopscotch or jump rope on the sidewalk, and sometimes we were allowed to go down the street and play in the schoolyard. Usually we'd disappear until the middle of the day, when my mother would holler out the door that lunch was ready. We went inside and sat at the kitchen table, or she gave us lunch on the stoop. I think it depended on whether lunch was peanut butter and jelly sandwiches we could handle without a plate or leftover goulash that needed a bowl. It also depended on whether there were other hungry kids around, because she was not the kind of mother who was going to "feed the neighbors' hungry brats."

I wonder if my mother always had so much work to do. When I went back into the house to use the bathroom, I saw her sitting on the sofa painting her nails or watching TV. I could tell how long she'd been sitting there in the chair across from the TV by the butts in the ashtray. Usually there were quite a few. Unless she had somewhere to go, her hair stayed in pin curls until just before Papa came home. My mother was a fan of *Queen for a Day,* and she called her TV shows her "one little luxury." Along with that one little luxury she also enjoyed her other indulgence, which was "a little wine." It wasn't a wine glass of wine; it was a tall beer glass filled halfway. When she watched her first show, she had her first glass. She was clever enough to keep that glass at half full even when she was steadily drinking from it. Her wine glass was one of those magic vessels that never went empty.

On that terrible summer day that changed my life forever, my mother came out of the house and announced she was going to the post office and then on some errands. I don't know why she had to go just then or why she didn't take us with her. I don't know either why she was dressed up with a hat, gloves, and high heels. She was carrying the patent leather purse Papa bought for her as a surprise, and, with the lipstick she'd put on and her hair combed out, she looked nice. She told me to watch Teddie Junior and made it clear that we were not to go into the house. She was convinced that wherever we went things got messy and dirty.

I was watching Junior, and he was good about listening. While I practiced jacks, he went out the front gate and as far as the neighbor's house three doors down because they had a beagle he liked. When Junior stood by the fence, the beagle jumped up to lick his hand, and all the while the dog's hind end would wiggle back and forth as if it was wagging its tail especially hard just for Junior. He was proud that the beagle didn't bark at him the way it did at strangers. That little courtesy on the part of the beagle, along with licks on his hand, made Junior feel he was part owner of the dog.

I had finally gotten past fivesies in Jacks, so I was feeling good, but I had to go to the bathroom. Sitting on a cool sidewalk didn't help, and I didn't think I could hold it until my mother came back. At first I told Junior to come inside with me, but he didn't want to, and it seemed silly to make him sit on a kitchen chair with orders not to touch anything while I went upstairs to the bathroom. I didn't feel right about leaving him alone outdoors either, because my mother had said I was responsible for him. I compromised. I told Junior to sit on our front steps until I came back. "Don't go wandering off," I told him. It seemed like a good plan.

I went up the steps two at a time and tried to go to the bathroom as fast as I could. Just as I was coming down the stairs and could see a slice of the front yard through the open door, I saw Junior running toward the sidewalk. I can still see the backs of his round legs and his sagging socks. If I knew how to draw, even today I could draw that part of the picture down to the detail.

That was the last thing I saw before I heard the screech and the thump, and then heard the wail of Billy's Gramma, who was sitting on their porch across the street. By the time I got down to the front of the house, it had all happened. I didn't see it actually, but I've been seeing it clearly in my mind ever since. How Billy came out in front of his house and called out to Teddie Junior because he wanted to show him what his grandma had brought him. It was a mitt with a brand new unscratched baseball nestled in it, like cheese in a mousetrap. And Billy shouted, "Hey, Junior, look! Look what I got!"

What five-year-old boy could resist that? Especially what five-year-old boy parked on the stoop waiting for something to happen? Junior did exactly what his instincts told him. Impulse overrode all the adult instructions about staying in your own yard, minding your sister, and never crossing the street without a grown-up. And who could have known that just at the moment when Teddie Junior ran out into the street toward Billy's house, a panel truck bringing a new chair for delivery to the Griffiths would swing around the corner and into our block?

I have two other images of Teddie Junior from those days. The first is his little body lying limp, draped over the curb after the truck picked him up and tossed him out of the way. Teddie's back and head are up on the curb, but his legs are still in the street, and his body is crooked as if someone didn't lay him down quite right. His shoulders and head turned one way, and his knees and feet turned the other. The life was squeezed out of Teddie like water gets squeezed out of a dishrag when it is taken in two hands and twisted one way by the left and the other by the right.

The other picture I have is Teddie lying on silk in a shiny wooden box. He is wearing a brand new first communion suit with a vest, and he has a tie of pure blue done perfectly into a knot under the collar of a sparkling white shirt. I think it was the first time, and I know it was the last time, my little brother ever wore a tie.

Laid across the front of Teddie's vest and tucked into his lapel, like a fancy watch chain, is a rosary. I know my mother put it there because the cross had the man on it. She was always very definite that an empty cross is not authentic. It was another way she had of declaring that her Italian family was better than Papa's Greek family. On that day in the funeral parlor, the matter of authentic rosaries didn't interest me nearly as much as wondering whether once Theodoro Constantinides Junior arrived in heaven his broken body would be straightened out again.

There is another detail about Teddie's brief moment of fame in the funeral parlor. On his left hand is Billy's brown leather baseball mitt, and in his right hand a brand new white baseball with perfect criss-cross red stitching. I know these are all real memories because I still have the black and white photo taken before they closed the box the last time. I'm not sure whose idea it was to put the mitt and ball in Teddie's hands, but I think Billy's parents offered them knowing that Billy would find no further pleasure in them. And I'm guessing Papa consented in one last attempt to believe that Teddie Junior died with happy visions as he ran across the street and into eternity.

My mother never got over Teddie's death. It's not that she became bitterer than before; she added a new theme to her self-pity. The mention of Teddie gave her a reason to sigh, and his picture on the table in the living room was a daily reminder that death had taken away her favorite child. It took the one who didn't mess up the house anymore. The day Teddie died got a new designation. It became the day "when Alethea let Teddie Junior get hit by that truck."

From then on I did what I could to get as far away as possible from my mother. I stayed late at school to wipe down the chalkboard and water the flowers on the windowsill in our classroom. I helped the kindergarten teacher wipe paste off the desks and carefully taped together the color crayons that had broken in the pressured fists of five-year-olds.

When finally I had to go home, I tried to stay out of earshot of my mother's miserable voice. Whatever room she was in, I tried to be in another. When the weather was bearable, I went outside to sit on the front steps. Bearable often meant tucking my purple knees as far as possible under my skirt and pulling up my socks as far as they would go. The excuse I gave for staying outdoors was that I liked to read my book out there.

Papa understood why I sat outside on the steps with my book. Sometimes when he returned from work, before he went into the house, he took off his sweater and draped it around me. It still felt warm. For himself Papa had another method of escaping my mother's poison. After dinner he walked down to the avenue and put his elbows up on the bar at Paddy's, where an accommodating bartender poured shots of Jack Daniel's when Papa nodded his head toward the empty shot glass in front of him.

On Saturdays Papa skipped Paddy's and went to the Spyridon Club, where he met his Greek friends and indulged in shots of Tsipouro with a chaser of Mythos. Some of the old guys still spoke Greek, and they'd take turns telling each other stories from the old country, indulging each other by laughing at exactly the right points in the story, as if they'd never heard it before. I don't know where my mother went on Saturday nights, but I know she wasn't home and didn't go with Papa to hang out with "those greaseballs that don't know a good grappa from a bottle of fruit juice gone bad." When she was being mean, my mother could be quite poetic.

When I was thirteen I got a job at the drug store, washing plates and glasses and scrubbing the long spoons for root beer floats. I made it my business to track down every splash and dribble from the milk shakes, and I buffed the thick glass banana split boats so that they gleamed, as if they had never been used before. I did my work to perfection because it was my pass for being absent from home until 9:10 every evening.

The drug store closed at 9:00, and it took me ten minutes to walk home, although after a while I learned that I could stretch it out until 9:30 by explaining that I had some things to finish up after closing time. Even Mr. Lintner accepted my strategies for stretching time. Some evenings when he left promptly at 9:00, he called back over his shoulder, "Alethea, make sure the door locks behind you when you leave." Apparently he trusted me.

I was a model child trying to do everything right because I didn't want to add any further sins to my ledger. I was desperate to believe that at the end of my life, my short list, with the horrible killing of Teddie, wouldn't seem so much worse than everyone else's long list with lots of itty-bitty transgressions. I figured my one big sin couldn't add up to that much more than everyone else's little nothings bundled together over many years.

I was nearly twenty-five before my dear friend Maggie confronted me about this cock-eyed thinking. "Let it go," she said. "Stop punishing yourself about Teddie. You've got to figure out the difference between sad and guilty or you'll be beating yourself up over this for the rest of your life." That was the day she used the word "peccadilloes," and later I looked it up in the dictionary. "Thea," said Maggie, "you don't have to count on everyone else's peccadilloes to counter your one big sin, because you weren't responsible for Teddie's death in the first place." That had never occurred to me.

Maggie was right. I have never gotten over feeling sad about what happened to my little brother, but I don't feel guilty about it anymore. Sometimes now I can see little Theodoro Junior sitting on the front stoop with sun glancing off his dark hair and a little bit of summer callous on his round knees. I can still hear his voice the way he would call out, "Hey everybody, look what I found!" That's what he would do if he discovered a nest in the hydrangea bushes along the front of the house or found an old rubber ball under the porch. I think of him now as a lucky child. He never had to figure out the difference between sad and guilty. He never had to grow old, but I still miss him.

I liked it when Maggie called me "Thea." Her voice didn't sound at all like my mother's when she would start out with, "Dammit all Alethea!" I liked having a name my mother never used. There's another reason I liked to be called "Thea." My Papa's Greek friends still called him "Theodoro," or sometimes just "Theo." I think it was my mother who watered the names down to Ted and Teddie Junior so we'd sound more American.

When I was thirteen and got the job keeping Mr. Lintner's soda fountain spick and span, I also started counting down the months until I could leave home. On my thirteenth birthday, which was the 18th of June, I calculated that I would have to live at home for sixty-one more months. Every month on the 18th I counted one down. I kept a piece of paper tucked under my mattress, and on the 18th I'd add another hatch mark. When I added a fifth horizontal slash, I could feel my heart do a somersault because it would take only a dozen bundles like that before I'd be free.

My mother found the paper when she was putting sheets on my bed, and she insisted on knowing what I was tracking. I know what she thought, because at the drugstore I worked behind the counter when it was busy, and the young guys came in to buy condoms in square foil wrappers. I'd also figured out what was going on those nights when the door to my parents' bedroom was closed, but I could hear my mother's giggles and knew they weren't sleeping. I didn't let on about any of this to my mother. I acted dense and kept her guessing.

When my mother was on to something, she was a pit bull. It made her mad that I was acting innocent, and finally, instead of asking any more questions, she took off after me with accusations and warnings. "Don't think you can fool me, little miss. I know why you come home late from the drugstore. Mistakes happen, and don't come crying to me. One stupid mistake and you'll end up paying for it for the rest of your life."

She looked at me with that dark look about which people say, "If looks could kill." It never dawned on me until years later when I told Maggie about this, that I was my mother's one little mistake, and it was for more than killing Teddie Junior that she never forgave me.

My mother was a childish sixteen year-old for the rest of her life. She became a mother long before she wanted to, and resented not having more time to flirt, and play, and test if men would notice her. That must have been a sacrifice for her, because my mother was one of those girls some people would call pretty, although I mostly remember that her nose was too big and her breath smelled like coffee and cigarettes. These were the things I could finally say out loud to someone else, once I began to tell Maggie about my family.

It took me nearly twenty years to ask where my mother was going that afternoon when she got gussied up and sashayed down the block, supposedly on her way to the post office. That was the afternoon when Teddie Junior ran into the street. Maybe she was going the same place she went on Saturday nights after Papa left for the Spyridon Club. Maybe that's why she was careful to come home early enough to get in bed before we heard Papa's unsteady steps on the stairs as he dragged himself home when the lights at the Spyridon Club went out at closing time.

When I talked to Maggie about my mother, I tried to imagine how different she might have been before she got jolted out of childhood. I don't have many pictures of her when she was young. There is one from her first communion. She is surrounded by her parents and her brothers, and standing behind her are two aunts who were nuns. My mother was a cute little girl.

There is another picture of my mother when she was a teenager. She is in a white bathing suit, posing on the front of a wooden motorboat. She is attractive in that old fashioned 1930's swimsuit way. In the picture it seems she knows it. It reminds me of her that day she walked down the sidewalk to the post office. She was all dressed up, and had a little sway in her hips as she walked in high heels. She was so different then, not at all like the mother who fretted about us always making work for her. The one who didn't like to share Papa's attention with us.

My mother was a flower that never bloomed. In a way she was like Teddie. One little choice changed everything. When I think of that, I know I should feel sorry for her, but I can't quite get to a place of sympathy that lasts. I do feel sorry for Papa. He stumbled into the trap too, and got taken by surprise just as my mother did, but he never stopped loving his wife and his children. Even after we lost Teddie Junior, Papa was always warm and kind. He never turned sour.

If I think about my mother too long, the sympathy evaporates, and I'm left with those other things. The edge in her voice when she said my name. The smell of her perfume when she got dressed up. That smug winner's look when my Papa playfully pursued her through the house before catching her and giving her one of those movie kisses, bending her back and nuzzling her neck before smooching her loudly. That's when she would cast a glance in my direction to make sure I understood she had won the competition for his affection. When Papa was being playful with my mother, I retreated to my room, trying not to hear them or think of them on the other side of the door.

My lucky break came the day Mr. Shawl called me to the guidance office at school. He pulled out paperwork for applying to colleges and assured me I would qualify for financial aid. I think he expected me to be disappointed that I would have to work on campus. Little did he know how much I wanted to work. Work was my refuge, and college was my escape.

In the dormitory I still lived in my cave, and I worried about being awkward and different. I hid food, just in case, and cleaned my room even when it didn't need it. I avoided friends who asked too many questions about my family. When someone commented about my dark curly hair, olive skin that didn't sunburn, or green eyes, I'd shrug but never admit that my one parent was Greek and the other Italian. On the rare occasion that someone asked if I had brothers and sisters, I told them I was an only child. It was easier to bear the insinuation that I was spoiled than to accept sympathy for Teddie's death.

A lot changed when I met Mark. He had everything I didn't have, including a family he went home to visit as often as he could because he liked them. He had religion; his family was Mormon. And he wasn't surprised that I stowed food away in my room, because his observant Mormon mother always stored enough food to last one full year. Others might find that a strange practice, but it made perfect sense to both Mark and me. One thing led to another, and we ended up with a plan to get married right after graduation.

I dreaded getting married. It wasn't being married that I dreaded; it was the wedding I was worried sick about. That had nothing to do with Mark. Before we got engaged he came home with me to visit my parents and took Papa aside to ask his permission. It meant a lot to Papa because that's the way it was done in the old country. Obviously Papa had never gotten around to doing that before he married my mother; nonetheless, this gesture of gallantry was proof to my Papa that Mark was a good man.

I knew I had to discuss the costs for a wedding. I'd been told by other girls in the dormitory that the parents of the bride were expected to pay for it, but I knew there was no way I could expect my parents to do this. The one time I broached the subject my mother's knee-jerk reaction was "Elope! It'll save you a lot of money. That's the way we did it." Papa stepped in and rescued me. "Don't worry about it, Alethea," he said. "We'll come up with it somehow. I'll take a loan if I have to. I've got only one daughter to walk down the aisle, and we're going to do this right."

Mark's family was generous too. They were apologetic because they had large families on both sides, and also friends and neighbors they wanted to invite. They wanted to include all the families that had invited them to weddings when their kids had gotten married. It was a swap, a two-way obligation. I was surprised how often Mark's mother said about friends they barely knew, "It would create hard feelings if we didn't invite them." I wasn't familiar with social systems built around avoiding hard feelings.

Once it was clear how long Mark's guest list would be, his parents stepped up and offered to pay for the reception. No matter how many people come to the church, it costs the same, but every time Mark's mother added someone to the guest list the cost of the reception went up. "That's our problem not yours, so we'll take care of it," Mark's dad said, and then he added the little addendum that probably made it worth it to him to pick up the tab. "Of course there won't be any alcohol, but if your guests would like coffee, tea, or lemonade we can make that available." Mark's Dad said that in a tone of compromise, but I picked up quickly that this was one more instance of "not creating hard feelings" with his parents' Mormon friends and relatives. Offering to pay for the reception was their way of having a "dry" reception and at the same time not causing hard feelings with my parents.

My parents couldn't imagine a wedding reception without drinks. How would guests build up courage to tell stories during toasts or get loosened up to go out on the dance floor? It took them a while to catch on that ours wouldn't be like the old style Greek weddings Papa was used to or the enormous Italian weddings of my mother's childhood. Once they realized the kind of wedding they were signed up for, my parents weren't in a position to argue. Their wallet didn't allow it. So we thanked Mark's parents for their generosity and let them organize the reception.

The day of our wedding is mostly a blur in my memory. I do recall my parents standing next to Mark's parents. My mother had a new dress, and she'd had her hair done at the beauty parlor. Papa wore a tux. Together they were a handsome couple. Uncle Stan, Aunt Sophia, and my cousins were invited, as well as Papa's Greek friends from the Spyridon Club. They were the guests most confused when they couldn't find the bar at the reception.

Toward the end of the evening, as Mark and I were making our exit, Papa kissed me goodbye and during a last lingering hug he whispered, "Well, even if it wasn't a Greek wedding, it was nice, don't you think?" He turned then and walked away without staying to wave goodbye to the bride and groom along with the other guests. I knew why. It wouldn't have bothered him to shed tears in front of his Greek friends, but he wanted everyone to know that Theodoro Constantinides knew how to behave at his daughter's American wedding.

I learned later from my cousin Shana that after the reception my relatives and Papa's friends reconvened at the Spyridon Club. He picked up the tab, not just for his guests, but for everyone at the club that night. I'll never know how he paid for it. It was one of the rare occasions that my mother went with him.

At the club Papa proposed a toast for his daughter and new son-in-law. There on home turf where having an accent didn't slow him down, he regaled his guests with stories and was finally able to shed the tender tears he had been holding back all day. As Papa reminisced, Uncle Stan and some of Papa's best friends pulled out their handkerchiefs to wipe down their faces. Their wives and daughters intercepted the teardrops on their cheeks with a delicate, but not hidden, side sweep of the index finger along the cheekbone just under the eye, which if done carefully does not leave lines in makeup.

Sometime toward the end of the evening before closing time, those still at the club joined in the Kalamatianos. This time my mother was at the head of the line with a white lace handkerchief in her right hand, while her left hand was held high by my Papa. Their friends joined with them, hand to hand, threading through the club in the effortless rhythms they first learned as little children when my mother in a lacey party dress and Papa in a first communion suit were drawn into the promenade of the generations. Finally it was my mother's turn to be the beautiful bride and Papa's chance to be a proud groom in the company of people who knew what a fine man he was.

I wish I could have been there to see it, although after all these years what difference does it make if I was there or not, because I do see it? The images my cousin Shana sketched for me soon after that evening at the club have gotten filled in with color and feeling. I hold on to this tender memory to assure me that not all was lost.

Decades later, after my mother passed away and Papa came to live with me, I asked him about the night at the Spyridon Club. He had recast his memory of the celebration and believed Mark and I were there with them at the club, finishing out the evening of our wedding day. I didn't correct him. He described old friends who were there and now were gone. "Oh, my darling Alethea," he said, "it was such a beautiful day and you were such a beautiful bride. It was the most beautiful day of my life except maybe for one other. That was the day just before we left for America. I stood with my Baba on the cliffs above the sea at Leonidio, and he said to me, 'Look carefully, Theodoro, and see it all. Whatever you see, take it with you, it is yours. This is yours to keep forever.' When I dream of heaven," my Papa said, "I stand on the cliffs of Leonidio and look across the sea."

Little did Papa know what he was doing that evening at the club when he took my mother's hand and danced, a man who would not bend to the insults of being an immigrant, who would not let his spirit be crushed by a thankless wife. He would not let the departure of his children end his life either. That night my darling Papa courageously threw the seeds of his dignity into the wind of the future, trusting they would take root in new ground, and he did it for me. For me and for Teddie Junior.

❖

Eleven

WHEN ROWLAND FINISHED READING Alethea's story, he left the manuscript on the table and went for a long walk. Strolling through the neighborhoods of Oak Park, he thought about a girl in Philadelphia, about her little brother, about a young woman escaping a bitter mother, and about her wedding day. He shuffled through his own memories of Alethea from when he was a boy. The girl of the story and the adult he remembered seemed so different.

Rowland had a fixed image, like a posed portrait, of Alethea and his mother drinking tea in the afternoon in the den on Woodward Street. Alethea was at his father's funeral too, mostly in the background but definitely there. Behind her back he'd mocked Alethea to his sisters. "She's permanently corseted," he'd said. "She probably sleeps in a corset." Alethea was one of those small, straight-backed women whose shape was more like a sturdy box than an hourglass, and she had a firm gait. It all added up to no nonsense, and she had probably learned to bear herself that way long ago as a young girl. She'd needed armor. The memory of his remark embarrassed Rowland. "Insufferable," he muttered half out loud to himself. "I wonder if my sisters remember that remark."

Rowland had never paid attention to the softer side of Alethea, her capacity for unsentimental love, her ability to persist and endure once she committed herself. She was the kind you could count on to show up when you needed her, but Rowland had never considered that he would ever need her. She wasn't the kind who complicated a difficult situation with a blizzard of words. She was a thoughtful presence. No wonder his mom treasured a friend like that.

On the way home from his long walk through Oak Park, Rowland passed the small florist shop his mother had always used. She didn't like ready-made arrangements. "They're too generic," she'd complained. "If you are going to send flowers for a special occasion the least you can do is pick special flowers." As Rowland stepped through the door and into the shop, he heard the bell on the door ring and wondered how often his mother had heard that same bell.

An older gentleman emerged from the back room to meet Rowland at the counter. "Good day," he said as he tucked the pencil he was holding into his shirt pocket and nudged up the glasses that had slipped down on his nose. "Looking for something in particular?"

"I need something for an older woman." The moment the words left his mouth Rowland felt foolish. "You probably don't need to know her age, do you? What kind of flowers am I looking for? I don't know much about flowers. Suggest something."

"Not seasonal then or for a funeral." The florist chuckled. He wasn't much younger than Alethea. His white shirt and tie were protected by a rubbery apron with fabric strips that held tools. Around his neck several long lengths of loose ribbon fell in soft spirals. "King protea," he suggested. "That's what you need. Where shall I send it?" The florist reached for his pencil and note pad.

"I want to deliver it in person," said Rowland.

"Considerate," the florist commented.

"What kind of flower is it?" Rowland threw out the question tentatively. He didn't want it to appear that he was questioning the florist's judgment.

"You wouldn't call *Protea Cynaroides* pretty. It's hearty, dramatic in the vase, long lasting, and dries well. It will last as long as you want to keep it. It's not fragile like orchids or roses. In the wild Protea has an indestructible underground stem with hearty buds that can survive wildfires and bloom again. It's a plant that demands respect." The florist's voice was reverent.

On the short walk home Rowland began composing what he would write on the card. Something about Protea and Alethea, but he couldn't make the lines work. His words felt thick and pointless. He was trying too hard to impress Alethea.

When Rowland arrived at Alethea's door with the Protea in hand, he was soft and tender. "I didn't know all those things about you," he told Alethea. 'I only knew you once you were an adult. That meant that you had the right to tell me not to run through the house or to take my boots off so I wouldn't track in mud on your shiny hardwood floors. They were always shiny, and you had nice rugs. I didn't think of you as having had a childhood; I thought of you as a force to be reckoned with, a force I admired, and one born with a lot of authority. Reading about you and your family, I understand better why Mom admired you so much."

"Thank you," said Alethea.

Rowland paused. "I don't want to overstep my bounds, but since reading your story I've read more in Mom's journals. She writes about a baby named Spencer." Rowland stopped there.

"It's okay to ask," Alethea reassured him. "Let me tell you that part of my story."

"WHEN MARK'S JOB TRANSFERRED him from Philadelphia to Chicago, I had to decide about looking for another job in a library. I decided to work only part time and to concentrate on having a baby. That baby was Spencer. When he was four months old I woke up in the middle of the night with swollen breasts, and I knew something was terribly wrong. He hadn't stirred for his feeding. I touched him. It's hard to talk about that night." Alethea cleared her throat and took a deep breath. "The feel of his little body was strange. It hadn't gone cold yet, but it was vacant. They called it 'crib death' in those days. I held my lifeless infant in my arms. I would have died for him, but he died instead.

Losing Spencer was the most difficult thing I've ever experienced. More difficult than losing my little brother, and more difficult than losing Mark, because we had our years together. The loss of Spencer was a disaster for our marriage. Mark and I handled grief so differently. As soon as he could, Mark went back to work, occupying himself with everything that had nothing to do with Spencer. I couldn't think of anything but Spencer.

One Saturday Mark said, 'Alethea, let me box up Spencer's clothes and take down his crib so you won't have to see those things every day.' I hadn't laundered the clothes Spencer wore the day we lost him. I'd folded them in layers of tissue and put them in the preservation box where I was keeping my wedding dress. I hadn't moved the items in his room, not even changed the sheets in his crib. Mark wanted to hide those things away in the attic.

Every effort Mark made to comfort me added to my fury. We didn't talk to each other beyond what was necessary. Eventually we tried to have another child. It wasn't love. It was desperate baby-making, and it didn't work. We visited doctors. That was agony for Mark, and he pulled away from me. He stayed late at the office and found reasons to be away from the house whenever he could.

You think when you marry someone you care about, and you have those feelings of being in love, you can face anything together. It's not true. Love is fragile. It's fury that's durable. When fury gets knocked down it bounces right back up. Under attack, love withers.

I was depressed, and the only person who understood me was Maggie. I raged with her about how unfair it was that my mother, a woman who never wanted children in the first place, popped out two of them with no effort. Meanwhile, no matter how much effort I put into making it happen, I couldn't conceive. Losing Spencer drew me into a contest with my mother, and once again she was winning.

Maggie stayed with me while I ranted, pounding my fists on the sofa cushions, and shouting loud enough for the neighbors to hear. She didn't try to quiet me down or talk me out of it. How could two people who both claimed to care about me be so different? Mark couldn't hear what I needed to say because, he claimed, he loved me and it was too painful. And Maggie could hear anything I had to say, because she was my friend, and she cared about me.

Finally Mark and I had the conversation that had been festering for months. 'I can't do this anymore,' Mark said. 'I can't manage my life around figuring out when to have sex so we can have a baby. I dread coming home to have you tell me it didn't work. I don't want to go to appointments to figure out whose fault it is or which one of us is flawed. It all disgusts me.'

'Well, get over it! Pull yourself together!' I told him. I had no sympathy for him.

'I want to love you,' he said, 'and I want to make love the way we used to. But I'm leveling with you, Alethea: I have the urge to get in my car and drive as far away from you as I can get.'

'That's a rotten thing to say to your pathetic barren wife,' I raged.

'Don't use those words?' he said. 'I want a normal life. I want that for myself, and I want that for you. This is ruining you. You've changed so much I hardly recognize you as the Alethea I married. This isn't normal.'

'Maybe we're not normal,' I shouted back. 'You think having a baby die is normal? Is it normal not to have children?' I was one breath away from punching him.

'You're not the only one who hurts,' Mark said.

'Act like a man!' I screamed at him. Like most men, Mark was a fixer, and he couldn't fix this. I used that as a weapon against him. If he wasn't as grief-stricken as I was, and if he didn't keep trying to fix this, then he wasn't a real man. It was a cruel thing to say. I felt like a slasher. I wanted him to bleed.

Mark began to sob from deep in his belly. Then he was terribly quiet, and all I could hear was breathing. At last he said, 'Alethea, I'll give you a divorce. You can go after what you want. Figure out how to have a baby. Do whatever it takes. But not with me. I can't do it.'

The next morning Mark got up, showered, shaved, ate breakfast, and went off to work the way he always did. All day long I mulled over taking his offer of divorce. At one moment I was close to accepting it, and then a moment later I couldn't imagine my life without him. When Mark got home, he said, 'Let's not drag this out. My offer stands. If you choose to stay with me, I'll be the best possible husband I can be. No excuses. You deserve a happy life. That's the best I have to offer. I'll accept what you decide.'

Mark wasn't a man who made fickle promises. Most wives I knew didn't have husbands who made promises like that. They might put the offer of a divorce on the table, but the promise to be the best husband possible without excuses? No way! Most men wouldn't think they owed their wives that. In the back of their minds they'd be thinking 'a man has a right to be a man,' and that would be their built-in excuse for always tipping the balance a little extra in their own direction. Mark wasn't offering that. He wasn't offering me an ordinary, mediocre, bumble-along marriage. He was offering a better than usual marriage, but one without children.

I made my choice. I decided to keep as much of what was good in my life as I could. I knew that meant I couldn't continue throwing everything precious into a sinkhole of bitterness. I thought about my mother and my father. I chose my father's way."

THE ENTIRE TIME ALETHEA was telling about Spencer and Mark, Row didn't look away once. When her voice trembled, he noticed. He reached over and touched her hand. There were tears in his eyes. "I'm so sorry, Alethea, so sorry for your loss," he said.

"Oh, Row. It still means a lot when someone says that, because even after all these years, I feel comforted when I'm understood."

"I always thought Mark was a good man," said Rowland. "I respect him even more now. I wish I could tell him I'm sorry for his loss too."

"He'd appreciate that as much as I do," Alethea assured Row.

It was a tender moment. Rowland had so often been skittish about feelings. He'd grown up with a father like Ross and a brother like Will. Men's men. Good men, but tough guys cloaked in that thick-skinned emotional leather that keeps feelings from getting through. Row was changing. Alethea could see what Maggie had always claimed was there, and she felt close to him.

Alethea tried to explain to Rowland how important his mother was when she and Mark lost Spencer. Maggie was the first person Alethea told when she suspected she was pregnant, and she admitted to Maggie how scared she was. She hadn't told Mark about her fear. To Maggie she confessed how much she dreaded going to the doctor, and Maggie told her every woman dislikes it. "Just focus on something else," Maggie said.

Alethea was surprised later that Maggie asked her what she thought about when she was trying to focus on something else in the doctor's office. "Putting mascara on," Alethea told her.

"Hold it, Thea," Maggie said. "You don't even wear mascara."

"That's the point," Alethea explained. "I tried to think of something that I'd never done before so that I'd have to concentrate. I thought about not poking myself in the eye. We laughed until we were nearly out of breath. Maggie understood. Over the years when one or the other of us was distracted during a conversation, we'd say 'are you trying not to poke yourself in the eye?' and it always relieved the tension."

In telling Rowland about her friendship with Maggie, Alethea didn't want to recall only the dark times, because there were also light-hearted times. That's why she decided to tell Rowland about the doctor's visit and what it meant for Maggie or Alethea to ask about not poking themselves in the eye. As she began talking about Maggie, the good stories kept coming, Alethea kept talking, and Rowland kept listening.

Maggie was smart and confident. When she decided to do something, she went the whole nine yards. After Mark's mother taught Alethea how to bake seven-grain bread, she taught Maggie, who practiced until her loaves were perfect. Maggie became passionate about bread. "Thea," she said, "do you ever stop to think that people have been eating bread with some sort of oil, like butter or olive oil or ghee, for thousands of years? While alchemists were trying to crack the secrets of how to create gold, women were preserving the mystery of how to sustain life. We're the original alchemists. Bread is a wonder." Sometimes Alethea had to go to the dictionary to look up words like "alchemy" and "ghee." She wondered how Maggie came up with poetry like that, right off the cuff.

Maggie was curious too. She saw magic in ordinary things, and it made being with her lively. Once during a huge rainstorm she led Alethea outdoors to stand on the porch, where Maggie threw her arms out wide and opened up her chest for a deep breath. "Thea," she said, "you have to be outdoors to smell rain. It's not the same from behind a window. We wouldn't want to miss this one, would we?"

"Before I met Maggie," Alethea told Rowland, "I was withered up like a dried seed, but friendship with Maggie was like water." In childhood after the death of Teddie, Alethea was convinced nothing remarkable would ever happen to her again, at least anything remarkable that was good. That changed when she met Maggie, who started calling her "Thea." As far as Alethea knew she was the only person who ever called her friend "Mags."

Once Alethea said, "Mags, I'm glad I met you. You introduced me to a different life."

"Thea," Maggie replied, "I'm glad I met you too. I need someone like you to keep me honest. People who came up like we did have a special kind of dignity, but only if we're willing to remember the things a hardscrabble life taught us."

"Hardscrabble" was another word that Maggie pulled out of her sleeve. Alethea didn't know the word before she heard Maggie use it, but when Maggie said it, Alethea knew instantly what she meant. It made her proud to be Maggie's friend. If someone else had said her childhood was hardscrabble, Alethea might have been insulted, but when Maggie did, she felt she'd been given an award.

"If a friendship lasts a long time," Alethea said, "there are bound to be difficulties. Life doesn't roll out smoothly, and friends get caught up in the mess. Once you get through the test of worrying that your friendship is not as perfect as you thought, you shift over into being grateful that it's durable."

Row was still listening quietly. "Is that what Mom's saying in her journal when she's remembering Spencer's birthday?" he asked. "There's one part I can't understand. She says she felt embarrassed by some things she said to you."

It was the right time to go on with the story. It wasn't easy for Alethea to keep talking, but she could tell Rowland was ready to listen, and she was hoping Maggie would approve.

After they lost Spencer and were struggling with infertility, Alethea was having lunch with Maggie, and she could tell Maggie was nervous about something. She was picking at her salad as if she couldn't find the right leaf. She kept resettling the curl that she tucked behind her ear. Finally Alethea said to her, "Are you trying not to poke yourself in the eye?" and Maggie knew what Alethea meant.

"I need to tell you something," she said. "I'm pregnant."

"Congratulations," Alethea forced herself to say.

"Oh stop it," Maggie said. "That's not the right thing to say. I've been scared to tell you. I feel guilty. Like I'm inconsiderate. You know what I mean. Tell me, am I being inconsiderate of you?"

"People aren't going to stop having babies so I won't feel bad," Alethea told Maggie.

That wasn't enough to settle the matter for Maggie. "After all you've been through. And after the way I added to the confusion. When I look back now I see what a terrible time it was, and I wasn't a good friend. I wanted so much for you to have a baby. I'm really sorry."

"You don't have to apologize."

"I don't want to hurt you. Tell me you believe that," Maggie insisted.

"Of course I do," Alethea told her. "I'll handle it. And I mean it, congratulations!"

Maggie's instincts were right. By the end of the day Alethea had her first bout of envy. She felt terrible about not having babies of her own, and she felt terrible about being envious of Maggie. Alethea's inclination was to pull away, and to Maggie's credit, she kept coming back to fix it. Alethea wanted that too, but it was harder for her.

Maggie had her baby. It was Jenna, beautiful little Jenna, and Alethea visited them the day Jenna was born. From the very beginning Maggie handed her over to Alethea. "I want you to be Jenna's other mother," she said. "I want her to be special to you and you to her. I'm giving you mother's rights. When you have advice, don't hold back. When I make decisions, I'm going to consult you."

"Like a godmother?" Alethea asked.

"No. I had a godmother," Maggie said. "She showed up on my birthday with barrettes or socks with lace cuffs, or something else a little girl was supposed to like. For the rest of the year I didn't see her. That's not what I'm asking of you. I want more, and I need you to promise."

This was so like Maggie. It was loving, and novel, and touched profoundly on all they had gone through together. All the loss and confusion.

A sweet feeling rose in Alethea as she told Rowland about Jenna. She loved Jenna in a special way, because Jenna reminded Alethea of Maggie, the young woman who stood out on the porch in the rain. The one who believed she was doing alchemy when she baked bread. "That bond that forms when you hold a baby on its very first day," said Alethea, "and you look into those eyes that are so deep with innocence, that bond goes to the heart." Her voice went quiet and her eyes drifted away. This time Rowland knew not to ask her if she was trying not to poke herself in the eye.

Alethea wondered if she could learn to love Row the way Maggie did. It would mean accepting his eccentricities and being able to ride the waves of his unpredictable feelings. She found herself thinking, "*Maggie, what do you want me to share with him? Let's do this together.* And then Alethea knew what she had to say. "Row, I have more to tell you, but for today this is enough."

"I'll look forward to it," he said.

Twelve

WHEN ROWLAND WENT HOME he reread the journal entry Maggie had written about Spencer. Later he slid the page under Alethea's door, and in the morning she found it there.

> *Today is the 30th anniversary of Spencer's death. I still think of him as a baby in a one-piece suit with snaps down the front. He is lying on his back and kicking his legs, practicing for the day he will ride a bike. My memories are out of date. If he were living now he'd be a grown man with car keys in his pocket and a wallet, but the image of the grown man is beyond my reach because I haven't had all the years in between to assemble it. I have the same stuck time frame for Steven, who will never live beyond his 20's. I'm sure Alethea also remembers Teddie this way.*
>
> *I still feel embarrassed about the proposal I made to Alethea after she lost Spencer. I had a temporary lapse of sanity. I take some comfort in Alethea's forgiveness. Today I am going to put that aside and be the friend Alethea deserves.*

Alethea decided to be honest with Rowland about what happened between Spencer's death and Jenna's birth. When it became obvious that Mark and Alethea were not producing a baby, Maggie came up with an idea that was totally off the wall. "I'll have a baby for you, and you can adopt it," Maggie offered. "People used to do that. Abraham's wife offered the maid to him so he could have children even when Sarah couldn't. I know this is a little far out, but we're good friends, and I know how much you want to be mother."

Alethea was stunned. "Mags, tomorrow you're going to wake up and think about the crazy thing you just said. You'll apologize to me, and I'll understand. It means the world to me that you would even think of doing that, but it's impossible. You know that, right? People don't give their children away."

"That's not true," Maggie said. "They do give them away, but it's usually to strangers. Some kids would be better off if their parents gave them away. Whatever reason other people do this, I want to do this because I know you'd be a great mother, and giving a baby to you would not be giving it to a stranger."

When Maggie had a plan she was hard to stop. She brought it up with Ross, and he was incredulous, but he didn't veto it outright. Instead he did what Ross always did. He listened as if he thought Maggie didn't mean it. When something didn't make sense to Ross, he couldn't imagine that it made sense to Maggie, because Ross was a man who believed in himself single-mindedly.

Maggie wouldn't leave it alone. She brought it up again with Ross, trying to get him to see her plan. He shifted his strategy, but the conclusion was the same. First it was "Aw, Maggie, you really hurt for Alethea, don't you? You're a good friend, but be careful saying things like that to her." On a second go-around it was, "You're leading her on, building up her hopes. You know it's impossible. People don't give their kids away. Don't get carried away with your feelings, Maggie; you've got to be reasonable or you'll hurt Alethea."

It made Maggie angry that Ross twisted the conversation around to make it sound like he was protecting Alethea. Maggie was convinced he wasn't considering Alethea in the slightest, because if he had been, he would have understood how desperate she was to be a mother. What made Maggie even angrier was Ross's assumption that he could close down the conversation before there was any back and forth discussion between them.

Maggie worked on Ross until finally he'd had enough. "What the hell, Maggie," he said. "Get a grip on yourself. Even if you're willing to give your kids away, I could never give mine away. As long as you're married to me, your babies are my children. I'm committed to them even if you aren't."

That was a comment Maggie couldn't forget. It stayed with her like shrapnel buried deep in her flesh. She stopped bringing up the matter with Ross, but she worked over the insult with Alethea. "How can he possibly think he's more committed to our children than I am? He announces that he has to travel for work, no discussion. The kids are definitely mine when he's gone. Any night he chooses to stay late for work, he's only a phone call away from freedom. On those nights I take over, and it doesn't matter how tired I am or what else I have to do. He can say what he likes, but it's obvious that his commitment is more flexible than mine. He should try being a mother."

Alethea didn't blame Maggie for backing out of her offer. She knew the instant Maggie came up with it, that it wouldn't work. On this particular matter Alethea was more like Ross than like Maggie. They were both practical and down to earth. Something else happened, however, that Alethea didn't expect.

After Maggie gave up the notion of having a baby for Alethea, she still held on to her resentment toward Ross. She couldn't get over it. The evidence was on Maggie's side in defense of her virtues as a mother, but that didn't heal the injury of Ross's comment. Often at the end of her litany of complaints Maggie would sigh and say, "I'm married to a man who's absolutely sure he's entitled to have the last word. You have no idea what it's like to live with a man so morally sure of himself. It's lonely."

When Maggie first brought up the idea of being a surrogate for Alethea, it seemed like such a far out idea that Alethea didn't mention it to Mark. They had enough difficulty as it was talking about infertility. But as the tension continued, Alethea thought it only fair that he know what Maggie had offered, even though it was water under the bridge. In addition, Alethea was concerned that sometime it would come up in a conversation with Ross, although later she realized that men don't talk about that sort of thing with each other. She didn't understand that then.

Mark was hurt that the conversation with Maggie had gone on without him knowing about it, and he was embarrassed that Ross had been brought into their personal struggle with infertility. He was sure Ross, who made babies so easily with his wife, would pass judgment on a man who couldn't give his wife children. "I'm the last to know what others are planning for my life," Mark complained. "Did it occur to you that I would have a say in an arrangement like that? You assume I would do whatever you decided?" That is what was going on when Mark offered Alethea a divorce so she could go ahead and do whatever it took to have a child, and that's when Alethea accepted his offer to make their marriage as good as it could be, even if it was without children.

Even after it was clear that Maggie would not have a baby for Alethea, there were other tensions for them to resolve. Alethea was sensitive about not having children, and after Mark's magnanimous offer Maggie was envious of Alethea's marriage. Ross was a good man, but when he was distant and unbending, it hurt Maggie. Alethea seldom went to their house anymore when Ross was there, because the forced politeness, after all they had been through, felt awkward. Maggie didn't avoid Mark, but she and Ross tended to soften their interactions with Alethea and Mark by counting on the buffer of other friends. These cautions created zones in their friendship.

Alethea told Rowland about Maggie's offer to have a baby for her, but she didn't tell him about what happened next. Ross went away for an extended assignment in Switzerland. Maggie and Ross had been there together when Laura was a baby, but now they had three children, and moving the entire family across the ocean was impractical. That didn't stop Ross. He went anyway, and Maggie stayed back to manage children, the household, and everything else on her own.

At first Alethea thought Ross's absence would make Maggie more available, but it didn't. Every day was overload for Maggie, and in addition she had a new friendship with a man she had met through her work. There was something in her life she wasn't sharing with Alethea; furthermore, Alethea preferred not to know about it. She was trying to focus on rebuilding with Mark, and that included not bringing her friend's dramas into the arena of their marriage.

Lunches with Maggie were boring because they talked trivia. Maggie fidgeted. She lost weight. She had a new hairstyle. Alethea missed the Maggie who would go out on the porch during a storm to breathe in air made fresh by rain. It felt as if the woman sitting across the table from her was a stranger visiting from behind a window. When Ross returned from Switzerland Maggie was still distant. It was sometime after that, when Alethea and Maggie had lunch together, that Maggie told Alethea she was expecting.

Jenna's birth was the beginning of a new connection for Maggie and Alethea. Much of the time they spent together was domestic and ordinary. Alethea delighted in doting on Jenna, and Maggie would take the opportunity of Alethea's presence to cook, or bake, or paint a wall. Meanwhile Mark made extraordinary efforts to fulfill his promise to Alethea, and she came to love him in a new way for that. That was not easy for Maggie because it was a harsh reminder of what she did not have. Her relationship with Ross was built around a practical division of labor, which included intentionally cordoning off feelings.

Maggie and Alethea remained good friends, but there was a new tenderness in their relationship. Not a sweet tenderness. Not sweet at all. It was tenderness like a sprain that you have to be careful not to land on wrong so you won't reinjure it.

Alethea didn't tell Rowland all the details of those strange months when Ross was away. It was too much to expose to a son. She decided she would leave open the possibility of telling him about it some other time, but only if it felt right. She would need to trust her intuition.

It crossed Alethea's mind that she was withholding the truth, and when Maggie held back the truth about her father, Rowland called it "lies." His view of truth was unfamiliar to Alethea. He had this notion that you wouldn't hold back anything from someone you liked. Secrets were the big threat. When all the other strands in bonds of fidelity had frayed, putting it all out there and speaking the truth was the last thread to hold.

Alethea too believed there was value in being authentic, and she understood the downside of deceits that victimized others. She was straightforward and had an aversion to cunning and manipulation. But she wondered, don't we get to choose what we share? Do we owe anyone else all our inner thoughts? Is the price of friendship that we no longer have privacy?

Alethea believed in privacy. She admired it. She remembered her father speaking with great respect for a friend "who kept his own counsel." She wanted to preserve her own belief that there is a deep inner space that is ours to keep or to share as we see fit. It is ours and ours alone to call forth if we will, and no one has a right to demand it. Call it old-fashioned if you like, but there is something about privacy that keeps life tidy and keeps people intact. She was still wrestling with this when she received an email from Rowland.

> Hi Alethea,
>
> Sometimes Mom had far out ideas and an enormous imagination. Knowing more about her now, I feel closer to her. I've been thinking about my own children. I want them to know me. I want them to know my mother and their aunts, their Uncle Will and my father. I'm not sure my kids are ready to sit down with me and hear all those stories now, and I'm not sure I'm ready to tell them. I'll have to figure out when the time is right.
>
> Yours,
> Rowland

> Dear Rowland,
>
> All the things you describe about your mother are things I loved about her too. Once in the middle of complicated times she said to me, "If I can't love sweetly, I'll love fiercely, but I refuse to give up on love no matter how hard it is." That's a bold way to live, and it takes a strong person.
>
> Yours truly,
> Alethea

Part IV

To Be Gathered Together Again

When you are sorrowful look again in your heart, and you shall see that in truth you are weeping for that which has been your delight . . . . You are suspended between your sorrow and your joy.

—*Kahlil Gibran*

Thirteen

ALETHEA CALLED TO CANCEL their next visit, and Rowland worried that he'd worn out his welcome, but she explained she was going away for the weekend. On Friday Lorraine's grandson was driving to Milwaukee for Lorraine's birthday, and he offered to pick Alethea up to take her along. He'd drop her back home on Sunday, but it would be too late for Alethea to get together with Rowland. "It's not ideal," said Alethea. "I'll have to stay over two nights, and I'm not comfortable in a strange bed or navigating unfamiliar hallways when I get up in the night. But I want to see Lorraine, and she's too fragile to come here to visit me."

"I'll drive you," Rowland suggested. "If we left early in the morning and drove back in the evening, you wouldn't have to sleep in a strange bed."

"That would be nice. It would give you a chance to catch up with Lorraine's children too. They'll all be there." Alethea smiled. "Those kids have been so loyal to their mother."

"Some families are better at that than others," Rowland observed. "What's the magic touch? What did Lorraine do to keep them close? Sooner or later when we see our kids moving toward the edge of the nest, all parents start to ask that. Will they leave and never come back? If only Lorraine could tell us."

"I didn't raise children," said Alethea with sadness in her voice. "I don't have an answer for you, but I can tell you that having children circle round you when you are old is certainly a gift. Lorraine is fortunate."

"I never knew her well," said Rowland. "She was nice, but I didn't pay attention to her beyond that. Kids notice what serves their own interests." As far as he was concerned, she was just another mom among all the others who lived in a house in their Oak Park neighborhood, drove kids places, and came to events at school.

"I still have a copy of the story I wrote about Lorraine's early years," said Alethea. "Would you like to see it before you visit her?"

"Definitely. I'd like that," Rowland told Alethea.

❖ Lorraine's Story ❖

Lorraine was born in Southern Illinois in an area so flat you might wonder if water had anywhere to run downhill. Her father owned his own farm, and so did most of the neighbors. When she was eight, Lorraine learned to drive the tractor. Two hours in the morning she'd go back and forth along the rows, turning carefully at the end, and calculating when she would be near the barn so she could turn in to let her brother Skip refuel and take over for the next two hours. When she walked back to the house, her lunch was on the kitchen table across from the empty plate that Skip had just polished off. It was a well-organized system of farm labor that included kids.

When Lorraine's shift on the tractor was over, it didn't mean her work was done. Off the tractor she was the family courier. She'd hear her mother call, "Lorraine, run this out to Dad," or "Lorraine, go to the barn and tell Chuck there's a phone call for him." Her uncle Chuck, single and in his thirties, grew up on the farm and never left it. Originally the farm belonged to Lorraine's grandparents, and when her Dad took it over from them, Chuck came along with the land, the farm implements, and the house. He had a second-floor bedroom that had been his when he was a boy, and it was still called "Chuck's room."

When Lorraine drove the tractor, her brother Skip teased her that she didn't need a license to drive a tractor. "All you need is proof you can fill that big butt-shaped seat with your own fanny."

His humor about the tractor seat was a way of teasing her for being slightly plump, but it also made Lorraine wonder who'd invented a tractor seat shaped like the imprint of someone's rear end. Chairs in the house weren't shaped that way. Furthermore, even though her mother could have filled the tractor seat very amply, she was the one member of the family who never drove the tractor. Skip's teasing made Lorraine wonder about that too.

During harvest season Lorraine's dad and Uncle Chuck kept the tractor going nearly twenty-four hours a day. Before supper on hot summer days, Lorraine and Skip sat on the porch rail that stretched across the shady front of the house. From that perch they matched the drone of the tractors with the puffs of dust visible across the horizon. They could name most of them. In the evening if it was still hot, they sat on the porch until after dark. Out across the fields they saw the eerie sway of light from tractors' headlamps, and they'd have a contest to see who could count the most. Although they made a sincere effort to count all the visible lights, they each added a few for good measure. By the time Lorraine was eight, she'd already figured out that the first person to give their count lost, and the second person to report won by a tractor or two. She learned early not to rush to be first in line.

Unlike some of his neighbors, Lorraine's dad didn't stop work on Sundays. He insisted that his wife and children go to church, but he and Uncle Chuck worked on through. The tired men with farmers' tans nodded off during the sermon, but their wives didn't nudge them during harvest season the way they did during the rest of the year. A farmer who sat down for more than a few minutes would be tempted to catch a few winks, and it was one of the few temptations kindly overlooked in their little church.

Summer Sundays in the middle of July, when there was not a hint of breeze, the little church, appropriately called "Crossroads Church," turned into a cooker. The expanding beams made cracking sounds like rifle shots, and the women in cotton summer dresses discreetly daubed streams of sweat before they dropped off their faces or ran down their necks to make wet spots on the floral fabric of their Sunday clothes. Some of the older women still used white handkerchiefs with lace edges, and between daubs they tucked them into their bosoms instead of their purses, knowing that shortly they would need their handkerchiefs again.

When the beams cracked and the daubing started, the janitor took it as a sign to open up the cathedral windows. Calling them cathedral windows was an exaggeration, but they were a style of window whose lower two thirds swung open on hinges while the top third was fixed and angled into a peak, a sure sign this building out in the fields was a church and not a school. It might have made sense to open the windows before the service, except for the uncomfortable trade-off between tolerating the heat due to closed windows and tolerating the flies hovering outside ready to rush in as soon as the windows were opened.

The janitor's chore was accomplished with a long pole that had a hook on the end. The first step was to pull open the high latch that locked the window. It's a mystery why the windows were locked at all, given the fact that for miles around when farmers parked vehicles in their yards they left keys in the ignition for convenience, and when they went to town they did the same, out of habit. They left their houses and barns open too, in case a neighbor needed to get in to borrow something. The church windows were locked for no other reason than that the locks were there, although the janitor said they were locked to keep them from blowing open during dust storms or heavy rain. That didn't explain why they were locked on sunny days and during mild weather, except for the fact that habits are easier to keep than break.

The janitor's second maneuver was to swing the window around to secure it to the wall, at which point he had to line up the loop on the wall and the catch on the window. The moment the janitor stood up and walked over to pick up the pole that was alongside the aisle under the windows, all heads turned to watch. It wasn't easy to land the hook at the end of the pole exactly on the window lock in just one try. If it took too many tries with the whole congregation watching, the janitor's hands trembled. Meanwhile the preacher talked on, although anyone who could break away from the drama at the window long enough to look back to the pulpit could see that the preacher also was watching out of the corner of his eye to see if the janitor could get the job done.

Years later, when Lorraine told the story of Sunday mornings at Crossroads Church and the janitor's struggle to open the windows, she chuckled about how little it took to entertain weary farm families. "It's not like we were used to much excitement, and church was more interesting than going up and down the rows on a tractor." She didn't chuckle when she told about the Sunday when their neighbor, who was sitting a few rows ahead of them, slumped over toward his wife during the service. He wasn't dozing off. He had a heart attack.

A funeral, which neighbors and church members were expected to attend, was an unwelcome interruption during one of the busiest times of the year, but no one mentioned it. Some did comment that it was fortunate "old man Stevens" didn't have the heart attack while on his tractor, because they could remember a farmer a few towns away who'd had sunstroke on his tractor and drove it through the wall of his barn. Some, who were feeling self-satisfied about having been in church that Sunday morning, piously commented that "old man Stevens" had picked as good a place as any for passing through the gates to glory.

In the barn, Lorraine's brother Skip and her Uncle Chuck, who had not been in church that morning, cracked jokes along with her dad about whether the Good Lord would have preferred to meet "old man Stevens" in his overalls and John Deere cap or dressed in his Sunday trousers and a white shirt pasted to his back with sweat. Of course they didn't crack these jokes when they were over at the neighbor's farm, along with the other farmers who were helping the widow bring in the crop.

Commentary was a style of conversation Lorraine heard often as she was growing up. One of the best at it was Filmore Jessup, who didn't have a place of his own but went from farm to farm doing implement repairs. He was usually the first to know the latest news. Some neighbors thought Jessup was a gossip, but he thought he was doing the community a service. In addition to reporting the latest as he moved among his neighbors, Jessup often added a lengthy excursus about the good or bad fortune of events. His analysis of breaking news was delivered with the piety of a weekday preacher.

After the high school kids, coming home from out-of-town basketball finals, rolled their car on the last curve before the county road went under the highway, Jessup did a careful analysis. If they had gone off the road on the second curve where the line of windbreak trees came to the road's edge, they might have hit one of those trees, and it would have been, as Jessup was apt to say, "curtains." As it turned out, all the kids survived, although a few had broken bones. Jessup was certain their good fortune had something to do with divine providence. Each time he repeated the story, he added a heartfelt "Thank the Lord," and also a reminder that "we never really know do we?" Jessup was not one to presume on divine mercy.

When Jessup repeated the story at the grain elevator, a farmhand was there who'd just moved into the area from Ohio. To Jessup's well-rehearsed story, the newcomer replied, "Hell no, you never can tell what'll get ya. Could be thin ice or a banana peel." Jessup didn't correct him, but from that time on he referred to the man and his family as "those unchurched folks who live over beyond the Tulvers." That was enough to put them on the map because the Tulvers were members of the Crossroads Church.

What Lorraine learned on the farm in southern Illinois stayed with her. High on the list of valuable lessons was her work ethic. As a kid she'd helped with the dishes, picked beans and tomatoes in the side garden, and collected eggs. Going to the hen house wasn't an adventure, the sort of thing hobby farmers do with their kids to educate them about animals and the place of humans in the food chain. Lorraine collected the eggs, because if she didn't, her mom wouldn't have them to scramble up when her dad came in from a night on the tractor. He was a hard-working man and expected someone to slide a plate of bacon, eggs, and pancakes in front of him for breakfast. That was Lorraine's introduction to the food chain and the value of chores.

Lorraine learned early that age had nothing to do with whether a child could take responsibility for a chore. If you could do it, you were expected to pitch in and get it done. That was the thing about driving the tractor. Lorraine's Dad didn't ask if eight years old was grown up enough to drive a tractor. Instead he told her to get in the seat to see if she was tall enough to reach both the pedals and the steering. He took note of whether she was strong enough to turn the wheel, and that's all he needed to know. He was raising his kids the same way he had come up out of the cradle and into the world of farming.

Lorraine's father was missing his left hand, but he wasn't the only farmer with part of an extremity missing. When she got to junior high and one of the other kids asked how *her* dad lost *his* hand, Lorraine asked her mother. It turns out he got it mangled in a grain auger. "Chuck and him weren't payin' attention. Goofin' off. That's when stuff like that happens," Lorraine's mother explained. Her dad was surprisingly deft with a hand and a hook. Sometimes, especially on hot days when the cup that held the hook to his arm got sweaty, he hung the hook along with his cap on the coat rack in the back entryway when he came into the house for lunch.

Twenty years later and in different circumstances, Lorraine wondered why her mother, who had so much else to tend, always made sure her Dad had plenty of ice tea in a jug when he was on the tractor. Her mother was meticulous about that long before people started carrying on about how important it is to stay hydrated. By the time it occurred to Lorraine to ask, her father had passed on and her mother was off the farm and in a retirement home.

"Oh, I worried alright," her mother said in a flat, matter of fact voice. "If he got thirsty and went back to the barn for something to drink, he might of lit into beers cooling in the fridge out there or brung em on the tractor with him. He managed pretty good with one hand, but if he'd lost the other one we would'a been done for."

Lorraine asked, "Was Dad an alcoholic?"

"Course not," and now her mother's voice wasn't flat or matter of fact anymore. It had an edge that was as good as saying, "Watch your tongue, young lady." Lorraine's mother could say a lot without saying anything. "Those men were hard-working, and they drank a little now and then to take the edge off. They don't need soft folk like you calling them drunkards." Lorraine didn't bother to defend her own work ethic. She knew that her Mom's definition of "hard-working" was a postal code and a rural route, but by then Lorraine was living in a city.

THE SPRING LORRAINE GRADUATED from high school she started going to town in the evening to the drugstore soda fountain. That's where girls met boys, and that's where she met Bart. He wasn't a local boy. Lorraine's neighbor, Harvey Langstrum, was in the army and stationed at Fort Leonard Wood, where Bart was one of his buddies. When their leaves came up, Bart came home on furlough with Harvey, because Harvey's home was a lot closer than Bart's home in Florida.

These clean-shaved boys in uniform impressed Lorraine. They smoked, cussed a little, and wore English Leather aftershave. Bart must have been impressed by Lorraine too, because several times he and Harvey dropped by the farm to make sure she'd be going to the soda fountain in the evening. Before the boys headed back to Missouri, Bart asked Lorraine to join him there. They'd save up money, and when he was due for a long leave, they'd have a real wedding with a reception to which they'd invite everybody.

Lorraine's parents weren't convinced it was a good idea, because they weren't impressed with Bart. Her mother noted that Bart was on the porch with Lorraine when Chuck came back from town with supplies, and Bart "didn't lift a finger to help." Her father's evaluation dug deeper. "Nobody around here knows him. Far as I'm concerned he's a pig in a poke." Meanwhile the letters and the phone calls kept coming. Once Bart tried to call collect, but Lorraine's mom refused the charges, and he didn't try that again.

Her parents' doubts didn't carry weight with Lorraine. They were the ones who'd taught her "if something needs to be done and you can do it, cut out the chatter and get to it." On a Friday morning in autumn well after the harvest, because Lorraine would never have wanted to leave the family in a lurch, she didn't come down for breakfast. When her mother went to check on her, she found a note on Lorraine's neatly made bed. It explained that she had hitched a ride to town with Judy Palmer and was taking the Greyhound to be with Bart. By the time Lorraine's mother read the letter, she knew that the Greyhound had left the station. When she told Lorraine's dad, his comment was, "Ain't much to do about it now."

When Lorraine arrived in Missouri things were not as ready for her as Bart had led her to believe. The apartment was a faded room on the second floor of a boarding house run by a woman who had mastered the skill of holding a cigarette in her mouth while talking. She could sort the mail or put out the garbage while talking non-stop, all the while the cigarette bobbing at the corner of her mouth. If she had to write a note or make a notation in the ledger where she recorded rents, she'd tilt her head and squint to keep the smoke out of her eyes.

That someone could talk so much was culture shock for Lorraine, who had grown up among quiet people, where there was an unspoken rule that if you didn't have anything useful to say, it might be better to say nothing. Her landlady's constant chatter made Lorraine miss the quiet evenings when five people sat down for supper at the kitchen table in her parents' farmhouse. The only sounds were forks on plates, an occasional buzzing fly that had been able to sneak past the screen door, a request to pass the salt, and then, toward the end of the meal, her mother's voice saying to Skip as she handed him a bowl, "Finish this up, son, there's not enough there for leftovers."

At the boarding house, two other couples also rented bedrooms on the second floor. The men were soldiers whose pay grade couldn't provide anything better. The floors squeaked and the walls were thin. On warm autumn evenings when bedroom doors were closed for privacy, the rooms were so stuffy it was hard to breathe.

The bathroom for all the boarders was on the first floor. Lorraine may have been raised on a farm, but it was a clean farm. In the boarding house, linoleum curled up around the toilet, and there was a nasty ring around the tub. The room was sour from towels and wash clothes overdue for the laundry and a good splash of bleach. The faded wallpaper fit in the category of things that cost to replace and might have to be left for later, but dirt could never be excused that way. Lorraine could hear her mother's voice, "A little soap and some elbow grease is all it takes to be clean. There's no excuse for filth."

Lorraine landed a job so they could save and get a real apartment, but it didn't take her long to realize that the only dependable income was hers, and it was barely enough to make ends meet. Bart never knew in the morning when he left for the base how long he'd be "working" in the evening. If Lorraine asked whether he'd be home for supper, he'd answer, "I'll be home when I get here. Don't bug me about it."

"Do you want me to keep supper warm for you?"

"Naw, I'll pick something up with the guys."

"We shouldn't be spending money like that, Bart."

"Stop nagging, babe, this is army life. Get used to it."

As months passed, Bart was showing up with less each payday. The crisis came the night Bart didn't come home until morning light was coming in around the worn edges of the roller shades in their bedroom. Lorraine was up and dressing for work. She asked him where he'd been all night, and he told her to mind her own business. She asked Bart how much money he'd lost, and he accused her of being a nagging bitch. What followed was a bizarre story about a card game. Lorraine knew he was telling the story to put her down. It was a stupid story. A mean one, poorly told.

Gilbert had been losing all evening, and then got dealt a hand he was sure would win. He reached into his pocket and pulled out the few dollars he had left, pushing every last cent he had into the middle of the table. Cranston grinned and decided to make the game more interesting. He told Gilbert he would see his bid and raise it by throwing in his girlfriend who was asleep in the next room. If Cranston lost the hand, Gilbert could have his girlfriend for a night, but Gilbert had to do the same. If Cranston won, he would go home to Gilbert's wife for a night. Cranston's girlfriend was okay, but Gilbert's wife was a real darling. The other guys were already imagining the fun they'd have telling the story.

Gilbert couldn't believe anyone would make a bid like Cranston's unless he had a full house or better, so Gilbert got up, left his cards and his money on the table, and walked away. When they turned Cranston's cards up, he had nothing, not even a low pair.

Bart repeated the story, adding embellishments and laughing. "You shoulda seen the look on that poor son of a bitch. He looked like he was gonna shit his pants, right there on the spot. Oh man, Cranston really stuck it to him." Bart was needling her, but Lorraine wasn't laughing. Like a lousy card player, he upped his risk. "Gilbert's a fool. I would'a seen through Cranston's bluff and not folded. No way, man. I would'a held on and left the table with all the money and a good roll in the hay with Cranston's babe."

That hooked Lorraine. "Shut up, Bart! You're disgusting."

Bart's laughter stopped. His shoulders came forward like a bull, and through clenched teeth he snorted, "You stupid little bitch. I'm the man around here. You shut up." He lurched toward Lorraine and slapped her, then staggered back and turned away from her. Before he could steady himself, she slipped into the hall and hurried down the stairs to the bathroom.

By the time Lorraine went back upstairs again Bart was asleep. Sweating. Snoring. His morning stubble was greasy, and she could smell his stinking breath from across the room. She gathered up her things and crept out to go to work. In the afternoon she dreaded going home again, but when she arrived Bart acted as if nothing had happened. Had he been so drunk he couldn't remember? It didn't really matter if he remembered or not, because Lorraine did. Bart had crossed the line, and she wasn't going to be slapped around by a drunk who didn't have enough sense to bring home his paycheck.

Each time Lorraine went for groceries she tucked away a few dollars, and she gave up coffee and lunch on her workdays. She squirreled away enough extra cash so she could do what she had done before. One morning instead of going to work, she packed her suitcase and went to the Greyhound station. This time she did not leave a note on the bed, and this time she bought a ticket for Chicago.

On the second bus, after she transferred in St. Louis, Lorraine sat next to a friendly young woman about her age, but Lorraine didn't feel like talking. By the time they were out of the station and on the highway her seatmate was paging through a magazine. Lorraine closed her eyes and pretended to doze, hoping she might be able to fall asleep, but she was restless. She reached into her purse for her wallet and flipped through her pictures. There were school pictures of Skip and her friends, and a picture of her parents taken on their twenty-fifth wedding anniversary. It was too big for the plastic photo holder, so she'd trimmed it down and folded it in half. Where she slid it into the picture holder, the smiling image of her dad showed, but not her mother. The picture was behind one of Bart in uniform.

Lorraine took out Bart's picture and tore it into tiny pieces, gathered them up in a tissue, and stuffed them into the ashtray on the armrest of her bus seat. She leaned her head back again, and that's how she stayed until the driver announced the next stop would be a fifteen-minute break. When they pulled into a bus bay alongside a drugstore, her seatmate got up and went inside, but Lorraine stayed where she was. Her seatmate returned with a coke bottle in each hand. They were opened and each had a straw. One she handed to Lorraine.

"Thanks," said Lorraine. "You shouldn't have."

"You're running, aren't you?" she said to Lorraine.

"I guess I am," said Lorraine.

"I know what it's like. You keep trying to figure out when you'll feel safe. You got on the bus, but you still didn't feel safe cause you wondered if you'd be able to get out of town. Now you're hoping when you get to Chicago you'll know for sure you've gotten away from him. It'll take a lot longer than that."

"Probably." Lorraine wasn't used to talking to a stranger about things so personal, and she didn't know what else to say, but the silence was awkward. "Thanks for the coke," she said. "Sorry I'm so unfriendly."

"Don't worry. I understand. I knew from the minute I saw you that you're scared."

"I wasn't born yesterday. I'm not scared," said Lorraine.

"Of course you're scared. You don't know where you're headed. You only know what you're running from. If you're not scared, you should be." For a statement so blunt her seatmate's voice was surprisingly kind.

Lorraine's throat felt tight. It had something to do with a stranger handing her an opened bottle of coke with a straw in it and giving her permission to be scared. If her mother were sitting beside Lorraine on this bus, would she have brought back an opened bottle of Coke for Lorraine from the station? Probably not. But that wasn't what was creating the tight feeling in Lorraine's throat. It was the next thought. Had her father ever slapped her mother? Had her mother ever wanted to run away? If her mother were next to her on the bus, would she give Lorraine permission to be scared? That's why her throat ached, and that's why she was trying not to cry.

"Do you have a place to stay in Chicago?" her neighbor asked.

"No."

"If you can't find anything else go to the YWCA. It's safe."

They fell into silence again. Lorraine glanced now and then at her neighbor's magazine, and her neighbor noticed because she said, "I've got another one. Want to have a look at it?" Lorraine wondered about this stranger who seemed to notice everything without even looking. Why was she being kind?

"Sure, that'd be nice," Lorraine said. She paged through the magazine, and paused at an ad for perfume with a French name and a round bottle that looked like it was wrapped with angel wings. How silly to suggest that angel wings or even angels were fragrant. Lorraine knew the scent of milky sweetness and manure that filled the milking parlor on winter mornings. She knew the smell of Skip's horse blanket and saddle. Her mom's Sunday dinners and kittens that slept in the hayloft smelled good. She could bring to mind the smell of cigarettes, beer, and nervous sweat when Bart had been losing at cards. That smelled bad. But she couldn't imagine what angels smelled like. Lorraine handed the magazine back to her neighbor and leaned her head back against the seat.

After they pulled into the station in Chicago and Lorraine was gathering up her belongings, her seatmate turned to her and said, "I know you'll be okay. You're strong, but that doesn't mean you have to turn down help when you need it." She reached out her hand, and Lorraine thought it was for a handshake, but instead she pressed a few folded bills into Lorraine's hand. "Take a taxi to the YWCA," she said. "This should cover the fare, and good luck."

As Lorraine watched the woman disappear into the station, she wondered where she was going and how it happened that they had taken seats next to each other on the bus. And then it dawned on Lorraine that the least she could have done was say "thanks" and ask the woman's name. Would she ever see her again? Years later, when Lorraine told the story of that day on the Greyhound bus and the kindness of a stranger, she said, "Sometimes I still look for her in a crowd."

❖

Fourteen

UNLESS ALETHEA HAD SHARED Lorraine's story with him, Rowland would never have given her a second thought. She hadn't mattered to him when he was a kid, and now she mattered only because Alethea needed a ride so she could visit an old friend. There are people we hear about second-hand, and we think we know them, but maybe we don't know them at all. We know nothing of what's behind the face, and we forget them easily because they aren't interesting enough for making up our own story about them. That's what we do, isn't it. We make up stories about people we know.

It occurred to Rowland that, when he got back to the classroom and was teaching literature to undergraduates, he'd introduce a story with an instruction that would make it more engaging. He'd tell his students, "Ask yourself what your own connection to this story is. Why does it matter to you?" He thought it was a good prompt, but when he imagined himself in front of a classroom giving it to his students, he had to laugh at himself. He was beginning to see how often his students were stand-ins for instructions he was giving to himself.

Lorraine's story wasn't interesting to Rowland because it was a good story. It was interesting because he wondered why his mom chose a friend like that. Rowland remembered her kids, and he remembered her husband, a coach at the high school, because he was the kind of man who definitely stood out in a crowd. Their grandmother lived with them too, and she was a character in her own right. Rowland was wary of her. But Lorraine? All he remembered of her was a quiet person who provided food and made plans with his mother.

Stuck in among his mom's journal pages Rowland found an entry that looked as if it had been written when he was four years old. That's when he hurt his shoulder at the park and had to go to the hospital.

I got to know Lorraine the day Row tumbled off the side of the slide. Although we both brought our boys to the park to play, I'd never paid her much note until that day. Row was turning around to go down on his belly, but as he grabbed the rail at the top there was a sickening pop, and he plopped to the ground. It took a full minute before he caught his breath and wailed.

By the time I was at his side, so was Lorraine, but she didn't move aside to let me take over. She knelt beside Row, took his face in her hands, and said, "You've hurt your shoulder little fellow (she used to call the boys that), but we'll take care of it and you'll be fine." She said it calmly, and looking up at her Row stopped howling.

I asked Lorraine how bad it was, and she said he should have it looked at. I suppose she learned that in nurse's training. It's good to have a nurse in the neighborhood.

Row's shoulder is fine, and now he has a new friend. He likes Lorraine's son Randall, and we've set up times for them to play at our house. Lorraine called and said, "If I walk Randall to the corner of the park, he can walk across by himself, but will you watch for him on the other side and help him cross the street?" I couldn't believe it. He's four years old, and she trusts him to follow instructions.

Our twins are about as well behaved as most four year olds, but I would never send them across the park alone. About half the time they forget instructions before they follow them.

Having Randall play at our house keeps my boys occupied. I'd worry if my boys were at Lorraine's house that they might break lamps or run through the screen door without opening it first.

That's already happened at our house. Maybe I should give Row some credit here, but the reason he hasn't punched out the screen yet is that he's always two steps behind Will. They're constantly competing with each other. I'm glad for Row that he's finally found a friend who's as smart as he is.

Tucked right in with the first journal entry written when Rowland was four years old was another one written after his dad died, more than three decades later. He wondered why his mom kept these two entries, and he wondered what else she had written about Lorraine over the years and tossed out when she began sorting the pages of her diary.

Since Ross's funeral I've had lonely days. Yesterday Lorraine called. She didn't ask if she could come over; she said she was coming to bring lunch, and she arrived with a warm shepherd's pie in a basket.

After lunch we went to the living room. She'd brought her knitting. I read a little, and then began to yawn because I've not been sleeping well. Lorraine took one of the sofa pillows and tucked it in the corner, and with a little pat signaled me to rest my head. I did, and she put the afghan over me. When I woke Lorraine was still there, in the chair, knitting.

We had tea before Lorraine left. As she went out the door she said, "Take as much time away as you need because grief is exhausting, but when you're ready for company again I expect you to call me. I'm here for you." She understands what I am going through since Ross died. She went through the same thing when her Jackson passed away.

Maggie's entries about Lorraine jarred Rowland's memories. Lorraine's husband "Mr. Davis" was Will's basketball coach. His first name was Jackson, but no kid ever dared to call him that. Mr. Davis' mother was Rowland's first coach in manners. Her grandchildren called her "MawMaw," and all the neighbors and their children called her that too when speaking of her behind her back, but they never called her that to her face. The only time Rowland ever tried that she set him straight. "Young man, I am not your grandmother and you may call me Mrs. Davis or Ma'am." She didn't tolerate head nodding either. Rowland went home after school with Randall one day, and his MawMaw prepared warm corn bread with melting butter and rivulets of honey coming off the sides. When she offered some to Rowland and he nodded "yes," she served the warm bread to Randall, but left Rowland staring at an empty plate.

At Randall's house there were cookies in the cupboard. Rowland knew they were there because when Lorraine was home she let the boys have a Little Debbie Oatmeal Cream Pie with a tall glass of milk. She said that if they drank the milk to the bottom of the glass it made the cookie healthy. Randall had skinny flamingo legs that looked like long sticks with bulges in the middle. His mother would serve him anything he liked in order to load calories, but Randall's MawMaw didn't approve of cookies because "growing boys need real food, and sugar makes your muscles soft. You keep eating that way," she said, "you'll get the sugar too." Rowland had no idea what it meant to "get the sugar" until Lorraine explained that MawMaw Davis had diabetes.

Rowland called his sister Jenna to check out what she remembered of the Davis family and their MawMaw. "I think she still haunts me sometimes," Rowland said. "I feel guilty when I eat sweets." He went on to tell about his recent visit to the Free Spirit ice cream bar in Minneapolis, where instead of ordering his favorite sweet cream custard with chocolate chunks and a caramel drizzle, he'd ordered cilantro and cucumber sorbet with pepper flakes. No gluten. No dairy. No taste either except for the heat. In humor he blamed MawMaw Davis.

"It's not fair to blame MawMaw Davis," Jenna objected when Rowland told her what he'd ordered, "but at least you're not blaming Andrea for everything anymore. That's progress."

Rowland owned up to the fact that he'd been trying to impress a new girlfriend. "These days in order to impress someone, you have to get the food right," he told Jenna.

ROWLAND CONTINUED SHARING MEMORIES about Lorraine's family with Alethea as they drove to Milwaukee. Despite the good times his family used to have with the Davis family, something had gone sour. Their families (Mom, Dad, and the kids) used to get together at each other's houses. The dads would grill in the backyard, and the moms would prepare the rest of the meal in the kitchen. They often ate at picnic tables. The Davis family had one in their yard, and so did Rowland's family. It was a good way to keep kids from trashing the house.

Then they didn't get together anymore. Rowland thought it had something to do with the dads. His dad and Mr. Davis used to sit together at basketball games, but after this "thing" happened, they barely spoke to each other. Laura told Rowland that Mr. Davis got in trouble with the police, and that their dad didn't want to associate with him after that. That didn't make sense to Rowland because Mr. Davis was a teacher and a coach. If he'd been in trouble with the police, the school would've fired him. "Do you know anything about that?" Rowland asked Alethea as they drove.

Alethea did know. Jackson added to their household income by officiating games for other school districts across the state line. Sometimes on the way home after a game he stopped off for a burger and a beer at a bar that had a television set so he could watch sports. Lorraine wasn't happy about her husband going to the bar when he had a long drive home, but he promised he'd limit himself to one beer, and she took him at his word. Elbows up on the bar watching a game on TV was the way Jackson Davis unwound after an evening of rambunctious high school athletes and their high-strung coaches. It was also his way of erasing from his mind the racial slurs hissed from the sidelines by spectators who didn't like calls he made on the floor.

One evening as Jackson pulled out of the parking lot at the bar, a cruiser pulled him over, and the officer ordered him out of the vehicle. Jackson asked why, and the officer said, "I'm giving the orders here, Rastus." When Jackson saw the name Rodriguez on the officer's nametag, it set him off. "Look who's calling me Rastus! They give you a gun and a uniform, and now you're a good ol' boy and get to talk trash to me. That quick you forget what they say about your sisters and your mother?"

The officer gave the order again, and this time Jackson got out of his vehicle because a second officer had stepped out of the cruiser and walked up to the driver's side of his car. When one of the officers pushed Jackson up against the side of the car to pat him down, Jackson pushed him back. The next thing he knew, he was on the ground, handcuffed with two officers on him. From the back of the cruiser on the way to the station Jackson was treated to the full recital of law enforcement trash talk by the cops in the front seat. "Hey, Rodriguez, you going soft or something. You should'a clubbed him, not cuffed him." And then Jackson heard Rodriguez reply, "Yeah. Bruised him up good. Do bruises show on black guys?" And then the first officer's reply. "Hell if I know. That's why we hired you half-black guys. You're supposed to know that stuff. Anyhow, why would I give a damn if they show bruises." And then Rodriguez again, "Sometimes you gotta show em who's boss."

Over dinner with friends a week later, Lorraine told the story. Jackson had already grown silent about it, but in the safe company of friends Lorraine needed to be heard. As she spoke of the insults and Jackson's humiliation, she was tense. The extra money Jackson earned officiating at the game hadn't covered the expense of getting his impounded vehicle back after it was towed from the side of the road. She was angry about that too. "It keeps piling on," she said.

Mark and Alethea were at the table that night, and so were Maggie and Ross. While Lorraine spoke, Ross listened, but when she finished, he turned to Jackson and said, "The law was on your side until you lost your cool and pushed the officer. You wouldn't tolerate that in a game if you were officiating, would you?"

"Exactly what do you think I should have done?" Jackson asked.

"You should've done as you were ordered and complained through the proper channels." Ross could be so confident when he thought he was right. As Alethea told the story, Rowland could picture his dad with his chin forward a little and his shoulders squared.

"Nice. Maybe that works for you, but there aren't proper channels on my side?" Jackson leaned back. "A black man files a complaint against a Latino cop who insulted him with a racial slur, spiced up with the f-word. Exactly who do you think would give a damn? Guys like you?"

"You'll never know," said Ross, "because you lost your cool and got thrown out of the game. You set yourself up for the trouble you get. What is it with you people?"

That was it for Jackson. He'd had enough. "You can pour a good wine in my glass at dinner, and you can sit next to me at games when I'm the coach and your boy is out on the floor, but that's as far as it goes. That big old line that runs right down the middle between your people and mine never moves a bit, does it? So now it's my people who are the problem. You mutha . . . ." And that's where Jackson stopped, got up from the table, took his coat, and left.

"That's how it ended?" Rowland asked Alethea.

"It wasn't a small disagreement over dinner," said Alethea. "It was a festering wound, and they never dealt with it."

"You're talking like a woman," Rowland said. "Guys don't talk things over, and over, and over. That's not what we do. They should've stopped mouthing off about it and let it go."

"Exactly who is we?" Alethea asked Rowland with her schoolmarm look.

"Men," Rowland said. "C'mon, you know what I mean." He didn't say anything more. For a few minutes Alethea was silent too. It was obvious they were both thinking about Ross and Jackson Davis. They were both trying to sort it out.

Jackson Davis was Will's basketball coach when he had conflict with two of the other players. As the boys were leaving practice one evening, they got into a fight, and Will got hurt. One of the other boys got hurt too. Ross came to Will's defense and complained that the other boys had been harassing him. He was sure Jackson had known about it, but had done nothing to intervene because it was a racial thing. He thought Jackson was protecting the other boys because they were black.

Jackson explained to Ross that the conflict was about Will's interest in another boy, and some of his players were bullying Will about it. Jackson thought it would be best to give the matter time to cool off on its own, to let it pass. "Boys will be boys," Jackson said.

"They do that stuff." But Ross wasn't buying it. He thought Jackson was insulting Will to cover up for the boys who started the fight.

The disagreement over dinner was a rupture. Ross found excuses to be absent when the neighbors had dinner together. Jackson showed up less often too. Maggie and Lorraine remained friends despite the feud between their husbands, and Randall remained Rowland's friend, but the families no longer socialized together at each other's houses.

"Did you and Mark get along with Jackson?" Rowland asked Alethea.

"We did. We always had Thanksgiving together. They invited us. Mark and Jackson were both fishermen, and Mark often went along with Jackson's teams for out-of-town games when not enough parents volunteered to chaperone. You might say their friendship was more work and play than talk."

"Mr. Davis knew Will was gay," Rowland said.

"Whatever Jackson knew, your Dad wasn't willing to hear it from him," Alethea replied. "It was a battle of honor. Pride against pride. Shame loaded on shame."

Rowland knew his dad could be stubborn. Most people didn't know that about Ross because he came across as a calm and in-charge guy. He didn't cuss, or spit, or put up his fists, and he had good manners. But he was unbending when he thought he was right. Rowland had expected better of Mr. Davis. The problems with Will had been difficult for Rowland too, and Mr. Davis had never taken a stand against bullying. It surprised Rowland to know that Mr. Davis had cussed out his dad. "It's bullshit," Rowland said. "Excuse my language, but it's really messed up."

Alethea looked out the side window of the car. There wasn't much to see, and apparently she thought there wasn't much else to say.

WHEN THEY ARRIVED IN Milwaukee and rang the bell, a middle-aged woman opened the door. "You remember Sissy, don't you?" Alethea asked. Rowland reached forward to shake her hand, and Sissy leaned forward to kiss his cheek.

"We've been waiting for you," said Sissy as she ushered them to an alcove in the living room where, tucked into the corner of a love seat, a very old woman was dozing. Rowland barely recognized Lorraine. She looked tired. Old and withered. Not at all like the woman who'd lived across the park from their house on Woodward Street.

Alethea sat down next to Lorraine on the love seat and took her hand. It was a thin boney hand with blue veins tracing through gray skin. Lorraine didn't turn her head until Alethea patted Lorraine's hand as a reminder that she was there with her. Then Lorraine slowly threaded her arm through Alethea's. There they were, two old friends, side by side.

Rowland chatted with Lorraine's children and grandchildren. Drinks and snacks passed through the room in the arc of the family assembled around Lorraine for her birthday. Alethea and Lorraine hardly spoke to each other, but no one else spoke to them either. No one wanted to interrupt their silent visit.

After a while Sissy went over and said, "Mama and Aunt Alethea, would you like something to drink?" Lorraine didn't reply, but Alethea said, "Yes, that would be lovely. Thank you, dear."

The drink perked Lorraine up, and after a few sips she didn't rest her head on the back of the love seat again. Instead she leaned toward Alethea and whispered something. Rowland thought he heard her say, "Estelle." He leaned in a little closer. "She hasn't gone back to that wretched man, has she?"

"No, she hasn't. She's doing well," Alethea assured Lorraine.

"And the children? I worry about Michelle. Poor little girl." It seemed Lorraine had old concerns bubbling up in the murky swamps of her mind. Alethea's arm tucked in beside her was mooring her to the past.

"The children are doing okay. Don't worry." Alethea's voice was kind.

"You've always been so good to them," said Lorraine. "Treating those children like your own. After all that's happened, they're lucky to have a dad like Mark." While someone else might have felt awkward saying this to childless Alethea, Lorraine seemed troubled by neither the sensitive topic nor the time warp.

Lorraine smiled. It reminded Rowland of the way his own children smiled when they were newborns. Maggie used to say those smiles were gas. Rowland always wondered if that was true. He always liked those smiles. They didn't seem to have a deeper meaning behind them. They were innocent and pure.

"Hm mm, Mark loves those children," Alethea replied. "Gregory's taken to baseball. Quite a little pitcher." Alethea's voice was not condescending. She'd practiced dealing with Mark's dementia during the last years of his life, and she was agile making time shifts to catch fragments. It seemed she knew exactly where Lorraine was, wandering around in the past. There was something so tender about the way Alethea accepted it as an earnest conversation.

Alethea gestured to Rowland to come over next to Lorraine. "This is Row, Maggie's boy. You remember? The twins?"

"How could I forget? Those boys. They were something." Lorraine grinned. "How is your mother doing?"

"She's fine," said Alethea. "Did you know she's retired?"

"High time," said Lorraine. "Tell her to come visit."

"I will," said Alethea as she cast a knowing glance in Rowland's direction.

Alethea sensed the visit had gone on long enough. It was time to bring Lorraine back to her safe cocoon in the bedroom. With ease, surprising for a woman her age, Alethea stood, but she didn't walk away. She turned and took the soft face of her dear friend in both her hands. "Rest well, my dear. May angels guard you." She said it in a soft voice as if she were talking to a child, and then she kissed Lorraine lightly on both cheeks.

Although her face hardly moved, Lorraine looked up at Alethea. She smiled and whispered something, but Rowland couldn't catch what she said.

After Lorraine was tucked in, Alethea and Rowland had dinner around the table with Sissy and the family. They reminisced about old times and told stories about their children. At last it was Alethea who said, "I could stay here all night enjoying this, but we have a long ride home. Row, it's time."

They said their goodbyes. Alethea collected kisses. Randall reminded Rowland that they should get together again before he left Chicago. Sissy made him promise to give her love to his sisters and Will.

In the car Rowland asked Alethea how his mom and Lorraine managed to stay friends if their husbands didn't want anything to do with each other.

"It definitely wasn't easy," she said, "but they found a way. They were determined women. That's different than stubborn, by the way. They were friends, and they weren't going to give it up."

"So the journal entry I read about Lorraine coming over to sit with Mom after Dad died is proof they never did give up, did they? You gotta admire that."

"Their friendship was steady." Alethea spoke softly. "Sometimes more than anything else that's what you need in a friend. Somebody who's steady. When Lorraine's children decided it was time for their mother to move to Milwaukee to live with Sissy, it was hard to see her go. Both your mom and I missed her, but we understood. She couldn't live alone anymore. She needed her family."

Rowland asked Alethea if she was sad that she and Lorraine hadn't talked much together. "You said that you wanted to visit her because you missed her. Is it disappointing that she didn't have much to say?"

"There isn't much new to talk about. What sense would it make for me to catch her up on the news? To tell her that I got new glasses last week or that Maggie's boy is living in her condo for the summer. That's not where our connection is. The past is what we have."

"I see that," Rowland said, "but it still seems hard."

Alethea continued. "We had a good life together. Lorraine was a peach. A real peach of a friend." Alethea put her head back against the headrest. "One day soon the phone will ring, and Sissy's voice will tell me that her Mama is gone."

"Hm mm," Rowland said. "Are you ready?"

"As ready as I'll ever be. It's a mystery." Alethea closed her eyes, and for the rest of the ride they were silent.

Fifteen

WHEN THEY PULLED INTO the parking garage of their building, Rowland said, "It's been a long day, but I'm glad we made this trip together." He offered Alethea his arm as they walked toward the elevator, and she took it, although she didn't need it. When the elevator opened to her floor, he stepped out with her. "It's late," he said. "I'd like to walk you to your door." She turned the key in the door, and he stepped in with her. "Aunt Alethea, can you give me a few more minutes?" he asked.

She turned to face him. "Have I earned a new name?"

"Long overdue," Rowland replied. "It has a good ring to it, don't you think? I liked hearing Lorraine's kids call you that." He followed her to the living room, and they each took a corner of the sofa. There was light coming through the windows from the street. The city hummed. A taxi honked. The living room felt like the inside of a car.

"Do you need lights?" she asked.

"No, this is good," he replied.

Alethea waited.

"How can I start? It's Michelle. I heard Lorraine say something about her."

"She always worries about Estelle and her children. It's an old loyalty." Alethea remembered the nights Estelle crept out of her house with Gregory and went to Maggie's house for sanctuary. When Gregory was colicky, if JR was trying to sleep, he'd threaten to shut Gregory up himself if Estelle didn't quiet him down. There was plenty to worry about, and those events of the past were still present for Lorraine. "Best to just let it be," said Alethea.

"I made it worse," Rowland told her.

"What do you mean?" Alethea asked.

"When we were fourteen, I got in trouble with Michelle."

"Trouble?"

"She had a crush on Will, but he pushed her away like he pushed all the girls away. He'd say he didn't like curly hair. Or he didn't like braces. Once he even complained that he didn't like cheerleaders because they thought everyone should admire them. Stupid reasons. Especially stupid because guys that age don't care about reasons. For a good time they'll look past anything. Not Will. He wasn't into girls, but that wasn't obvious back then. Everyone was still trying to find the girl who could get his attention."

"Oh my," said Alethea. "That must have been hard for you."

"Girls wanted me to get Will's attention for them. If it didn't work, they'd settle for me because I offered a shoulder to cry on. I knew it was Will they wanted, but getting his rejects was better than nothing."

"You've always blamed yourself for not measuring up to Will, haven't you?" Rowland could feel Alethea looking at him, but he didn't look back. He knew it was true, but he didn't like hearing her say it.

"That's how the problem with Michelle started. She settled for me too. We were into sex, you know, not exactly the kind that makes babies, but we messed around a lot. Tried everything else. You know what I mean?"

"More or less."

"There's another thing," Rowland continued. "I started doing drugs with Michelle. At first I bought weed for her. Later she bought for herself, or traded sex for better drugs. Sometimes she'd share with me, and I feel bad about that. I got her started, but when I quit, she didn't. I don't know what she uses now, but the last time I saw her she wasn't looking that good."

"She struggles. That's for sure," said Alethea.

"Michelle wanted to do other stuff that could get us into big trouble. Really stupid stuff. Once she followed me into the men's restroom at the library and started taking off her clothes. I was scared shitless because I thought we were going to get caught. She didn't care about getting caught. Actually I think she wanted to get caught. She wanted attention. I don't want to pretend I'm a victim, but she had me cornered."

Alethea was listening, staring at the floor. She didn't interrupt.

"I was the pot head, and Will was Mr. Clean." Rowland gave an embarrassed chuckle. "Will knew what other guys said about Michelle, and he thought it was weird that I was hanging out with her. We were like cousins. Our moms were close, and when her mom was gone Michelle stayed at our house. One time Will caught me fooling around with Michelle in our bedroom, the one I shared with him. He ordered me to leave Michelle alone."

"How could he order you to do anything?" Alethea asked.

"He was the alpha. Not just with me, with my sisters too. Definitely with Steven because he was a lot younger. It was obvious that Will was Dad's favorite, and he always took Will's side. We were younger than Laura, and even though we were twins and I was born first, that didn't matter. In our family, Will was it." Rowland recited it like a memorized speech. It was clearly not the first time he'd said it.

"And your mother? Did she go along with that?" Alethea asked.

"Not so much. She tried to make it up to me, but that didn't feel great either."

"Complicated. I can see that." Alethea said.

"My fights with Will got worse when I got mixed up with Michelle," Rowland admitted. "She was messed up. Really, really messed up. She smoked. Lots of kids did, but one time she begged me to hold her lighter under her hand to see how long she could stand it. I didn't want to, and she screamed at me and said I was gutless. She clawed her own arm until it drew blood, and then she told everybody she got those scratches defending herself from me."

Alethea was starting to look uncomfortable.

"Do you want me to stop?" Rowland asked. "Is this too much?"

"No. Go on. Say what you need to say."

"I wanted to get away from Michelle," Rowland said sheepishly. "I ignored her at school. She got into it with other boys, and they bragged about it. They'd say, 'C'mon, Row, tell us. What'd you get off her?' I made stuff up, but Michelle ratted me out. She told the other guys I didn't dare to do the stuff she wanted to do. That started a rumor that Will and I couldn't handle girls because I was Will's boyfriend. The guys put brown bananas in our lockers and said stuff about us when we passed them in the hall. Once bullies put the target on your back, it gets worse and worse."

"Is that when Will got into that fight at school?" Alethea asked.

Rowland described for Alethea how first Will attacked him. They were walking across the park, and Will tackled Rowland, twisting his arm behind his back. "You perverted little bastard," Will said. "You're going to tell Michelle your sorry, and you're going to take her to the dance." He told Rowland that if he didn't make it right with Michelle, he'd break his arm. Will was shaking with rage, and Rowland believed he meant what he said. He was scared of Will, who was unpredictable when he got mad. Rowland didn't doubt Will could break his arm if he were mad enough.

Alethea looked puzzled. "Why didn't you ask for help?"

"Help? Are you kidding? Mom and Dad would've killed me if they found out about Michelle. If they found out about the drugs, they would've had me locked up." Rowland paused then and looked like he'd seen a ghost. "Steven got into drugs with us too. That's where he got his start. First from me, and then from Michelle. I did that to my little brother."

"Oh, Rowland," said Alethea. "How could that have been going on and no one knew. Who was watching out for you?"

"If my parents ever found out, I don't know what I would have done. I thought about killing myself." Rowland paused and took a deep breath. "I'm not being dramatic. I really did think about it because I was desperate. Dad had a gun he kept in a lock box in a drawer. I took it out once, but I couldn't figure out the combination."

"I'm so sorry." Alethea reached across and touched Rowland's arm, but only for a moment before she drew it back again.

There was a pause, and Alethea said nothing more. Rowland took that as a sign that she was still listening. He tried to explain to Alethea that he apologized to Michelle like Will had ordered him to, and lucky for him, she didn't want to go to the dance. When

Rowland told Will, he said, "If I ever hear you've treated another girl like that, I'll smash in your ugly face." It was a few days later that Will got into the fight with the guys at school. Will got a fist in the mouth, and one of the other guys had to go to emergency. Most of what Rowland remembered about those days is that his dad went to meetings at school and his mom cried a lot. Soon after Will refused to share a room with Rowland anymore.

"That's the fight I remember," said Alethea, "and I remember your mom crying. She was a mother bear. She would have taken on any enemy to protect her children, but once her children were hurt it all seemed to cave in on her."

"I hurt Will." Rowland told Alethea. "I hurt Michelle too. And Steven. It feels as if I made a lot of trouble. Between my dad and Mr. Davis too. I'm like Michelle's dad. We're bad news. Trouble follows us around."

"Row, listen! You are *not* like him." Alethea punched out every word. And then she said, "Tell me you hear me!"

"I feel so guilty."

"You mix up guilt and sadness," said Alethea. "You wish you could have done something different. You'll have to sort out sad from guilty, or you'll be beating yourself up over this for the rest of your life. Row, your mistakes are your mistakes, but not everything was about you. There was a lot more going on than you knew."

Rowland took the small pillow out of the corner of the sofa where he was sitting and put it on Alethea's lap. Then he let himself sink over toward her and rested his head on the pillow. She put her hand on his shoulder. He could feel the warmth of it. With her other hand she lightly stroked his hair. It occurred to him that he should pull himself together, get up, and head home. He'd already dumped too much on her. Everything was quiet except for the grandfather clock against the wall in Alethea's living room and the cars going by on the street below. "Can I stay here tonight?" he asked her.

Alethea got a pillow and quilt from the bedroom and made a place for Rowland on the sofa. Then she walked to her own room and closed the door, but she left the light on in the hall. Early in the morning Rowland folded up the quilt and stacked it in the corner of the sofa, tiptoed to the door, and let himself out.

Sixteen

THE MORNING AFTER IS hard. Rowland called Alethea to ask if she needed anything from the bakery or the grocery store. Of course she knew he was calling to reconnect after their conversation, but she was sweet about it. She told him she needed milk, a half-gallon, not a gallon. And from the bakery she asked him to bring cheese danish. Two would be enough. A little later, when he showed up at her door, she invited him in to share the danish, and she asked him to change the bulb that had burned out in the hallway. She'd already tried to reach it by standing on a chair, and she'd left the chair there for him to use.

They sat quietly at Alethea's dining room table sharing coffee and danish. Rowland broke the silence, asking Alethea if she thought it odd to communicate by email even though they lived two floors away from each other.

She nodded a slow yes before she answered. "Email's arm's length, isn't it? It's like there's an invisible header at the top of the screen that says, 'I want to communicate with you, but only a little, and I want to control it.' That's the way it feels to me at least."

"That's one way to read it," Rowland agreed. "There could also be an invisible header that says, 'Let me reach out this way in case I'm interrupting something, because I don't want to be a bother.'"

"I'm not used to thinking that way," Alethea observed. "Your mom was always welcome at my door, and I was always welcome at hers. We never used email. I liked it better that way, but then, your mom and I were old-fashioned. If she showed up at my door while I was ironing, I'd say to her, 'I'm ironing. Come in and chat with me while I work,' and she might stay for a while or she might tell me that she was on her way to the farmer's market and wanted to know if I needed anything. We treated each other like extended family living in the same big house with different rooms. The doors on our condos weren't there for our friends. They were only there to keep strangers out."

"It must be a good feeling to have *someone* who always welcomes you if you show up at the door," Rowland said. "That's pretty rare."

"You're always welcome at my door, you know," Alethea replied. "I don't want to be forward, Rowland, but as you know, I've never had a son. Getting to know you means a great deal to me, and I don't take it lightly. I'd be grateful if you'd think of my door as always open to you."

Somewhere in the back of his head Rowland could hear his sister Laura reminding him that he can be high maintenance. "I don't want to wear out my welcome," he said, "but it means a lot to me too. I've missed Mom this summer. Can you imagine you'd ever think of my home as yours? When we visited Lorraine I could tell that's how the members of her family feel about each other."

Alethea laughed. "You'd have to be more specific about the welcome at your home. I'd need an address."

Rowland laughed too. "I know. That's a dotty comment coming from a guy who doesn't have a home and is temporarily living in his mother's condo. But I want you to feel that I'm approachable. That wherever I am, if you need me, you'll let me know. Maybe that's not about owning a house or me giving you keys. I want to be someone you can count on."

"I'm glad we got that straightened out," said Alethea. She looked at him with a clear gaze, like she was reading his face, and then she broke into a smile. "That means a lot to me."

For the rest, they kept their visit light. Rowland told Alethea he'd decided to make a trip to Minneapolis because he had things to take care of that he didn't want to leave until the end of summer. It turned out that it also was a good time for a vacation with his son Zach. They'd hike. He expected to be gone a few weeks, and he promised to contact Alethea when he returned.

At the door when he left Rowland said, "Take care of yourself, Aunt Alethea, and no more climbing on chairs." Then he hugged her. She isn't very big, and he wrapped both arms around her and held her for a moment. It was comforting even though a little awkward the way a first time often is.

ON THE TRAIL HIKING with Zach, Rowland thought about his mother, and he thought about Alethea. He thought about the stories he'd discovered over the summer. Not only did he know things about others he'd not known before; he'd noticed something about himself. He'd discovered that once you get to know other people's stories, you can't insulate yourself entirely from them anymore. You can try to distance yourself from them with judgment, but they're no longer neutral. And if you let yourself be touched by them, they overflow and erode your own. There's no way to get new stories back out of your memory again so that you can reclaim your previous illusions. When he got off the trail Rowland wrote a message.

Dear Aunt Alethea,

I've had time to think. While we were going over Mom's journals you said you were not sure you could count on me because my motives were hidden, and you didn't trust me to be fair to Mom. That you would think I'm too selfish to show proper concern for my own mother shook me up.

Someone else told me something similar last spring. It was the woman I was seeing when the semester ended, before I headed to Chicago to stay in Mom's condo. My departure was thoughtless because I made no agreement to stay in touch with her. I'm wondering now why I did that?

I've had dinner with Polly in Minneapolis. She told me my refusal to introduce her to friends or tell her about my family has been a red flag. That's why she made no effort to get in touch with me during the time I've been away. She could have emailed, but she didn't because she's not interested in dating a secretive man, and she wonders what I have to hide. After what you said to me, that was another sucker-punch.

I'd like to invite Polly to Chicago so I can introduce her to my sister and to you, if you're willing. Polly is clear that she will not stay with me at Mom's condo. It's about boundaries she says, and she intends to keep them in place until she's sure about what's going on with me. I told her I'd arrange a bed and breakfast for her.

I want to be open with you about what's happening with me, and I look forward to seeing you soon. I'll return at the end of next week.

Yours truly,
Row

When Rowland returned from his trip, his mother's journals were still on the table, and the box was still on the floor. He packed up the journals and put the box in the closet of the den where his mom had left it for him. "Is it possible," he asked Alethea, "that we half remember things for a long time as if they are unimportant, then they surface again and we finally understand what they mean? Can we really know something and not know it at the same time?"

"I suppose so," said Alethea. "We shouldn't be too harsh with ourselves about that. We're not ready to know everything at once. When the time is right, the pieces fall into place. Maybe they don't fall perfectly, but certainly we see things we couldn't see before."

"Instead of trying to figure out Mom's life," Rowland told Alethea, "I want to figure out my own."

While he was hiking with Zach, Rowland tried to remember what his life was like when he was his son's age. He mused about going with his friends to Frank's Hut for hotdogs and fries. Bad food. Garbage. The booths were upholstered in naugahyde so that in summer, when he wore shorts, the backs of his legs stuck to the bench. He remembered too the scratching sensation when his legs rubbed across the cracks in the material. The place was a dive. Kids smoked there, and the mix of deep fryer grease and stale tobacco smoke was filthy, but kids thought hanging out at Frank's proved they were living on the edge.

There was a guy who hung out at Frank's and wore a camo jacket year round, even in summer. If kids wanted to buy weed from him, they walked over to his table, slipped him some cash, and went back to their own table. He'd make them wait, and then, when he was ready, he'd go to the restroom and on his way back saunter over to their table and make a drop. Usually it was joints wrapped in colored newsprint. The transaction was completely obvious, but it was choreographed to create an air of underworld intrigue.

When Rowland thought back to the times at Frank's, it occurred to him that buying pot for himself was a rite of passage. It was a declaration that whoever he was, his parents didn't own him anymore. It also asserted that his clean-cut, athletic twin was not more worldly-wise than he was. Considering his young self from the purview of a middle-aged man, Rowland could see that these were deceits, but he could still remember how they felt and how much he had wanted to believe them.

Rowland expected Alethea to register disappointment when he told her about his memories, but she looked at him instead with an open face that told him he could keep talking if he wanted to, and she would listen to him. "It makes me wonder about my own kids," he said.

"That's good," said Alethea. "You should worry. Fathers should do that. It isn't fair to leave it all to mothers."

"Do you wonder, though, why some things stick in memory and other things are completely lost?" he asked her. "Have you ever wondered about that?"

"Memory, of all the powers of the mind, is the most delicate and frail," said Alethea.

"Who said that?" Rowland asked.

"Ben Jonson. I know exactly what he means. My mind is like a closet; every time I clean it I discover a few things I've forgotten were there. There are other things in that closet I know have been there all along. I never forget they're there, but when I look at them again I wonder why I hold on to them."

"My mom wasn't pleased that we hung out at Franks. When we came home she'd tell us we smelled bad. Her nose told her where we'd been." Rowland laughed. "That's an example. Why would I hold on to that, of all the things I could remember? Once Mom made Will and me put on sports coats and shirts with collars to go to Estelle's Tearoom for lunch. She wanted to teach us manners so we'd know how to behave in a restaurant. The whole time, Will and

I were eyeing the plate glass windows that faced the street, hoping our friends walking by wouldn't glance in and see us there with our mother having tea. Mom meant well, but for us it was like being put out in the town square in stocks. It was the perfect setup for being the butt of a joke. It's been thirty years since I last thought about that."

"You know who really liked Estelle's Tea Room?" Alethea asked. "My father, an old Greek from Philadelphia. He came to live with us after my mother passed away. Every day he walked down to Estelle's to get coffee and read his newspaper. When he arrived, the newspaper was waiting for him on a table near the window where the light was good. The short while my father lived with me has left precious memories, and Estelle's kindness to my father is woven through them."

"How did Estelle end up opening a restaurant anyway?" Rowland asked. "And who would have thought of opening an English tearoom in suburban Chicago?"

"It's a long story," said Alethea.

"I'm sure it is. Not for today?"

"Better for another time," said Alethea.

Seventeen

ROWLAND OFTEN THOUGHT ABOUT his mother and her friends while he was doing busywork at the dining table in Maggie's condo. He'd set up his laptop there, spread out his books, and turned the table into a desk. Sometimes as he was considering how to respond to an email or bored by the volume of uninteresting university mailings he felt obligated to browse through, he'd lean back and look at the table. He couldn't count the number of meals he'd been served at this table, nor could he remember a dining room without it in any of the houses in which his family had lived.

The patina of the table was a remembrance of things past. A depression on the edge along one side reminded Rowland of the time he threw a flashlight to Will instead of walking across the room to hand it to him. On the spot where Steven used to sit, he'd left fragmented forms of letters pressed into the wood during his struggle with homework, when he'd grab the pencil like he was wrestling with it and pressed so hard that the lead sometimes went through the paper. Worn patches marked where Rowland's dad sat and where the arms of his host chair pressed against the side of the table when he sat up close to serve the plates after he carved the meat.

Rowland didn't think of the table as belonging to his father; he thought of it as his mother's table. She was the hospitable one. Gathering people around a board furnished with good food was a gift she shared with her family and with her friends. Rowland had a flash of memory about an evening when his parents were out and a babysitter was getting supper ready. Out from under her watchful eye, all five children crawled under the table and signed their names with a large permanent marker Will had found in his dad's toolbox. The signatures were still there. Rowland checked.

It occurred to Rowland that his mother wasn't the only homemaker with a dining table. Scrambling through his memories of houses and tables, he could visualize dining rooms in the homes of his mother's friends. In a house across the park from their house on Woodward Street, the Davis family had a dining room with wainscoting and high windows. Estelle's dining room, in the apartment above her restaurant, was too small for anything besides the large table and the assortment of chairs that didn't match except for the identical needlepoint cushions on each seat.

Rowland had gotten to know Alethea's table again during the weeks when he'd been sitting with her at it while they worked on his mother's journals. He could remember another room that table used to inhabit when Mark and Alethea lived in a big three-story house. That dining room was in a remodeled porch, and from the living room there were three steps down to the table that stood in front of huge windows facing into the garden. Above the buffet was a large painting of a troubled seascape, and at the shoreline was an over-turned boat on which an angel was seated. Rowland remembered gazing at the painting during meals when adult conversations got boring. He recalled the ray of sunlight cutting through dark storm clouds at a certain slant so that it bathed the angel in golden light.

At the very moment he was musing about the angel and the certain slant of light, the present broke back into Rowland's consciousness again, and he realized he was at his mother's table in her condo in Oak Park. Lorraine and Estelle's dining tables were gone, and their houses were occupied by strangers. He felt an ache when he considered that the table at which he was sitting wasn't his mother's table anymore either, and soon he'd have to decide what to do with it when he emptied her condo for the last time.

Rowland's curiosity about his mother's friendships was driven by his own lack of friends. He was like a hungry man cued to food. He still didn't have an answer to the question he'd put to his mother the time he'd asked how she made friends. Were all these remnants

of pages and furniture the parts of his mother's life he was supposed
to pack away and put to rest? Would a therapist tell him to get over
his mother and move on?

Rowland's meandering thoughts about friendship were driven
by an aching void that gnawed at him. Rowland squirmed when he
remembered going out for dinner with a faculty colleague from the
Sociology Department after a late afternoon committee meeting.
As they walked out of the building, they negotiated a plan to meet
up at the Last Chance Bar for a burger and a brew. They were
both divorced professors living in dull apartments with empty
refrigerators. "At least we're not those guys who go bowling alone,"
Rowland had joked. He'd enjoyed showing a sociologist that he was
well read, but his remark embarrassed him now. When he thought
back on that brief exchange, he could see that he might as well have
gone bowling alone.

Rowland was good at socializing. He gave himself credit for
that. He was the guy who could go alone to a conference, and in
the evening after meetings go to the bar and always find someone
to talk to, usually a complete stranger. Several months before,
while Rowland was alone at his own kitchen table doing email
on his laptop, he became aware of a hollow feeling. He'd already
had dinner. He knew it wasn't hunger. *Am I lonely?* Quickly he
substituted the word *"alienation"* because at least that implied there
were plenty of others like him who were victims of the same social
blight. To fend off the feeling, Rowland opened up the contacts
on his phone. He didn't have to go far through the list to identify
people to whom he could send a text to set up a foursome for golf
or an evening to watch sports at the bar. But he didn't feel like golf
or watching sports. He wanted something more, something else
that he didn't have a name for, just like he didn't have a name for
the feeling in the pit of his stomach.

Rowland was changing. His sister Laura joked about finding
women for him to date, but instead of playing along with the
banter, he told her he was serious about a woman named Polly
Tropos, a colleague at the university. He admitted uncertainty
about whether Polly would still be interested in him, because he'd
been a cad earlier in the spring when he was seeing her regularly.

Nonetheless, he hadn't giving up hope that she would give him a second chance. Laura was taken aback by how transparent Rowland was in admitting this. She was probing for something she could tease him about, but found instead that it wasn't fun to spar with someone who wasn't sparring back.

Jenna noticed too that Rowland was changing. He seemed sweeter and less competitive. He talked less and listened more. She referred to the "old Rowland" and the "new Rowland" when she talked to Alethea about him. She wondered if this was the effect of living in their mom's condo, and she joked that maybe Rowland was absorbing Maggie's good karma left in the walls. Giving his new girlfriend credit for changing him seemed too easy, because Jenna hadn't met the new girlfriend yet, and both sisters had learned from experience to keep expectations to a minimum when Rowland was jumping into a new infatuation.

Since his mom's death, Rowland had a growing awareness of how important Will and Laura were to him. He could hike with Will, and he could talk business with Laura. He'd begun to feel closer to Jenna over the summer too, although he'd never said that to her directly. He wondered if she felt the same, because Jenna was warm and kind with everyone. On those few occasions during the year when Rowland got together with his brother and sisters, if the kids were all there, he'd sit at the edge of the circle, and then he could feel briefly that life is good and that he belonged somewhere. He'd get back a whiff of that contented feeling he'd had as a little boy under the library table.

Rowland reminded Alethea of her promise to tell him the story of Estelle's tearoom and how Maggie's friends had created the tradition of gathering for long dinners at each other's tables. He didn't admit to her that his interest had something to do with his own loneliness.

"I haven't forgotten that I promised," Alethea said, "but let's begin by going back a little. I want you to know the real story. No need to idealize. In the end our friendships were a good thing, but along the way sometimes they were ragged. If we had known in advance how hard life would be for each of us, we might have hidden from each other and never become friends. Fortunately we lived through one hard thing at a time, and in the process discovered that having friends meant that when it was our turn to be beaten down, the others were there to pick us up."

WHEN ESTELLE AND JR arrived from England, they moved into the neighborhood where Maggie and Ross were already settled on Woodward Street. On summer days with children out of school, the backyards were a playground. On weekends families gathered to grill. By evening when mosquitoes came out and children were salty from a day in the sun, they were ready for sleep. Lorraine's kids bunked in with Maggie's, JR and Estelle's settled into their own beds across the yard, and on the screened porch at Maggie and Ross's house the adults gathered to finish out the evening with a nightcap.

"Remember how much Gregory cried when he was a baby?" Rowland asked.

"Colic," said Alethea. "Poor little guy."

"Was Estelle a good mom?" Rowland asked.

"She wasn't a happy mother. We didn't know the extent of that at first when she was trying to protect her children from JR's temper. He was a bully, but Estelle covered for him because she needed friends and couldn't risk letting her neighbors know what her husband was like. She thought if others knew what went on at her house, they'd avoid her."

JR was a different breed of dad than the other men in the neighborhood. His children were an inconvenience to him, and he let Estelle know it. After Estelle got to know her friends well enough to trust them, she confessed she took Gregory down in the basement when he cried at night because she was afraid to disturb JR. If Gregory kept crying, she held a cloth diaper over his mouth for a second or two. Not enough so that he couldn't breathe, but long enough so that he had to stop howling to catch his breath. Later when Estelle confessed to her friends what she'd done, she cried and blamed herself. "I'm a terrible mom," she said. "That I ended up with three babies doesn't make sense. The stork must have blown off course in a wind storm and dropped them at the wrong house."

One night Estelle came to Maggie's side door at midnight with a fussy baby in her arms. She wanted to quiet Gregory by walking him in his buggy until he fell asleep, but she was afraid to go out alone, so Maggie went with her. In the morning Maggie told Ross about it, and he complimented her for being a good friend, but that's not what Maggie wanted from Ross. She wanted him to speak to JR and set him straight. She wanted a man to tell JR that Gregory wasn't crying on purpose, that babies are restless sometimes, and that JR should grow up and not make it worse for Estelle. "Honey, don't get too involved," Ross said. "Men protect their own families, and it's not a good idea to interfere with anyone else's."

One time when Sissy Davis went over to babysit for Estelle and JR's kids, she got the time wrong and showed up early. The kids were playing on the porch, but Sissy could hear voices. "What do you do all day?" Sissy heard JR shout.

Then Sissy heard Estelle. "I don't have time. I have to get ready. Can't you wear one of the ones I've already ironed?"

And then Sissy heard, "Ow...Ow...don't! Stop! Let go of my hair. Just give me your shirt."

Sissy knew this wasn't right, so she ran home to tell Lorraine what she'd heard, and Lorraine went back herself to stay with the children. Sissy didn't babysit for Estelle and JR again after that, but Lorraine wasn't someone who'd walk away and forget a friend who was in trouble.

Other stories leaked out. JR ranted when he was drunk. If there were dishes left in the sink at the end of the day, he'd wait until the middle of the night and get Estelle out of bed to make her wash them. Years later after her parents were divorced, Michelle told Alethea how her dad terrorized the family. If he was mad he'd smoke cigarettes, drop his ashes on the floor, and order Estelle to clean them up. Once JR told Estelle to kneel in front of him and apologize for being lazy. When she hesitated he slapped her, and the children saw it.

"Why did she let him get away with it?" asked Rowland.

"It was that way in more households than you'd guess," said Alethea. "I can't justify it at all, but it happened. Each home was a fiefdom, and interfering was a violation of privacy. Men were raised to believe they were kings in their own castles. Your dad was far better than most, and he would never have hit your mother, but he had his own streak of privilege that she accommodated in order to not cause trouble."

"Did Mark treat you that way?"

"Never," said Alethea. "Never, ever. And Jackson never behaved that way toward Lorraine. She would not have tolerated it, but it was more than that. He cherished her, and she was loyal to him. They had something special. Sometimes, off the cuff, he'd pick up his glass and propose a toast to Lorraine because she'd made him a lucky man."

The final blow for Estelle came the night Michelle knocked at Maggie's side door. She was in her nightgown and barefooted. "Something's wrong with my mom," she said. "She's in the basement. She's crying."

"Is she hurt?" Maggie asked.

"I think so."

"Where's your dad?"

"Sleeping."

Ross was away, and Maggie was afraid to go over alone, so she told Michelle to tuck in with Laura, and Maggie called the police. When they went next door, they found Estelle in the basement, naked and bound to a support column, with her hands tied behind her. The floor was cold, and she was shivering. One of the officers covered her with his coat, and after they unbound her, they told Maggie to stay with Estelle while they went upstairs.

On the upper floor JR was in bed, barely conscious, with an empty whiskey bottle beside him. The two other children were awake. Gregory was in his crib whimpering, and Nate had climbed in next to him to comfort his little brother so he wouldn't make noise. The police took JR with them, and Maggie called Alethea and Mark to come over and stay with Estelle because Maggie had to go home to be with her own children.

What happened that day at Estelle's house happened to the whole neighborhood. Estelle's friends felt guilty that they had not intervened sooner. They knew something was going on even if they didn't know the extremity of it. Once it all broke loose they felt responsible to create safe harbor for Estelle and her children.

"Did they all assume that?" Rowland asked. "No one walked away? It's a lot to expect of friends and neighbors."

"Friendship, if it's more than putting on a show, is for better or worse. The only way to escape the worst would be to forfeit the friendship. You don't get to cherry-pick the good times." Alethea spoke calmly as if what she was saying was obvious to anyone who'd ever been a friend.

"Did you know that from the beginning?" Rowland asked her.

"No. We didn't know what we would face together."

"If you had known would it have made a difference?" Rowland asked.

"I don't know. I'm not an idealist," said Alethea. "I'm glad we didn't know what was coming. By the time there were hard times to face, the friendships were already forged. I wouldn't have wanted to go through my life without friends. Certainly not without those particular friends."

JR DIDN'T COME HOME again after he was charged. Estelle needed income, and she found a job waitressing in the evening, but childcare was a problem. After months of daily rescheduling and piecemeal plans that fell through, Mark and Alethea invited Estelle and her children to move in with them in their large house a few blocks from where Maggie and Ross lived on Woodward Street. While Estelle worked evenings, Mark and Alethea were there for the children.

As a young woman in England, Estelle had loved her first job working in the tearoom, and she knew she was good at it. She was convinced that if she could open a tearoom of her own she could support herself and her children. Money from the sale of the house after her divorce would get her started, and she would name her place ESTELLE'S.

To tend the children while she worked, Estelle asked her mother to come and live with them. Her mother did visit, but from the day she arrived she made it clear that she had matters she needed to wrap up in England before she could settle in with Estelle and her children. Soon after her mother returned to England, Estelle's brother Randolph also came for a visit. Mark and Alethea welcomed him. He was an interesting guest, and often they'd linger together at the table after dinner, entertained by Randolph's quick sense of humor and comic stories about his work as a chaplain at a boy's boarding school.

Randolph was less charming to his sister, often behaving like a district supervisor carrying out a review. He criticized her children's manners and disapproved of how Estelle managed her money. Her job waitressing in the evening meant that she was often away over dinner, and Randolph thought this was neglectful. He also had serious doubts about the tearoom. "It's poppycock," he said. When he saw the stunned looks of the others at the table he added, "Show some common sense, Estelle. A restaurant is far too much of an obligation. Your life is complicated enough as is."

Toward the end of Randolph's visit, he informed Estelle that their mother would not be "taking up tenure" with Estelle. He spoke of Estelle's request for help from her mother as an invitation, as if Estelle had offered her mother a job, and Randolph was conveying the message that his mother had declined the offer. Estelle was incensed. Living in America Estelle had learned to be straightforward, and she accused Randolph of nosing in on something that was not his concern.

When Randolph cleared his throat, it was not always because it needed it, but rather a signal to Estelle that he expected her to pay attention. He noted that his mother was an attractive woman. Age had softened her appearance so that, while she was no longer as "striking" as she had been when she was young, she might still be described as "lovely." There were pauses here and there in Randolph's delivery, during which he was allowing the message to sink in. Employment at the funeral parlor gave their mother financial security, which was no small matter because her dissolute husband had left her in poverty. Randolph laid out his case like a lawyer. As he spoke he sipped his after-dinner scotch, and his face flushed.

Estelle broke in. "I don't like thinking of my mother as a kept woman, and I resent your influence in persuading her not to come to America to live with me and be a grandmother. You would rather she be a second-fiddle in the undertaker's household than a family member in mine. I'm offended."

"Put your own concerns aside," Randolph pushed back a little from the table. "Do you think the mistake of marrying a man who proved to be a wretch now condemns Mother to spend the rest of her life alone? Her employer capitalizes on her predicament a bit. I'm willing to admit that, but Mother also benefits a great deal. She's provided for, and that's something for which you and I should be grateful."

Estelle stared at Randolph in disbelief. She expected him to be ashamed of what he'd said. He took another sip of scotch, held it out a little to check how much was still in the glass, and poured a little more. He did this in a choreographed display of gentlemanly control. Those at the table watched in silence, as if they all knew the rule about not interrupting a man who is "refreshing" his drink.

When Randolph picked up his glass again, Estelle took advantage of the pause. "You've got it wrong. You're totally off! Maybe you're used to thinking that wearing your collar backward makes you right, Randolph St. George, but it doesn't. It makes you arrogant."

Randolph watched his sister speak, and when she finished he cleared his throat again. "Your insults don't change the obvious conclusion, little sister. Mother has made up her mind."

"No you've made up her mind for her, " said Estelle, "but I have a question for you. Why can't you let off polishing up the story to make it look good while you're actually saying that you approve of Mother's decision to be a mortician's mistress?"

"Don't be moralistic, Estelle," said Randolph dismissively.

The silence hung for a moment before Estelle replied, "Moralistic? And you're a clergyman? Really Randolph, I would have thought better of you."

"It has nothing to do with me being clergy; what is at issue here is ordinary common sense. Do you have any idea how hard it is to be a clergyman? Even when you're right, you're wrong. And when you're wrong, you're doubly wrong. There's no upside to this profession. You don't get to think about things the way ordinary people do. You never get to be practical. You're always expected to be above it, floating about in the ether of righteousness. Just once I'd like permission to be like every other man."

"Of course. Go ahead. Be like other men," said Estelle. "That's not saying much, by the way." She sneered. "The least you could do is try out your experiment being like other men when it's not at the expense of your own mother? Why did you become a vicar anyway, if all you expect to do is utter the same old rubbish?"

Mark and Alethea had never seen Estelle wound up like this. She leaned over to get a sip of water from her glass, and her hand trembled. Years of being scoured by JR's bullying had worn away her will to be nice at all costs. "You're drunk, Randolph," she said. "Like father, like son."

Randolph pushed his chair completely away from the table and stood up. "Keep your righteous indignation to yourself. You want to know why I became a vicar? The pension is good; that's why I became a vicar. Sometimes practicality tips the balance, and you have to take advantage of whatever is offered, but that shouldn't surprise you. Like mother, like daughter."

Estelle blanched. Mark and Alethea didn't understand how this could be the knockout punch, but Estelle didn't say another word as Randolph excused himself. "I think I'll retire," he said. As he left the room he nodded toward Mark and Alethea. "My apologies. I do appreciate your hospitality. I'm sorry you've had to endure our family squabble."

Estelle did not discuss the matter again with Randolph before he returned to England, where his wife and his work were waiting for him. His departure was distressing for Estelle, but only at first. With clarity about what she could and could not count on, she set her sights. "My family feels like an old boat," said Estelle. "It used to be tethered up to the wharf, but the ropes rotted and it floated out to sea. It's still out there somewhere, but it's not mine to tend anymore." From time to time Estelle exchanged letters with her mother, who always seemed to write about the weather, as if the climate in England mattered to Estelle, who responded with her own news about the weather in Chicago and anecdotes about the children.

WHEN YOU'VE SURVIVED A crisis, you might think everything should settle down, and life should return to normal. From time to time Estelle would say exactly that. "It's a relief to move on. Hard as this life is, at least I know what to expect." But she was wrong. She couldn't have predicted what happened next. Within the year Lillian, Randolph's wife, was diagnosed with cancer, and her decline was rapid.

Randolph had always been proud of Lillian, but he'd never felt that he deserved her. He'd married up and dreamed of proving himself by becoming the vicar of a prestigious parish in a university town. Instead his appointments were to dull places, his last the chaplaincy at a boy's boarding school. He'd had nothing better to offer Lillian than the fussy life of a chaplain's wife in an out-of-the-way place.

After Lillian's death Randolph was depressed. He couldn't stand preaching to restless boys or listening to them mumble high church hymns in chapel. He grew impatient with their ambitious parents, and on a number of occasions his interactions with them lacked tact. After he bungled along for what his employer judged was an abnormally long time of grieving, he was offered "a compassionate retirement." That is the way the headmaster put it on the day he informed Randolph it was time to go, but when Randolph told Estelle what had happened, he said, "I've been sacked."

Estelle was still living with Mark and Alethea. The restaurant was up and running, but the build-out of the family's living quarters above it had stalled. Organizing the apartment remodel was too much for Estelle, and fortunately for her, Mark and Alethea were in no hurry to see the children leave. When they learned the news about Randolph's job, they encouraged Estelle to invite him for a visit. Grief had softened Estelle's anger toward her brother, and they had room for him. "I'm the only family he has," Estelle said, "and he needs a change of scenery. I accept your offer. You're great friends."

During his visit, Randolph and Mark worked in the apartment above Estelle's restaurant: painting, refinishing floors, fixing and replacing what was worn and broken. Mark had skills and a garage full of tools, and Randolph had time. At the end of the day, when Mark would stop in on his way home from work, he would find Randolph with dust on his clothes, scrapes on his knuckles, and ready to admit the satisfaction that came from working with his hands.

Several times Randolph delayed his return to England, first to finish the remodeling and later "to ease the transition" when Estelle and the children moved into the apartment. He helped the children with homework and drove them places, and on rare occasions he helped out at Estelle's restaurant when an employee failed to show up and they were short-handed. As Alethea recounted the events, Rowland could remember Randolph, an eccentric foreigner who wore a sweater with leather patches on the elbows, old-fashioned glasses, and an odd tweed hat, which he sported even when the weather wasn't cold.

With Randolph there to back her up, sometimes Estelle made plans, counting on Randolph to watch the children but not checking with him first. Randolph didn't appreciate it. He worried about money, and it perturbed him that Estelle was cavalier about spending. He criticized Estelle for letting the restaurant and her social life take priority over her children. Randolph was known to complain in humor, "I'm staff at the manor. Lady Estelle gives the orders," but his humor was less obvious when he would add, "I have a life too and sooner or later I'm going to need to return to England to attend to it."

"Did Estelle neglect her kids?" Rowland asked.

That was the hard question Alethea didn't want to answer. She tried to explain to Rowland that being a single mother was demanding, and running a restaurant was exhausting. She tried to commend Estelle for always setting time aside for her friends. She'd created a tradition of Sunday night meals served around her table. They couldn't meet every Sunday, but they met regularly enough that they all came to count on it. When her friends would rave about those evenings, Estelle would remind them "I'm awkward with affection, but I'm confident about cooking. The best part of our dinners is what my friends bring to the table."

"Let me say this," said Alethea; "if I recall the young woman who first came from England with JR, and I put that next to the woman she became, it's nothing short of remarkable. Nonetheless," Alethea sighed, "she wasn't a natural mother. She wasn't as bad as she thought either. There were other things for which she was more gifted."

"Whoa," said Rowland. "That's judgmental. You wouldn't hold a single dad to that standard of perfection would you?"

"I wouldn't. We're more willing to forgive men for their parental shortcomings. Still somebody has to be there for children." Alethea got a far away look. She could remember an evening when their circle of close friends was gathered around the old oak table in the dining room of Estelle's apartment. Mark was there with Alethea. Maggie had come alone. Lorraine was there with Jackson. Randolph's friend Thomas, who had been joining their dinners quite regularly, was also there that night.

Randolph was meticulously gracious in attending to the guests when they arrived, but not quite as talkative as usual. Estelle was sober as she finished the last details in the kitchen, where Lorraine was helping her. It was following the meal as they were beginning dessert that Estelle mentioned an argument with Randolph about Estelle's children. "They're spoiled," he'd said. "They're out of control. How can I leave them and return to England unless I know someone is tending to them?"

"Maybe I'm not maternal," Estelle told her friends, "but I love my children, and I'm trying to earn a living." She choked up. "I'm not a perfect woman, and I've got unfortunate baggage, but I'm doing the best I can." She looked directly at her brother. "Why can't you see my good intentions, Randolph? Feel free to leave. Go back to England if that's what you want. You don't have to justify staying because I'm a failed mother."

Randolph closed his eyes and shook his head to tell Estelle to drop it. That dismissive gesture that a father makes to interrupt a child's inappropriate remark. It set Estelle off. "I'm not a saint, and I don't do everything exactly as you expect, but your judgment wears me out. Decide, Randolph! Make up your mind! Can you bear to live with me and my children without being a crank all the time?" She paused for a second and then went in for one last blow. "Do you want to be here or don't you?"

Randolph was silent. If you're sure you're right, silence is as good a response as any. It's like having the last word with no effort.

He got up from the table and gathered plates, which he brought to the kitchen. Those at the table could hear water running and cupboards opening and closing.

Estelle's friends, sitting with her at the table, did their best to keep the conversation going, but it was awkward. They wondered if Randolph would be joining them again. Perhaps instead of coming back to the table he would go to his room and begin packing. They considered wrapping up the evening and heading home even though they hadn't finished dessert.

"I remember those tense minutes," Alethea recalled as she was telling Rowland the story. "It wasn't exactly a donnybrook, but it also wasn't a slight disagreement that could be swept under the carpet. It occurred to me that within the next few days Mark and I would be saying a permanent farewell to Randolph. Maybe this was the transition point. Perhaps he would be heading back to England for good."

Then the door to the kitchen opened, and Randolph returned to the dining room. As he passed Estelle where she sat at the end of the table nearest the kitchen, he stopped and rested his hands on her shoulders. He bent forward and kissed the top of her head. "I'm sorry," he said. "I know I'm harsh, and you deserve better. You've offered me a home, and it's been hard for me to admit how desperately I've needed it."

Estelle smiled, a pained smile, to acknowledge him there. And then she tipped her head to the side and rested it against the hand he had placed on her shoulder. "You deserve better too," she said. "This is your home. I don't know how I'd manage to make a home without you. Please don't leave. What is it about us, Randolph, that makes it so hard to say what's so obvious?" She smiled up at him, and Randolph walked to the other end of the table and took his place. When they glanced at each other across the table, his eyes were shiny and her chin trembled.

When Alethea told Rowland about that night, she said, "It was one of those way outside of the ordinary moments taking place under the most ordinary circumstances. The evening had started out just as so many others around the table with friends. None of us anticipated that this one would be any different. But on this particular evening something happened. There was a swerve and things took a different course. It was a small thing, but no one missed the power of it." Alethea looked up at Rowland.

"Ever since that night," she continued, "I've tried to figure out what changed in the room when the conflict that had built up was eased, and we were all touched by the forgiveness and the generosity that came flooding back. It was palpable. Was there coincidentally a slight power surge? Were the lights a little brighter for a moment? Did the air conditioning kick in at just the right instant to give a burst of fresh air?"

Alethea saw Row's puzzled look. "Of course, I know, that's not what it was, but it felt that real. What happened between Estelle and Randolph was a sprite of holiness that danced through the room and touched each one of us. It passed from person to person like a current of goodness going around the circle. We all knew it for what it was: to need forgiveness and be forgiven, and commit once again to what we knew was best." Alethea whisked a tear off her cheek, but she did not drop Rowland's gaze. "You see, something like that happened time and again around the table with our friends. Something very simple would melt away our deceits, and then we'd be quickened. Oh I know that's an old-fashioned word that must sound silly to you. But I know truly that's what it was. We'd feel life moving among us. And the remembrance of it still makes me shiver. I can't explain it, but I can say it changed us, each one of us."

Rowland sat transfixed listening to Alethea tell about dinner at Estelle's. He was amazed by how transparent Alethea was as she offered him the remembrance of things past. This same Alethea could in other circumstances be so staid and careful. He wondered if his mother would have told him this story if she'd lived long enough, if she'd had more time. Would he have been willing to listen, or would he have cracked a joke or closed her down the way he had on that dark day in Cordoba. Why had he been so fearful of his mother when in her tenderness she offered to reveal to him what he so badly wanted to know? Maybe it could only be Alethea. Maybe he could only bear to hear the stories second hand.

Eighteen

"It never ends," said Alethea. "The stream of life keeps going, and we're still in it." She wanted Rowland to understand that her friendships didn't end with funerals. Her relationship with Maggie flowed on into the conversations she was having with Rowland, and it flowed on in her connection to Jenna. Her visit with Lorraine had been a day with Lorraine's children and grandchildren. Estelle's children would always be important to Alethea, and so would Randolph. She had lived alongside these families, and they were woven into her thoughts every day. That's not to say that the transitions had been easy, or to deny the days marked by pain.

Alethea thought back to a beautiful Tuesday in autumn a few years before when she drove Estelle to the hospital to check in for an outpatient surgery, a minor procedure. By the end of the day, events had swerved in a direction no one could have anticipated.

Even when Estelle was not at work, the tearoom was on her mind, and that morning as she waited for her surgery she was running through her checklist. Randolph would man the cash register and welcome the regulars. Michelle would handle orders for take-out. The new kitchen manager could be counted on, and the woman hired to supervise the crew of servers was reliable. Reviewing her mental checklist was Estelle's way of calming herself. Her restaurant had grown up. She was no longer "queen of the daily crisis." That's what she had called herself on chaotic days when the restaurant first opened.

Alethea kept Estelle company in the preoperative holding area; Michelle was planning to join them after the lunch rush. When

Michelle arrived Estelle was sitting up in bed wrapped in warm blankets and wearing a disposable cap. Every hat Estelle ever put on her head looked cute on her, including this one. Apart from the IV line running into her arm, nothing about her indicated she was going into surgery. She could have been waiting for a spa treatment or a massage.

When Estelle's gurney slid away through the swinging door to the surgical suite, Michelle and Alethea blew her kisses. Estelle looked back and said, "In a little bit then, loves."

Michelle and Alethea settled into the family waiting area, where videos about health and diet ran endlessly on a screen, and fish swam in circles in a shiny aquarium. Alethea burrowed into a book she'd brought from home, and Michelle played a game on her phone. It was an annoying game because her phone made clicking sounds and little beeps, but Alethea didn't say anything. Michelle needed distraction.

Close to the two-hour mark, a nurse in scrubs came to the desk and then over to where Michelle and Alethea were sitting. She told them the procedure was taking longer than expected. Alethea asked her why and the nurse said the doctor would be able to explain that to them later. She turned then and left in a hurry as if she needed to get back to work.

"Do you think it's serious?" Michelle asked Alethea.

"I hope not," Alethea replied, trying to sound calm.

Michelle was pale. "I have to go to the bathroom," she said, getting up and taking her purse with her. She was gone long.

When she returned and sat down, Alethea put a comforting hand on Michelle's back. She could feel little shivers. "What's going on?" Alethea asked her.

"Diarrhea. I'm nervous," she said. Her eyes were dark like a lake at night, and she picked at a small scab along the line of her chin. She had a large bottle of water, and kept twisting the cap off, taking a few sips, and then twisting the cap back on. Her worry seemed extreme. Alethea wondered about the drugs Michelle swore she wasn't using anymore.

It seemed awfully long until the nurse reappeared to say the doctor would be coming in momentarily. She wasn't cheery. The doctor began with what sounded like a memorized speech. "I am sorry to have to tell you . . . ." Alethea looked at Michelle and saw panic. The next words that caught her attention were "a reaction to anesthesia we didn't anticipate," and then after a jumble of terms, the words that struck home like a hammer blow to the head, "we were not able to revive her." There with the doctor at a round table in a pastel room with beach and mountain scenes, Alethea felt like she was driving a car that had lost its brakes and was headed toward the edge of a cliff. She held out against what she was hearing, still hoping she misunderstood him.

"Dead?" she asked the doctor.

"Yes," the doctor nodded. "There was nothing more that could be done."

The doctor sat quietly, watching them. Michelle burst into tears, and Alethea held her. "I assume you'd like time with Estelle alone before the funeral director arrives," the doctor said. "Take a few more minutes here together, and then we'll come and get you."

Estelle hadn't said which funeral home she preferred; she hadn't been planning to die. She'd been planning to go home and settle in to be pampered by her daughter and her friend. Alethea had made chicken soup for her, and Michelle had picked up a bouquet of freesia because they were her mother's favorite. The bouquet was still in the car. Estelle loved the way freesia smelled. She described it as the fragrance of expensive English perfume that's gotten old and is a little off but still plenty nice. Alethea had chuckled to hear Estelle describe a delicate flower that way, because to Alethea it sounded more like Estelle describing herself.

Michelle looked like she'd been dropped off in a foreign country where she didn't know the language. "Do you know anything about funeral guys?" she asked Alethea. "Do you have connections?"

Alethea couldn't help thinking of Estelle's mother working for a mortician. "I'll check with your Uncle Randolph," she told Michelle, "and I'll ask the nurses to make the call. Meanwhile you should call your brothers. And I'll call Maggie."

When Maggie answered the phone and Alethea told her what happened, she said, "Give me a second. I'm having trouble believing this." The phone was silent, but Alethea could tell Maggie was still there because she could hear her breathing. Then she heard her whisper "Oh, no. Please, no. Oh no. This can't be." Her voice went silent, and then her strong everyday voice came back. "Where are you? I'm coming. At least let's be together."

While Alethea waited for Maggie, she thought of that night years ago when Estelle was bound to the pipe in the basement and JR was drunk upstairs in his bed. She thought about their children, especially little Michelle, who had always tried to be so brave. How unfair it was that Estelle was dead and JR had outlived her. There was no way friends could rescue Estelle this time.

Once she knew Randolph and Maggie were on their way to the hospital, Alethea asked Michelle if Nate and Gregory were on the way too. "I haven't called them yet," Michelle said in a panicky voice. "What should I say? Can't you call them?"

"Do you have their numbers?"

Michelle's thumbs went into action, and seconds later two contacts appeared in Alethea's text messages. If she hadn't been there, she wondered, would Michelle have sent her brothers text messages to let them know their mother was dead?

A FEW WEEKS AFTER Estelle's funeral, Michelle called Alethea and asked to come over. When Alethea opened the door and saw Michelle, she was shocked. Michelle was gaunt and thin and blotchy. "I can't get Mom out of my mind," she said. "I keep thinking about her and my dad." While they sat together in Alethea's living room, Michelle talked about the families in their neighborhood and how they used to gather on the patio at Maggie's house. Ross grilled the meat while the moms brought out the other food. Michelle had just seen those friends again at her mother's funeral, and it had jarred her memories loose.

Michelle talked about her dad too. Not at the funeral, because he wasn't there, but he was on her mind. She was trying to put together a shattered picture. She remembered times on the patio when her dad called her over and said, "Michelle, run over to our house and get me one of my beers out of the fridge; I don't want to dry up Ross's supply." She'd run home as fast as she could to get the beer her dad preferred, and she felt oddly proud that she was doing something for which she could win his approval. "Am I going totally wack or something?" Michelle asked. "Why do I remember stupid stuff like that?"

Michelle reminisced about Halloween. Ross waiting for the children at the sidewalk while they went up on porches to trick or treat. She couldn't remember if her dad was there or not. She recalled Mark putting training wheels on her bike and running along side her when she learned to ride without the training wheels. Michelle remembered how the neighborhood kids lit sparklers on the Fourth of July, and how Jackson Davis told the kids to put the sparklers in a bucket of water when they were done, not on the deck or in the trash because there might be a spark left that could start a fire.

"Where was my dad?" Michelle asked. Alethea didn't get a chance to answer before Michelle went on. "I can't remember that Mom was there either. Who the heck brought us up? Was Mom always busy doing her own thing?" Michelle was agitated.

Alethea had the urge to calm Michelle down, to tell her that Estelle had done everything she could for her children. She loved them. There was no doubt about that. Then Alethea thought better of it; she didn't want to add to the confusion of Michelle's tangled memories.

"My dad hit my mom," Michelle blurted out. "I saw him do it. I was scared he'd hit me too. Did you ever see him do that? Did you ever see him hit the other kids?"

"I know he hit your mother," Alethea told her.

"He called Mom names. Once Nathan called me a slut, and Dad slapped him. When Mom said that Nathan learned that word from Dad, he slapped her too." Michelle took a huge breath like a diver about to go under. "Who protected us from Dad? Why did Mom let him get away with so much? Why didn't Mom stop him?"

That's when Alethea said, "Oh honey, I'm so sorry you went through that."

"There's another thing," said Michelle. "My dad let me drink beer. He put vodka in the orange juice and thought it was funny. One time when he did that, Gregory got really hyper and staggered around and Dad laughed. Mom cried. Why didn't Mom tell him not to do that? Or maybe she did. Is that why he got kicked out? Do you think Mom made him leave because of us?"

Michelle changed the subject abruptly. She talked about school and night courses. It was hard for her to study. She felt tired a lot. She had to use medicine to sleep because her nights were terrible. Just as abruptly Michelle changed the subject back again. "Do you remember Nana?"

"I do," Alethea replied. "I remember when your nana visited, and we all lived together at our house. Do you remember that?"

"She was the best," said Michelle. "She let me wear her lipstick, and sometimes she put nail polish on my toes. She took care of me. After she went back to England I missed her. I wanted to go with her, but she said I had to stay with Mom and help her. She told me to wait until I was grown up, and then I could come to England and live with her."

When Michelle left, Alethea watched from the window of the living room until she saw her appear on the street below. She looked fragile. Lost. As Alethea watched Michelle wandering off down the street, she did what she often did when she was alone in her condo. She turned inward to talk to an old friend. *It's so unfair, and I don't know what to do about it, but I'll keep loving Michelle the best I can. That's what I'll do for you, Estelle.* And then another odd thought broke into the stream. *"What is it about death that makes us so determined to defend those we love?"*

On that day after Michelle's visit, Alethea wept. For Michelle and for Spencer. For her little brother Teddie Junior too. She wept for Maggie's Steven, and this time she also wept for her own mother who was a teenager who never grew up. She wept because she was missing Estelle, her dear friend who understood sadness about everything broken and lost, her friend who understood tears held back so long they finally merge together into a big sighing stream.

When Alethea sat with Rowland at the table and tried to explain to him the grief that flooded through their circle of friends when they lost Estelle, she said, "I had yet to discover that Estelle's story didn't end the day she handed it over to us at her funeral. It's still being recounted as a story so different than the one by which Estelle would have expected to be remembered. Someone else gets to assemble her story. Some of it will be told by Michelle, and it probably won't be told well. Some of it will be held by her friends. And some of it will be remembered by you, Rowland."

Was that the right thing to say to Rowland? Was it fair to put that weight on his shoulders? After all, he was still dealing with the loss of his own mother. Alethea was still musing about this several days later when she found some pages from Maggie's journal that Rowland had slipped under her door. Apparently Rowland had come by while she was out.

I wonder if Estelle's passing has breached the sturdy fortress our circle of sisters provided for each one of us. It gave us strength in terrible times, and much happiness too. When I saw Estelle at the funeral home, it was hard to leave, to turn and walk out of the room and leave Estelle there in a box. So alone. What I have now are memories. Cups of tea, good humor, and trivial things that are delightful. There were sweet times. And I want to remember beautiful evenings we enjoyed at her table. What a gift those hours were. The comfort of friendship and not feeling alone.

Tonight when I opened the door and walked into my own living room, I saw the paperweight Estelle gave me when Steven died. When I thanked her for it, she said, "You know the most beautiful glass requires ash?"

I held the paperweight. I could feel the smooth coolness of the glass in my hand. It was solid, and it caught the light. Estelle seemed near. I see now what I must do. I'll ask Alethea to go with me to visit Randolph, and I'll give him the paperweight. While we are there I will ask my two dear friends to honor Estelle by continuing the tradition of dinner together. I'll invite them for dinner at my table. Our circle mustn't be broken. The people we love will come and go from it, but the circle must live on.

Part V

Beyond the Solitude

There is no insurmountable solitude. All paths lead to the same goal: to convey to others what we are. And we must pass through solitude and difficulty, isolation and silence in order to reach forth to the enchanted place where we can dance our clumsy dance and sing our sorrowful song—

—*Pablo Neruda*

Nineteen

MY MOTHER WOULD LAUGH if she knew I've been keeping a journal of my own during this summer of living in her condo and reading what she left for me in that carton with a note. My jouornal isn't in a bound book with blank pages, nor is it tapped out on an old Underwood typewriter. It's less visible than that. I compose on my laptop and file it in a folder named OAK PARK. It seems long ago that I got a call from Laura asking me what to do with Mom's teeth. Summer is passing quickly, and I've only begun what I came here to do.

Living in the middle of something and not knowing about it is a peculiar thing. When do our eyes open? How long do we remain like baby animals that can't see yet? Small, fragile, and confined to our own little nest. Children don't catch on to everything while they are busy growing up, but this has to change if we don't want to be infants forever.

I mentioned this to Alethea. "Maybe that's what it means to honor our parents," she said. "They don't have to earn it? We owe it to them to grow up and discover that life didn't begin with us. I had one parent who was easy to love and one who was difficult, but to each of them I owe the respect of knowing their story."

"That's mind-twisting," I told her. "It sounds like doing public relations for our parents. Revisionist history."

Alethea didn't pick up on my critical remark. She went on to something else that was on her mind. "I wasn't your mom's only friend, and I'm not the only one still standing on two feet. There's a remnant of our friends that still gets together. We catch up on ordinary things. Randolph tells us about the opera. Thomas tells us about a new bird he's spotted. Lately he's been filling us in on Proust. We tease him about being a fan of endless stories. I tell them about you too, and our visits together. I promise you, I'm discreet. Would you like to join us? Think about it and let me know."

I DECIDED TO EXTEND my stay in Chicago and live in Mom's condo until the end of my sabbatical. I wanted to invite Alethea, Randolph, Thomas, and my sister Jenna for dinner. If I planned it for a weekend, I could also invite Polly to come to Chicago for a visit so I could introduce her to the group. I liked the idea of having dinner around the dining room table in Mom's condo.

Alethea gave me the paperweight that changed hands from Estelle to Mom to Randolph and to Alethea, and now it's mine. I put it on the windowsill where it catches light, and it reminds me Mom is still here. Sometimes I look at the paperweight and wonder about the way Mom connected light and awe. I sit in her reading chair by the window, and I wonder if prayers have gone up from this place. She hasn't left completely, and this summer I've been seeing a lot her.

I've been seeing a lot of Alethea too. This morning I dropped off items for her that I'd picked up at the farmer's market. I knocked on her door, and as she opened it she said my name. "Rowland." Her voice went up in a little leap of delight, and it landed softly as she smiled. It struck him as an old-fashioned gesture, as if she were announcing my arrival. I stepped through the doorway and extended my hand, which she took as she raised her cheek to me, and we gave each other a two-cheeked Greek kiss. She's the only person I've ever greeted this way, and I like it. That's the thing. If I thought it was cool to give Greek kisses, of course I could do it with perfect choreography. But admitting that I like it, admitting that it means something to me, that's the new part. I still get a strange feeling if I imagine that Will and Dad are watching, but I'm getting better at pushing that aside.

Greeting Alethea reminds me of Mom. I feel her cheek brush softly against mine. Hers is warm and soft. Almost always I shave before visiting Alethea, and I wonder how a grown man's freshly shaved cheek feels to a motherly woman. The curiously sentimental places to which my mind wanders still make me squirm sometimes. Tenderness is new terrain for me. I don't know much about tenderness unless it's laced with sex.

When I think of Mom tucking me in at night, I realize how much of the past is lost. The good goes out with the bad. Loss has taken on new meaning for me. I've always known about lost manuscripts. I've read articles in which scholars bemoan the beauty of the past lost through fire, flood, and war. Much more has been lost through simple, stupid neglect. In my class lectures each semester, I recount my own experience during a trip to Romania where I visited an ancient Roman bath and discovered that a farmer was using it to corral goats. I sneer about the neglect and make snotty comments about the goats lacking appreciation for the ancient mosaics on which they shit.

I've never before thought of lost treasures beyond those that might be prized in museums and rare book rooms. It's never occurred to me to include in this lost past all the forgotten men and women who were people like me, ordinary people erased from memory by time. The truest moments of their plain lives came and went. Each one born, each one living for a time, each one dying and forgotten. But that's not all. Lost with each one is the memory of moments too tender to express, too lovely to admit. What if I didn't remember how Mom used to put her cheek against mine?

What if I had never learned about Spencer's death, or Mom's offer to have a baby for Alethea? What if I had never found out about Alethea's loyalty to Michelle or known about the friends who rallied to Estelle's side when JR was terrorizing her family? It's not something I'm entitled to know, but it's a privilege to know it, isn't it? If I never were told the story, wouldn't that be my loss?

This makes me think of Dad too. He was a guarded man. Did Ross love Maggie, and did Maggie love Ross? Does the sheer will to endure qualify as love? My parents had blind spots for each other, although I didn't know what they were when I was living there beside them. Maybe their blind spots were nothing more than freckles on their love. Children and grandchildren, loyalty through illness, the hard work of providing for and tending, did that all add up to true love?

If I push myself forward through time and think about my own children and their future, I wonder what they will see. What will they know of their own story? Will they recollect only a failed relationship when they remember what happened to Andrea and me?

And what about Doc Barnes and my grandmother whom I confuse with Emily Dickinson? I never met them face to face. I want to capture as much of them as I can. I want to throw a net of words over them. No, that's not right. I want to wrap a cloak of honor around them.

What's happening to me? What is this? Homesickness? Longing? Nostalgia? What name can I give to this oceanic feeling that overcomes me when I glimpse my own place in the stream of life, a stream that was there before me and will keep going after me? I've never thought of my own life this way before. Is this the dawn of aging? Is my own youth over and done, and is this what is coming next?

That thought broke my reverie. I got on the phone and asked Polly, who studies classical languages, "Do you think it's possible to be intimate with the past?"

"It is possible," she said. "It may begin by assembling what we know about the past, or think we can find out about it in texts. But the real intimacy comes when we live what we've learned from it. The real intimacy begins in 'aha' moments in which something we've known for a long time finally dawns on us. Are you writing an article?" she asked.

"No, just having a thought. Talk to you later."

I didn't know what else to say to Polly at the moment because a memory of my dad was battering its way into my consciousness. I told my brother Will once that I'd rather be knocked unconscious than share feelings with Dad. Remembering my remark makes me shift in my chair, as if a scorpion is crawling across my back. It's a mixture of remaining frozen and still so the scorpion won't bring its tail around and wound me, and right beside that sadness because I don't know Dad. I promise when the time is right I'll tell Zach about how Mom hummed to me at bedtime when I was a little boy. I'll begin there, and then I'll tell Zach much more. I want to give Zach the chance to be a different kind of man.

I thought of calling Polly back, but instead I called Alethea. "I'd like to accept your invitation to get together with Mom's friends. I'd like to get to know Randolph and Thomas too."

"Good idea," she said. "I'll set it up."

Twenty

"IF I INVITE FRIENDS for dinner around my table," I asked Alethea, "will it be possible to recreate the tradition Mom had with her friends on Sunday nights? Will we have good moments, good talks, and the good karma thing? I wonder if that was only possible in the past because things were different then. Has so much changed that it's not possible anymore?"

"You'll only know if you take the chance and do it," Alethea replied. "It's not an equation you can work out on paper. Try it! What do you have to lose? Of course, you'll need a home and a dining room table. A restaurant or a conference room don't create the right atmosphere. Balancing pizza on one knee and beer on the other while the big screen TV is broadcasting sports in the background doesn't set it up right either. If you're going to do it, make it a real dinner around a table."

"I have a home, and I have a dining room," I told her. "It's Mom's, but I'm sure she'd approve. If I wait until I return to Minneapolis, it'll be easy to lose my enthusiasm and put it off so long it'll never happen."

I took the leap and invited Polly to visit me in Chicago. She liked the invitation, but she insisted she'd find a bed and breakfast because she didn't feel ready to stay with me at Mom's condo while we were sorting out our relationship.

I asked her what it would take to change her mind. Somewhere in the back of my own mind an evil gremlin whispered the word "diamond," and somewhere else in the back of my mind the evil twin of that gremlin whispered "Hell no!" Meanwhile, clearer than either of the voices in that inner debate was a calm voice telling me through the telephone, "Time, Rowland. It takes time. It's too easy to spend a night in your bed and conclude from that more than it means." I recognized that voice. It was the voice Polly uses when she's sure of herself. "I've become old-fashioned," she said. "A year ago I was willing to think the way we did when we were kids, figuring that if it makes us happy we should go for it. Now I'm more inclined to think like Aristotle."

"What the shit, Aristotle?" I thought she was playing me.

"Yeah, Aristotle. What the shit right back to you," she said. "He figured out two millennia ago that 'friendship is a slow-ripening fruit.' I'll bet if he were around so we could ask him, he'd advise us that lust is ready for harvest too soon. You're sexy, Rowland. Very sexy. You were a year ago, and you are now. But the slow ripening fruit? That's another matter entirely."

"Whatever," I said. "Even if you're right, it's corny to quote Aristotle right after I've invited you to my bed. If you don't want to sleep with me, just say 'no thanks,' and I won't argue with you." I knew Polly could be pompous, especially when she was making the point that she understood something I hadn't figured out yet. I wondered if I'd have to learn to love that too. I decided to keep my mouth shut and let her have the last word.

"Well, at least we're clear, then," she said. "I'd like to come to Chicago."

JENNA HEARD THAT POLLY was staying at a bed and breakfast, and she invited Polly to stay with her, but it was Alethea's invitation that Polly finally accepted. I planned the visit carefully. Alethea agreed to invite Randolph and Thomas for dinner. I recruited Jenna to help prepare a table with casual elegance using serving pieces she'd inherited from Mom's household.

Polly was the unknown guest for the evening, and I enjoyed introducing her to the others, although they already knew who she was. "Father Thomas and Father Randolph, I'd like you to meet my very dear friend, Polly Tropos," I said.

"I thought she was your girlfriend," said Randolph. "Why so formal?"

"Oh Randolph," said Alethea, "this isn't the 1950s. People don't have girlfriends and boyfriends anymore. At least that's what Rowland tells me."

"You're right, Aunt Alethea," said Jenna. "We don't even have significant others anymore."

"What do you have now?" Randolph asked.

"Beats me." Jenna blushed. "I don't know what adults have. Kids have hook-ups."

"That sounds like refueling airplanes midair, " said Randolph. "I didn't mean to embarrass you." He patted his middle, as if he were enjoying a good meal.

After more small talk, Randolph asked Polly about her work. "It's complex," she said with a deflecting gesture. "I study ancient languages that aren't interesting to anyone but classicists."

"Try us out," said Randolph. "Thomas and I studied Latin as bored schoolboys, and Alethea is a librarian. We're all good at pretending we know a little about a lot of things. I promise we'll compensate for ignorance by being curious."

"You'll find it dull," said Polly, looking uncertainly at me and then at Jenna.

"It's okay," I told her. "Go ahead, impress them."

"I do onomastics," said Polly. "That's a bad start already, isn't it? When I tell people what I do, they think it's a medical procedure."

"So what do you do?" Jenna asked.

"I study ancient names," Polly explained. "Linguists use onomastics to study how languages evolve over time."

"Give us an example," said Thomas, brightening up. "By the way, 'onomastics' is an interesting word. I'm hooked."

Polly gave a well-crafted elevator speech about a name that first appeared in Mycenaean Greece nearly four thousand years ago. Later the name appeared in Crete. In the poetry of Hesiod the woman is identified as a midwife. "You're probably wondering why anyone would study this. Who cares, right?" said Polly, still feeling apologetic for steering a dinner conversation onto a topic more suited for a conference.

"Oh not at all," said Randolph, "but now I'm wondering what the name is."

"It is Eileithyia. That's an early spelling. Later the spelling changed to Ilithyia."

"That sounds like Alethea," Jenna observed.

"That's why tracing is difficult. Not everything that sounds alike is the same. Eileithyia's name means 'she who comes to aid.' She was a midwife. Alethea's name means 'truth.' By the way, in mythology Alethea was the daughter of Chronos, the god of time, and she was the mother of Virtue."

Along with impressing Randolph and Thomas, whose attraction to the obscure was like the appeal of honey to ants, Polly's comment had gotten Alethea's attention. "When my parents chose a name for me, they had no idea what it meant. My mother wanted me to have a name no one else had, and Papa approved because it sounded Greek."

"I thought your mother was Italian," said Thomas.

"She was. You're right," Alethea responded. "Don't try to make sense of it."

"You're lucky she didn't go for the Latin form and name you Verity," said Thomas. "Your name has a better ring to it."

"So it must have been fate, then," said Polly. "Sometimes people make things happen without knowing why. They're tools for fate working its way." I looked closely at her. I couldn't tell if Polly was serious. "In Alethea stories," she continued, "there is usually a true Alethea and a false one, a deceiver. The true one wins out, but not without a struggle."

"So that's what you mean by fate? In the long run the right side wins, and what happens is what was meant to happen? Obviously not a modern story," I said.

"Right you are," said Polly. "It isn't modern. The notion that certain things are meant to happen fascinates me. It's more compelling than the modern idea that everything is accidental and random."

"Yes! Yes!" Randolph patted the tabletop as if he were voting in parliament.

"How did the two of you ever meet, you and Row?" Jenna asked. "You're a match. I mean in an odd way. You're both brainiacs.

A lot of people wouldn't be able to understand either one of you. It's nice you found each other."

"Fate," I said. "I had to teach a section of world literature to freshmen the first year of my appointment. I wanted the job, so I said I'd do it. Trouble was, I didn't know anything about early literature, the heroic epics of Greece, the drama and poetry of Rome. So I went over to the Classics Department and sat in on a course. And there she was, the one and only Polly Tropos."

"Were you teaching, Polly?" Thomas asked.

"No. I was observing too. Student theater was doing the *Odyssey*, and I was hired to create program notes. I figured if I listened to students discussing the poem in class, I'd be able to write better notes."

"Sure. Rewriting good literature to make it say what you want." It was hard to tell if his comment was a jab or a joke because Thomas often said things with a deadpan expression.

"Did it work?" Randolph asked.

"So, so," Polly admitted.

"And that's how the two of you met," said Alethea. "And here you are. It's been such a special summer. First getting reacquainted with Row and now meeting you." Alethea could toss out compliments without seeming overdone. It was an entitlement of age, and it reminded me of Mom.

At the end of the evening after the other guests left, Jenna lingered to help clean up. "How about lunch tomorrow? I'm going to Greektown with Aunt Alethea and Polly in the morning. We'll visit the National Hellenic Museum, and afterward we'll pick up Greek pastries for Polly to send to her mother. We could all have lunch together when we get back."

"Whoa. Polly's my guest. Where did this itinerary come from?" I felt upstaged.

"We just made it in the kitchen," said Jenna without apology. "Alethea's father was Greek, and so is Polly's mother."

OVER LUNCH AFTER WE met up again, Alethea told about her father leaving Greece as a young man. "He was thoroughly American and proud of it," she said. "He served in the Army, never failed to vote, and always took off his hat and put his hand over his heart when the National Anthem was played, but he never gave up thinking of himself as Greek."

"Why would he let go of that?" Polly asked. "So few people know about Greece. The history is thousands of years deep. Where else do you have villages that have been doing the same traditional dances for hundreds of years? When I see a Tsakonikos, I feel like all my ancestors are in the line of dancers. I'm proud to be half Greek."

Alethea began telling a story that I'd heard before. I didn't mind hearing it again. It was her story, beginning with events that happened before she was born. She told how her father stood with his own father on the cliffs above the sea, looking down at their village, looking out over the water, and realizing soon they would be leaving Greece to emigrate to America. Alethea's voice trembled slightly as she imitated her father's accent repeating the words his Baba said to him. She explained that her father always repeated it twice, first in heavily accented English for Alethea, and then in their Tsakonian dialect out of respect for his father. "Look carefully, Theodoro, and see it all. Whatever you see, take it with you. It's yours. It's yours to keep forever."

I glanced across at Polly. Her eyes were watery. I looked back toward Alethea and noticed the blush on her face. "My mother would love that story," Polly said.

"It's so seldom," said Alethea, "that I find someone who understands the place from which I come. I was born in America, but I never felt completely American because my parents weren't. We were just a little odd."

"I know that feeling. I know it so well," said Polly.

"I've always been confused about where my true home is," Alethea continued. "I feel at home in my condo. No doubt about that. I enjoyed the big house where Mark and I made a home together. He remodeled it to make it just right for us, and we shared it with people we loved. The row house in Philadelphia where I grew up never felt like home. It's the address on my birth certificate, but it's a house full of painful memories. The truth is, deep down, my home is the cliff on which my father stood with my

Pappou. I've never been there, and don't know exactly where it is, but it's my original home."

Polly got up from her chair, came behind Alethea and embraced her, resting her head gently alongside Alethea's, and laying her arms along Alethea's like a cloak. They were oblivious to the fact that they were in a busy restaurant at lunchtime. They lingered together in that embrace, not conscious of time but only conscious of place, a place somewhere else through which they were connected.

I looked across at Jenna. Her eyes were shiny too. What did Jenna know about Greece? Or immigration? What did she know about this connection between Alethea and Polly, like a spark where two live wires touched? That's the thing about Jenna. She seems to understand people with so little effort.

Sitting in the restaurant, in a public place, watching Polly hug Alethea, I felt uncomfortable. I knew I was witnessing one of those precious moments around the table, but I also felt the urge to shut it down. I wanted to move on. To change the subject. To get back to a normal conversation for a public place. I considered beckoning the waiter to refill the coffee. Then it occurred to me what that odd restless feeling was. *A Barone man would get the coffee cups topped up. But I don't want to be like my father. I don't have to be like Will either.*

Twenty-one

Soon again I invited Polly to come to Chicago for another visit. She accepted. This time I suggested that Zach travel with her so he could visit Jenna's son Philip. The cousins are the same age and have good times together. I invited the boys to stay with me at Mom's condo, and Alethea invited Polly to stay with her.

"Do you think it works to mix generations?" I asked Alethea. "I'll have the boys help me cook. That way they'll have some skin in the game. I've been promising to show Zach how to make Coquille St. Jacques. It's flashy on the table and not hard to prepare. The guys will enjoy going with me to the fish market."

When all were gathered at the table, just as I was about to reach for the salad bowl to begin serving the food, Alethea asked Randolph to say grace. He did it effortlessly, and I could tell it wasn't the first time he'd ever said grace at a gathering. When he finished, he gazed at the food set out on the table and asked, "Do you boys know why we serve scallops on shells?"

Randolph went on to explain how a clamshell became the symbol for a saint, who was supposedly buried in Santiago de Compostela. "It's St. James," Randolph explained. "All over the world people and things are named after him: San Diego, Santiago, St. Jacques, Jacob, James, Jimmy, Seamus, Iago . . . once it gets going it spreads. For the last five hundred years people from all over Europe have been hiking to the site to honor the saint. And here we are honoring him at dinner."

Thomas was listening. "Don't be too impressed, guys," he said to Zach and Philip; "these shells on our table weren't fished out of the sea in Spain. Rowland probably bought them on Amazon. It's still a fine meal, and you two are good chefs, but don't be taken in by a charade."

"I like tradition," said Randolph. "It doesn't matter to me if the shells are produced in a factory in China. They mean something if we decide to let them mean something. My friend Thomas here is so concerned with the real thing, he ends up with nothing. I'm satisfied just to have a reminder."

"That's called discernment," said Thomas. They were all relieved to hear a chuckle in his voice. Thomas could be overly serious. "Randolph needs stories because chaplains are expected to entertain. Did you know he was a chaplain when he lived in England?"

"Thomas likes to trim me down to size when I get carried away with stories. I suppose that's why I need a friend like Thomas," said Randolph. "What I've not figured out is why he wants a friend like me."

They all looked at Thomas, who seemed put on the spot. He paused and then said, "I like Randolph's company for the same reason people like having radios in their cars."

"Background noise?" asked Randolph.

"Something like that," said Thomas with a twinkle in his eye. "A rescue from tedium."

"What were you doing in England?" Philip asked Randolph.

"I was born there and grew up there," Randolph replied.

"Did you work there or here or wherever?" Philip asked. The young boys were leaning into the conversation, and I was proud of them.

Randolph was not quick to admit to strangers that he'd been a clergyman. He preferred to tone it down, neutralize it, with a ready collection of stories about the goofy pranks of boys who attended the boarding school where he'd been chaplain. The families from which the boys came weren't particularly religious by conviction, but they were seriously religious by tradition. The parents wanted their boys to know how to behave at religious events, because any grown man with a prominent position could be expected to attend an investiture, a dedication, a christening, or a funeral now and then. They'd hired a chaplain to teach religious etiquette.

Although teaching boarding school boys how to behave in a chapel was the primary role of the chaplain, bundled in with that was Randolph's presence as a listening ear. That was the part of his work he valued most, even if it was not included in the job description. He talked with boys because he cared about them. "I never dreamed when I was ordained I'd be required to hear the confessions of teenagers," Randolph said in humor.

That caught the attention of both Zach and Philip. "Seriously?" said Zach. "Like was that a school requirement? That's pretty weird."

This evening with two young guests present, Randolph explained that usually schoolboys' confessions were dull. One stole a watch from another. They all cheated on tests if they got a chance, and they lied to their parents about the hours of study they put in when their grades were drifting down. Only a few felt guilty enough to confess their misdemeanors. The real villains, the bullies and slanderers, seldom confessed. Zach and Philip agreed with Randolph on that. They said it was that way at their schools too.

Randolph went on to tell about the saddest confession he'd ever heard. It was the story of a lad who came to Randolph to confess that he'd pulled the legs off a spider. He described his sin in detail, telling how he caught the spider, trapped it in the box in which his mother had sent biscuits, and then pulled off the first leg while watching to see if the spider could navigate without it. Then he pulled off the second leg and watched the spider struggle.

As the boy recited the details of his sin, Randolph distracted himself by guessing how many legs a spider could lose before it was incapacitated. The story dragged. Randolph worried that the lad would make him late for afternoon tea, where imported cheese and expensive sherry were served. It might be packed away by the time he got there. He looked the boy in the eye to see if he was finding an end to his story, and that's when Randolph realized how genuinely remorseful the lad was. This was not a homesick boy making up a transgression so he would have an excuse to visit with a kind adult. This was a boy with a burdened conscience.

Zach and Philip weren't missing a word. Randolph skillfully worked the imaginations of his listeners with images of the boy's pale, dry hands with nibbled nails, torturing the spider. He described the pale pimply boy with irritated, crust-rimmed eyes. And then Randolph admitted that something happened to the chaplain as he listened to the boy's confession.

"When I was a lad I didn't harm a spider, but I did pull the wings off a fly one time. Actually I did it more than once," Randolph admitted to them. "It's dreadful to bully a creature so small it can't fight back. By listening to someone else's confession, I was made to see my own capacity for cruelty. This boy unearthed something I'd buried decades before. I'd never thought of myself as cruel. Lazy maybe, or dishonest, but cruel was not on my list of sins."

Randolph described how the boy waited with quiet expectation for the chaplain to absolve him of his guilt. "We'll pray," said Randolph, "you and I, admitting our faults." When they finished Randolph absolved the boy. "Go your way and sin no more," he said, but the boy continued peering at Randolph. He wanted something more from the chaplain. Randolph felt compelled to add, "Come back again when you have more to confess because by then I will have more too. Sitting with our misdeeds alone is difficult, and I'd be grateful for your honest company."

The friends at the table were quiet.

"What ever happened to that boy?" Zach asked.

"He became a member of Parliament," Randolph said with a chuckle.

"Seriously?" Philip asked.

"No, I'm not serious," said Randolph. "I have no way of knowing what happened to him, but why not? Is there any reason a repentant sinner wouldn't make a good Member of Parliament?"

"I've heard that story before," said Alethea. "Actually I find it dear."

"I agree with Alethea," said Thomas. "The best stories bear repeating." He paused, as Thomas often did to measure what he was about to say next. No one interrupted him. "That's why some of the best stories last for thousands of years. They get repeated." He glanced over at Polly, who met his eye. She understood.

Randolph looked at Zach and Philip. "This is the way it goes sometimes. Good conversations go in circles. It takes a while to get to the point."

"Randolph has other stories, but let's save them for dinner tomorrow night," said Alethea. "I'm cooking and you're hosting again, aren't you, Rowland? Isn't that what we agreed? Send the boys over a little before you're expecting the rest of us so they can help me carry the food."

Twenty-two

WE GATHERED AGAIN FOR dinner in the evening, and Randolph said grace. The boys lost no time reminding Alethea that she had promised a story. She explained that Skip was the brother of her good friend Lorraine, and that Lorraine had been their grandmother's friend too. Skip was a career soldier, who sometimes visited Lorraine's family when he was on furlough. He was there for dinner the night that Randolph first told about the boy at the boarding school making his confessions. "That's important background for this story," Alethea said.

Zach and Philip nodded as if to tell her to skip the background and get on with the story.

"Okay," said Alethea, "I'll just jump in."

"I had something like that with Lorraine," Skip had said after he heard Randolph's story. He recounted how he tried to talk to his sister about something he'd done when they were kids, living on their family's farm in Illinois. He still felt guilty about it. Lorraine told him to forget about it because it was nothing. "She doesn't want to know how sorry I am," Skip complained, "but it doesn't help if somebody says that what you did is too small to be sorry about. You still feel guilty."

"Aw Skippy," Lorraine said, "That's different. Sometimes you just have to let it go."

Skip was a quiet fellow, and it was unusual for him to claim an audience at the table. This night was different. He had his own story to tell, and he wanted to be heard. He wanted to apologize for teasing Lorraine when she was little. He took advantage of her innocence, laughing at her when she made blunders and sometimes intentionally mixing her up. He fed her misinformation, and then ridiculed her for believing it.

At church they sang a song called "There is a Balm in Gilead," but Skip persuaded Lorraine that the words were "There is a bomb in Gilead." He made up an elaborate story based on the fact that when fields flood, seeds carried by the water self-plant. Big words he'd picked up listening to his Dad at the farm co-op got woven into the story. Words like seed "deposition" and "methane build-up." The bottom line was that flooded fields make problems for farmers. Skip told Lorraine that if the seed deposition got out of control, the only solution was to set off a bomb and turn all the soil upside down. Once Skip got going he couldn't stop. He even used the words "a bomb that heals seed sick soil."

Lorraine was all ears. She asked if it could happen on their farm. Would Dad and Uncle Chuck have to set off a bomb to rescue the farm? Skip told Lorraine that the bomb was a secret. Most of the time it works fine, Skip explained, but now and then something goes wrong and creates an explosion with enough power to break all the glass in the house, and maybe even the neighbor's house. The windows, the dishes in the kitchen, and Mom's pride and joy china cabinet in the dining room where she kept the Sunday dishes. It was serious stuff. Mom shouldn't know about it because she'd worry too much. Furthermore, if anyone found out that Skip blabbed, he'd be in big trouble with his dad.

Lorraine kept the secret, as far as Skip knew. Then he began to feel guilty because Lorraine had questions. She wanted to know where Dad would get the bomb. Skip told her Dad would get it from Monsanto. Lorraine wanted to know if anyone would tell them before Dad set off the bomb, and Skip said that one day it would just happen. He told her that the bomb would come in a special container that was black and had skull and crossbones on it. From then on when the farm co-op delivery truck pulled into their yard, Lorraine ran out to check what it was carrying. Skip knew she was looking for the black container.

What finally planted Skip's guilt for good was the day Lorraine began to cry in church. She was standing next to her mother while they were singing "There is a Balm in Gilead." Skip knew exactly what Lorraine thought her mother was singing, but by then he was into the lie too deep to admit it.

The evening Skip told this story at dinner, after hearing about Randolph's confession shared with a boarding-school boy, Skip wanted to make amends. A deeply humbled forty-six year old man wanted to apologize to his sister for being mean when he was a boy. He needed to tell his little sister that he'd made her life unnecessarily miserable, and that he was terribly sorry.

"I don't want you to feel bad about this any more," Lorraine said. "Skip, I'm fine. No damage done. I remember all the stuff about the bomb. First I believed it because all sorts of people were talking about the bomb when we were kids. They were building bomb shelters. But when you said it came from Monsanto I knew there was something wrong with your story. The bomb everyone else was talking about came from Russia. So I knew you were making it up. I figured we were having fun. It was a game, not a lie, Skippy. Don't you see? It's okay."

Skip wasn't buying it. "Why were you crying in church then? I saw you with my own eyes. You were standing next to Mom. She was singing, but you weren't. What was that about?"

"Oh, Skip, that was completely different." Lorraine shrugged her shoulders. "I don't know how to explain it, but don't you remember that Sundays were special? On Saturday Mom took a bath and pinned her hair. It was the only day of the week she did that. On Sunday morning we had a different routine. She was still telling us what to do. 'Wear clean socks, Skip! Lorraine, wear your blue dress today; it's chilly out!' She was still giving orders like she always did, but they weren't weekday orders. They were the kind of orders she gave when we were looking forward to something special." Skip nodded in agreement.

"Then off to church we'd go," Lorraine continued. "Mom in her Sunday dress and nylons. Remember her high heels? Not very high, but they made little round holes in the dirt in the yard, and they made little round dents in the kitchen linoleum in front of the sink. Mom had a big rhinestone pin on her dress. She wore white gloves, but not until we got to church if she had to drive the truck. In church Mom seemed happy. Something about her was different when she was there. She liked to sing. Her voice was nice. Sometimes it warbled a little, and I wondered who else could hear it. I stood next to her, though, and she held the book out to me at my level so I could see it and hold one corner. We'd sing together."

"Why did you cry in church? You still haven't explained." Skip said.

"Well wait. I'm trying. After church we'd go home. Mom put the roast in the oven before we went, and when we got home, she didn't change out of her Sunday clothes. Instead she put on an apron. Then Dad and Uncle Chuck would come up to the house from the barn, and she'd say to Dad, 'Harv, please, clean up. It's Sunday, you know. Do it for your kids.' And he would. He went in and took a bath. While he was relaxing in the tub he whistled. Then he'd come out all clean in his dress pants and a fresh cotton shirt. His hair was slicked back because it was wet, and he seemed happy."

"He needed a break," Skip said. "But that's beside the point."

Lorraine explained that once everyone was around the table and the food in the center was perfuming the room so their mouths were watering, their dad said his Sunday dinner prayer. "Take care of the hungry, the sick, and the missionaries in the foreign fields. Give them what they stand in need of. And bless this food and this family." The prayer was always the same and so was the dinner: Roast, potatoes, beans, applesauce, sometimes rolls, and then dessert. Because it was Sunday, their dad didn't go back to work right away. He took a nap on the sofa. He called it his "Sunday snooze." For once he wasn't under pressure. Their mom went to the kitchen to do the dishes, and Lorraine went with her. While they were cleaning up, they'd sing a hymn. One from church in the morning. Sometimes it was "By the Sea of Crystal." Their mom liked that one especially. All afternoon the tablecloth stayed on the table. It didn't come off until after supper. Then their mom checked to see if it needed to go into the laundry. If not, she folded it back up and put it in the drawer for the next Sunday.

"I remember all that, but you're dragging this out, Lor," said Skip. "What are you avoiding? You still haven't explained why you cried when Mom sang in church." There was impatience in his voice.

"That's the part I can't explain," said Lorraine. "It was a feeling. It was the feeling of being next to her. It was the feeling that this wasn't a day like all the rest, like all the rest that were dull. It was the sound of her voice, even though she warbled. I guess I liked Sunday. Maybe I was crying because I was happy, and happy goes too deep for words. That deep happy is hard to hold in."

"My God," said Skip. "I don't know what to say, except, I still want you to forgive me. I did what I did. I thought I hurt you, and I didn't say anything about it for thirty some years. I need to know that you understand that I'm sorry."

"I hear you, Skip. I understand." Lorraine blinked hard. "I love you too, Skip. I didn't say that either for thirty some years."

Skip didn't say anything. He'd never learned what to say when someone said "I love you." He'd been a bachelor for a long time. Maybe no one had ever said "I love you" to him. Skip was not like kids who send each other text messages. One says "LU" and the reply says "LU2."

" I have clear memories of that evening when Skip was with us at the table," Alethea said. "How Thomas reached over and put a hand on Skip's shoulder, and Skip didn't pull away. Randolph said to Skip, 'You're a fine man, Skip.' My dear Mark, quiet Mark, sat with his hands folded and looked across the table gently at Skip. Lorraine and Skip had soft loving looks on their faces. Something was happening. By the time Skip and Lorraine were done talking, Maggie's eyes were brimming with tears. And when I saw Maggie, I teared up too. But what was it? It was such a little thing. Such a little moment. Still we all remember it."

When Alethea finished telling about the evening around the table with Skip, Randolph and Thomas were quietly looking at her, but Jenna was looking at me.

"Do you have regrets sometimes?" Jenna said very quietly to me.

"Yeah," I admitted.

"Me too," said Jenna.

"What would Dad have done if he'd been there that evening at the table with Skip?" I asked Jenna. "Alethea didn't mention if he was there, but I figure he wasn't. He would have found some way to close it down. It would have been too much for him."

Jenna smiled. and replied, "I wonder what Will would say if he were here with us now."

Would my Dad have cleared his throat and said, 'I could use a refill on the coffee?' Would Will say 'Thanks for a nice evening everybody. I need to call it a day because I have an early appointment in the morning?' *Who knows what they'd say,* I thought to myself. *People change. We all change. Who am I to judge?*

Twenty-three

THE BOYS ENJOYED THEIR introduction to real dinner parties at a real dining room table. They were fine hanging out with old folks, and I was surprised by how patient they were with heady talk. The next time Zach had a Friday off, he invited himself back to Chicago to visit his cousin Philip, and they offered to help me cook dinner again.

At the end of the meal Jenna was bringing the last of the dinner plates to the kitchen and getting ready to serve the dessert. Randolph was snooping through the table of contents of a book on Chaucer that I'd left on the coffee table. Thomas was standing near the window with Zach and Philip. The three of them were deep in conversation.

Alethea and I were still at the table, paused there. I tipped my head toward the window, toward where Thomas and the boys were standing. "Seems they've discovered something in common," I said. "Thomas is a puzzle for me. I know he's intelligent and well read, but he seldom says much, and when he does it's often to question what someone else is saying. Look at him now, though. He's getting on famously with those kids. What do you make of him?"

"It may be hard for you to see the gold in Thomas," Alethea answered. She sensed I had reservations about him. "If you quibble with Thomas you'll discover he's a skeptic. He doesn't accept anything without checking it over many times, and even then you never know if he's convinced. But in the worst of times you couldn't ask for a more loyal friend." Alethea was challenging me. "Thomas isn't a talker. He's a doer. When it matters most, he shows up."

Alethea went on to tell me that Thomas stepped up when Randolph had bypass surgery. Estelle was already overwhelmed by the restaurant and kids, and there were complications that extended Randolph's stay in the hospital. Every night that Randolph was in the hospital, Thomas was there. He slept on a lounger in the corner of Randolph's room. It wasn't easy to sleep with machines buzzing and nurses coming in every ten minutes, but Thomas stayed anyway. Rock-solid, loyal, and keeping watch. No drama.

Alethea had her own experiences with Thomas and loyalty. "When my dear Mark was fading," she explained, "Thomas visited him nearly every day. Mark was restless and confused. Visits were awkward, and some of our friends drifted away because they didn't know what to do when a man who'd always been a gentleman began losing control of himself. Thomas didn't let it bother him. He sat quietly with Mark, and it calmed Mark to have him there."

"Did Thomas get along with Mom?" I asked.

"Mostly. Early on there were rough patches. They were so different in so many ways, but over time they got past those things."

"Has he always been single?"

"Thomas was a priest. Marriage wasn't an option for him," Alethea explained.

"Is he still a priest?"

"I don't know exactly how that works." I could tell she was hedging.

"Did he get fired or defrocked or something?"

"If you need to know more you should ask him yourself," Alethea said. "Ask him if you're interested in his answers, but don't ask him if you're just being nosy." I got the point.

WHILE ALETHEA AND I were talking, there were little bursts of laughter from the other side of the room near the windows. "What do you suppose they're talking about?" Alethea asked me. We listened. Zach was telling what he'd discovered about owls on the Internet. On his phone he had a video of an owl ripping prey apart and swallowing it in big chunks. He told how owls eat skunks and snakes and later hork up the bones in pellets. The great horned owl was Zach's favorite because it could take out an eagle.

"He's discovered nature, red in tooth and claw," I said to Alethea.

"Tennyson?" Alethea asked.

"Maybe. Or Darwin," I said.

"I prefer Tennyson," said Alethea, "to faintly trust the larger hope."

"I doubt those kids are ready for that," I said. "They'd get the part about red in tooth and claw, but they'll probably leave the part about a larger hope for later. At this age they have no idea they'll ever need it."

"And you?" Alethea smiled the way she sometimes did when I was patronizing about religion. "Hope or no hope?"

"Let's leave that and the birds to Thomas," I replied trying to steer our conversation back to neutral territory.

Zach was holding forth about owls, but Philip brought Zach up short when he told him that a peregrine falcon can take down an owl. "No, no way," said Zach, "falcons aren't that big. Great horned owls weigh more than falcons, and an owl can crush a falcon in its talons." Zach had no intention of sacrificing the glory of his owls, but Philip wasn't going to back down and let his falcons take second place. He insisted that a falcon flying 150 miles an hour in a dive can knock out a bird twice its size. The two young guys were debating like fans with teams pitched against each other in playoffs.

"It looks like they've set Thomas up to judge the debate," said Alethea. "Lucky for them Thomas is a birder."

"Lucky for them he's a priest," I said. I was still feeling annoyed by the way Alethea had closed me down when I asked about Thomas. "Neither of these young guys will give up easily. They're both true believers. Let's see how Thomas handles that."

Before the contest was finished, Jenna called us all back to the table for dessert. "Tell these boys the story about Mr. Bodaway," Randolph said to Thomas. "I think there's an owl in that story somewhere."

"Randolph, you've heard it before," said Thomas, "and so has Alethea. I'm not one of those old men who monopolizes conversation at the table by repeating himself."

"That little jab is directed at me," said Randolph as he looked around the table and grinned. "I don't apologize for repeating myself. In fact I proudly repeat myself, and each time I add a little bit to the story to liven it up. Thomas, on the other hand, is a purist. He tries to shorten the story with every repetition, until finally it's so short there's nothing left to say."

"Speak for yourself," said Thomas.

"How many times can a story be repeated before changes slip in?" I asked. "It's natural that it changes. That's the way it is with oral tradition. Repetition clarifies the basic narrative and structure, but then accretions sneak in and the story shifts under the weight of time."

"So which is it, Rowland; is repetition good or bad?" Jenna asked. "And what are accretions anyway? You and your big words."

"Thomas, be a sport," Randolph urged. "Tell your story. The boys will enjoy it. If you don't tell it, I may be tempted to tell it for you, and it won't be as good."

"Do you know what they're talking about?" Jenna asked Alethea.

"Yes. I've heard the story a few times. Once when Thomas first told it and a few times after that when Randolph repeated it. Randolph likes the story because he's still trying to figure it out." Alethea gave Randolph a knowing look.

"Will you tell it, Alethea," Jenna asked. "Is that okay, Thomas?"

"Approved. Let's hear Alethea's version of my very own story. We've already heard Randolph's." Thomas chuckled.

"While Alethea tells the story, why don't you go to the kitchen and open another bottle of wine?" Randolph instructed Thomas. "That way Alethea won't have to see you wrinkling your brow or be distracted by skeptical snorts when you don't approve of a detail she's added or when you think she's skipped over an important one."

"Oh, no you don't, Randolph. If Alethea's going to tell my story I want to be present to hear it," said Thomas. "Shouldn't it be that way? If you're going to tell someone's story, isn't it only reasonable to invite him to be present to hear it?"

"As you can tell," said Alethea, "we have different opinions around this table at times."

"This is like being back on campus," I said. " Half the meeting gets wasted debating procedure. Just tell the story." I was the host, and I thought it right that I chair the meeting. Besides I wanted to hear the story. I was curious about Thomas, even if all I could get about him was secondhand.

WHEN THOMAS WAS A young priest, he confused being spiritual with being cool. His hair was long and shaggy, and sometimes he celebrated mass in sandals and didn't bother with vestments. He wore blue jeans, a sweater with elbows worn thin, and cuffs with loose threads. He wasn't too spiritual to notice such things. He was aware of his attire and proud of it; it showed he identified more with ordinary people than with cassocked clergy.

Young priests in the diocese were expected to offer mass at various locations: hospital chapels, temporary housing for migrant workers, and the Veterans Home. The latter was a dreaded assignment because parishioners with squealing hearing aids fell asleep in their wheelchairs before the mass was finished. Thomas didn't mind taking his turn, but his superior kept sending him back. That he found insulting.

Thomas received a message from his superior suggesting that after mass he stop by and visit Mr. Bodaway, who lived on the second floor. Thomas replied to the message by asking if Mr. Bodaway was Catholic. The message that came back said "Sometimes, but don't expect him at mass."

On the first visit Thomas tried to strike up a conversation with Mr. Bodaway by asking him questions about his military service. All he got was "Hmm hmmm." Thomas thought the old man might be deaf, or maybe he'd had a stroke and didn't speak. Several weeks running after mass, Thomas dropped in on Mr. Bodaway. He wasn't unfriendly, and he nodded to Thomas in recognition, but he never uttered a word. Thomas didn't see the point of the visits, but he did as his superior instructed him.

One Saturday evening from the hallway outside Mr. Bodaway's room, Thomas heard voices. Mr. Bodaway was telling two young boys who were visiting him how he learned to whittle. His grandfather carved beautiful birds, and Bo wanted to do that too, so his grandfather gave him a knife and a block of wood. When Bo tried the knife, it hurt his hand because there was a large crack in the bone handle.

Time after time Bo expressed his desire to learn whittling, and time after time his grandfather gave him the knife with the crack in the handle. One day when Bo visited, his grandfather showed him a new owl he had just finished carving. It was magnificent, and his grandfather asked Bo if he would like to have the knife that whittled that bird. Thinking he had finally passed the test of patience, Bo told his grandfather that with a new knife he was sure he could whittle something as fine as the bird in his grandfather's hand. His grandfather handed him the knife with the cracked handle.

"This knife has proved already that it can find a bird in the wood," his grandfather told him. So Bo took the knife and became a fine whittler with a callus on his hand that matched the break in the handle of the knife. When his own children asked him how he got that callus, he told them he got it from a knife that knew how to whittle because it had worked in the hand of his grandfather and his grandfather's father, and other carvers before them.

That's where Alethea paused the story. As she had been telling it, I'd glanced over at Thomas. Actually I'd checked the palms of his hands. There were no scars.

"Do you still visit Mr. Bodaway?" Zach asked Thomas.

"No. He's made the journey to the other side," Thomas responded.

"What did he tell you about owls?" Zach wanted to know.

"He taught me that the owl is silent when he flies. When you see him do not look at him, but look where he looks, because he can see in the dark." Thomas looked directly at the two young boys as he spoke.

The conversation around the table went on to other things, but Thomas got up from the table, walked to the window, and looked out into the night. I got up and stood beside him to see what Thomas was looking at. All I saw was the city. A park. Shadows of trees. Specks of light in the buildings on the other side of the park.

Light streaming along the building on the other side of the street as a car turned the corner. A man walking a dog. A taxi. "What do you see?" I asked Thomas.

"What do you see?" Thomas asked me.

"Nothing special," I told him. "The same things I see out this window every day."

"That's what I see too," Thomas said as he turned back toward the table.

"Does that disappoint you?" I asked Thomas as I walked beside him.

"No," Thomas replied. "That's plenty."

Twenty-four

THE POSTCARD FROM CORDOBA was still on my writing table, reminding me of questions I'd waited too long to ask. What did Mom mean when she wrote: "I now know the meaning of AWE." I'll never get the chance to apologize to her for my unlaundered remark on that day in Cordoba when we stood together surrounded by the columns of the Mezquita, but I wish I knew what she meant.

The time didn't feel right for bringing up the matter with Alethea. Our conversations had taken a different turn, and I didn't want to interrupt our progress. Since getting to know Randolph and Thomas better, I considered reaching out to one of them to discuss what Mom meant by "awe." They both had experience dealing with the religiously confused. I could assume they'd understand my questions.

I weighed my options and settled on Thomas. I feared that if Randolph sensed my discomfort, he'd crack a joke to lighten the mood and get me off the hook. I knew Thomas wouldn't do that. He was the soberer of the two. When I called Thomas to ask if we could talk, he cordially invited me to visit him at his apartment in a senior complex.

The apartment was small and spartan. There were no knickknacks around, and nothing hung on the wall. It had the atmosphere of a dorm room before students move in. The part of the apartment that seemed lived in was a very large desk against one wall. It held a laptop and printer, several stacks of books, and an assortment of papers. The bookshelf next to the desk was well-stocked with heavy-looking volumes. In the opposite corner of the room was an efficiency kitchen, and next to it a sturdy table with two chairs. Thomas led the way to the table and motioned me toward one of the chairs. He took the other. "What brings you?" he asked.

Not wanting to skirt around the issue, I told him about my trip with Mom to Cordoba and our exchange at the Mezquita. I repeated for him what she said to me about prayers going up from that place and being surrounded by light. It was more difficult to repeat what I said to her about the prayers not doing much good, but I didn't round off the ugly edges. I admitted to Thomas my comments about mindless tourists and their motives for visiting old sites so they could send postcards or brag to their neighbors about their vacations when they got back home.

"Let's put aside what your mother said for a moment and begin with what you said," Thomas responded after listening attentively. "It was reckless. Would you agree? Is that a fair assessment?"

I nodded in agreement.

"The thing about reckless moments is that they open the door to what we've locked away, to what we're hiding." Thomas inhaled deeply and then exhaled slowly. "The truth escapes along with the reckless words. I know that myself, all too well. So what is the truth you would have expressed more carefully if you'd sorted it out?"

"Mom had something I don't have," I said. "She had the ability to believe in mysterious things. On the one hand I admire that, but sometimes it looked too easy. When I got near it and looked at it up close, it seemed naïve. Maybe even cowardly, like she didn't have the courage to put it to a test. It didn't only happen that day in Cordoba. It happened other times too. She embarrassed me with her simple-mindedness. I'd shoot back with a humorous remark to deflate her claim. I usually could take a pot shot at her without sounding too mean because she had a good sense of humor. By laughing I could hide if I meant what I was saying. That day in Cordoba what I said was humorless. I wish I hadn't said it."

"Well, said or not, is what you said what you truly think?" Thomas was tracking with me, but he wasn't cornering me. There was kindness in his voice.

"What I said is what I think, but only part of it." I parsed out my words slowly.

"What else do you wish you'd said?" he asked. "What's the other part of it?"

I looked over at Thomas. He was listening intently, but not poised for the kill. It felt worth taking the risk.

"It's hard to explain. How could she be so confident that she was onto something? Don't get me wrong. Mom wasn't preachy; she wasn't twisting my arm. She was careful about what she revealed in those situations. No recklessness on her part. But as careful as she was, she wasn't tentative. In her own quiet way with a soft voice she made it clear that she was all in. She believed something." I looked across at Thomas to check whether he was approving or disapproving. "Am I making any sense?" I asked him.

"Yes," he replied and waited for me to go on.

"Did you know Mom well?" I asked him.

"I think I did," he replied.

"Then did you see this in her too?" I asked. "Did you ever talk with her about it?"

"I saw it in her at other times," he replied. "And in the interests of being truthful, she did tell me that she was profoundly impressed by her visit to Cordoba, but she didn't tell me about her conversation with you. That doesn't surprise me. She was always very respectful of her children's privacy."

"You're a priest. Do you have . . . what shall I call it . . . religious confidence? I asked him.

"I'm less like your mother and more like you," he admitted. "The whole matter of truth is hard for me." He cast his glance out the window for a moment, and then looked back and caught my gaze again. "I mean that. At times it's very hard for me."

"Did Mom know that about you?" I found relief in thinking that I wasn't the first skeptic with whom Mom had ever wrestled.

"She and I once had an argument about it," Thomas said. "The sparks flew. She won." He nodded reflectively. "I didn't overcome my tendency to question everything, but I did get a good look at her confidence. I felt ambivalent about it, just as you did. Just as you do. But in the muddle of our argument, and it went in circles, one feature was clear. She believed some things are true, and she stood her ground."

"What do you mean then, that she won?" I asked. "She dug in and held her ground, but it sounds like you did too. Isn't that the way it goes with religion? In the end we all have our own opinions?"

"It's more than that," Thomas said. "She had found a way of looking at the world that I wouldn't allow for myself. I thought it was compromising. But I could see it in her. Your mother was a time-traveler. She could think her way back into another time when people were less skeptical. Before everyone became disenchanted. Those were times when people were so surrounded by religious symbols, events, and language that there wasn't much room to doubt."

"Pre-modern?" I asked.

"No, not necessarily. That's too extreme." Thomas was slowing me down. "Imagine living in an Italian or Spanish city built around a towering cathedral with plazas named after saints, festivals celebrating their stories, doorways marked with crucifixes. Imagine times when barely a week went by without a christening, a wedding, or a funeral attended by the entire neighborhood. Imagine not a day passing without men and women in religious attire swishing by you in the street and greeting you by name, because they'd known you from the day you were born. Where was there room for doubt in that world? Those who lived there may have questioned for a moment; they probably had their dark times. But their dark times were not like our dark times because they immediately got folded back into the rhythms and patterns of belief."

"You think they were better people?" I asked.

"I'm not suggesting that they all lived saintly lives. They didn't. There is plenty about the past that is regrettable. Saints are sinners and so are ordinary folks. They lived the same messy lives that people always live. What they professed and how they lived were far from perfectly matched. But when they got tripped up, when they got confused, all those reminders around them helped them get back on their feet again."

"You really think that's what my mother was like? She wasn't that medieval. She was very tolerant and open-minded about a lot of things." I was feeling defensive for her.

"No, slow down. That's only half the story. Compare that setting to our own. You know what I mean. We've both put in our time on university campuses. Assert that you believe anything to be true, except maybe what's in vogue this week, and ten critics will pop up to challenge you. They'll ask you to prove it, and they'll show you that your case is a house of cards. Not that they have answers. They'll let you know that those who question are smarter than those who come to firm conclusions. They'll drop a pile of examples at your feet to remind you that people who think as you do are unenlightened. If you look around then to see who has your back, who will step up to help you keep your balance, you discover that you are on your own. That's the hard part. The loneliness of conviction and the ubiquity of doubt.

"I understand that," I told Thomas. "It's our luck to live in an age of incredulity. We shake off the yoke of authority, and now it's up to us. But what's up to us? Whatever it is, it seems like a far stretch."

"That's what I mean," Thomas said. "That's what your mother and I argued about. It started when I told her that it was witless of her to grab onto something and assert it's true unless she could back it up with proof."

"And? What's so extreme about that?" I asked.

"She came back at me and accused me of holding on to incredulity like it's an old bone I can't stop gnawing until finally I have no teeth left." Thomas didn't smile as he spoke. "I knew she was right, but I had no idea what to do about it. So I challenged her to give me an example of something she knew she could believe and didn't have to doubt or scrutinize."

"What did she say?" I truly wanted to know. I felt ready to hear it, determined not to respond to Mom's voice from the grave the way I had responded to her standing next to me at the Mezquita in Cordoba.

"She didn't answer me right away," Thomas said. "She told me she needed time to think. First, because she wanted to be sure that she was telling me about something she knew from the bottom of her heart. She didn't want to churn out a hypothetical example. And second, she had to decide if she could trust me not to give in to my knee-jerk reaction and try to talk her out of it. That second reservation stung because I knew what she was saying."

"So she dodged the question and blamed you for her failure to answer it?" I said.

"No," said Thomas. "You see that's the crux of what made Maggie and me so different from each other. I could let her venture an answer and knock it down, as I always did when I encountered people too confident about what they think is true. In that case I'd end up with nothing. But she had something I didn't have. Some sort of trust in truth. And she wasn't a fool. So I figured I'd better button my lip and hear what she had to say if I wanted to get out of my own skeptical trap. Seriously, I was getting tired of it myself. It was getting me nowhere."

"Did you ever get your answer?" I asked Thomas.

"I did. Maggie came back to me a few weeks later and said she was ready to answer my question if I was ready to hear it. I told her I was. Her answer was totally unexpected."

"What did she say?" I asked Thomas.

"I'd like to tell you," he said, "but I need to know that you will listen to it respectfully. You don't have to agree with it all, but will you try to set your skepticism aside? Can you do that?"

" I can try," I told him.

"This is what I am certain of," said Maggie. "I know my mother loved me. I know it without a doubt, even though she died too soon, she wasn't a perfect person, and there were many things about her I never got to know. This I know for sure: she loved me. I know it because I experienced it sitting on her lap with her arms folded around me while she was singing good night songs to me."

"That's all?" I asked Thomas.

"There's more," he said.

"That's not all I know for sure," Maggie said. "I know I love my children. I've not been a perfect mother, and there are things I would do differently if I could do them over, but I know for certain that I love them and have loved them from the first moment I saw them. It is deep in me, and I have no doubt about it. From that safe place on my mother's lap I learned the meaning of truth, and that first experience carried forward so that I was able to trust other moments in my life that were equally real. I learned from her to believe what is true."

"How did you respond to that?" I asked Thomas.

Thomas looked uncomfortable. "I told her that I'd accept that as true. Her mother loved her, and she loved her children. But what about people who accept something as true and it carries them off in terrible directions. What about those people who got caught up in the charisma of the Führer and ended up being death camp guards?"

"There you go again, Thomas," Maggie said. "That's what you do. You are more interested in ferreting out the bad stuff than reaching for the good. You believe the bad is bad, and that's the right thing to do. The bad is horrible enough that it's impossible to argue against that. But do you believe the good is good, or does that seem too risky for you? You are so determined never to be deceived that you can't trust anything. What about the price you pay for that lifeless view? Think of what you miss."

"Is that what you mean when you say she won?" I asked Thomas.

"No, I didn't drop it there," Thomas said. "I came back at her with the usual response. I asked her if she ever had doubts."

"Of course I do," Maggie said, "but I also make sure that I circle back again and again to those places, those people, those experiences where I first felt touched by what I can trust is true. Sometimes it's like watching fireflies on a very dark summer night. There's a lot of darkness, but even though they are very brief and very small, it's the fireflies that capture my attention. They soften my heart. They remind me to keep watching for what is good and true, not because I sorted it out in an argument with a smart guy, but because sometimes experience, precious and good experience, is convincing. And, Thomas, that's about all I can say about it. We each have our choice to make, but being a skeptic is not as neutral as you think."

"That's heavy stuff," I told Thomas when he paused for a moment. "Did your friendship survive it?"

"Did your mother keep loving you after you attacked her moment of awe in the Mezquita in Cordoba?"

"Of course. Mom was a mother bear," I told him and chuckled a little.

"Of course, our friendship survived," Thomas said without a hint of a chuckle. She included me in the circle of her friends. I began to join them for dinner."

"How did you fit in with them?" I asked. "Mom's friends, the ones she said were sisters. A few of the husbands too. And then Randolph. Were you comfortable with all of them? Was there room for a skeptic?"

"At first it was hard to set aside my impulse to question everything. But I could see that they had something I didn't have. The hardest times for me were the times when I felt jealous. I listened and watched as they lived out their friendships. They stood by each other in the hardest times. They were all time-travelers, in the same sense that your mother was. There was something they trusted because they'd lived it in another time. They carried that surety forward with them from the past into the present. What they first knew to be true without a doubt, they could still believe even after time had tested them. Around them I began to have small glimpses of what the world looks like to those who believe. And I became quieter."

"And you keep showing up?" I asked him.

"Yes. They've made me part of their circle."

"Thomas, there are other things that happened on my trip to Spain with Mom. I think I need to deal with them."

Light or dark?" Thomas asked.

"Dark," I admitted.

"For now stay with the light."

"I'd like to visit with you again sometime," I said. "Are you open to that?"

"Of course," he said. "You're always welcome." And I could tell he meant it.

Twenty-five

IT WAS TIME TO empty the last items from Mom's condo. I'd been getting rid of things no one wanted, but I'd decided to keep some of the kitchen tools. I'd also decided to keep Mom's dining room table with two extra leaves and eight chairs.

Before the movers were scheduled to arrive, I planned one more dinner in Mom's condo with Alethea, Randolph, Thomas, and Jenna. I also invited Polly to come for the weekend, and she asked to stay with Alethea but offered to remain a few days extra so she could drive back to Minneapolis with me.

Jokingly I observed that Polly's eagerness to come for the weekend probably had more to do with the prospect of another visit with Randolph and Thomas and less to do with her generous offer to help me pack up and drive back to Minneapolis. "I do love seeing them," she said. "Where do you find people willing to discuss Greek mythology and onomastics. You've got to admire those old guys. Their minds are still going full tilt, and they've been thinking about a lot of things for a long time. Thomas is living proof that still waters run deep."

Over dinner Randolph and Thomas told Polly that since her last visit the two of them had been reading Hesiod's *Works and Days*. They chuckled about "neat-ankled women," and Randolph cracked a joke about fresh young women with lovely cheeks. More risqué were his comments about misbehaving gods. After a few warm-up volleys between the two old men, they turned to the thoughts of a poet whose view of the world saw it in decline. They were serious. "Has it always been this way?" they asked. "Do thoughtful observers always conclude that the state of affairs in the world is headed downhill?" There would have been enough to keep the conversation going all evening, but this time Alethea took charge and suggested that instead of giving over the evening to Hesiod and fretting about an unknown future, we should claim it for ourselves and share with each other what we were looking forward to in the months ahead.

My own dreams that Polly would be the ideal woman for me had taken a sensible turn. It wasn't that Polly didn't match my expectations; it was that my own expectations had become modest. I wondered if I could be a suitable partner for Polly. Deep down somewhere I still played with fantasies of ideal partners, but as soon as my thoughts went there, I'd dash my own hopes with fears that romance is a hopelessly old-fashioned leftover of an unenlightened past. It wasn't that I didn't want to be with Polly; it had something to do with the fact that I didn't want to make a commitment to being with Polly.

Frankly, I was wary about making commitments to anything, but spending time with Alethea over these months had unsettled my arrogance about that. I knew that soon I'd be spending my days among academics again, where language about gods and loyalty would be replaced with hymns to science and explanations of true love reduced to neurotransmitters in the primitive brain. Instead of expressing my dread directly, I did what I have done so often. I said something opaque that was only vaguely related to what I was thinking. "Maybe I should become a chef and host group dinners," I said when we were gathered around the table for our last meal. I meant it in jest, but I was brought up short when the others around the table nodded in agreement and began tossing in stories of people who at midlife made career changes and took up work that was more suited to their gifts and temperament.

I'd set myself up for this moment of misunderstanding when a day before I'd told Polly I was going to buy a house with a good-sized dining room. After settling in and furnishing it with Mom's dining set, I'd start inviting guests for long conversational dinners. I thought I was telling Polly that I intended to be more sociable, but I didn't mention that I intended to do this with her. Polly didn't frown, but she didn't smile either. She wrinkled her brow and told me she wasn't opposed to the dining set or lovely dinners, but my way of proffering the plan didn't include her in it as more than an occasional guest.

I got huffy. "Dammit all, Polly Tropos," I said. "I feel like I've got a collar around my neck, and you've got the leash."

Polly stayed calm. Amazingly calm. She told me directly that she was not negotiating a relationship with me, she was giving me feedback about the messages between the lines of my communications. "I just want to be clear," she said; "if you're making plans that include me, then it would be nice if you included me in the planning. If you don't intend for me to be part of the planning, then I prefer to be cautious in making assumptions that you intend to include me at all."

"Dammit again, Polly," I said. "I don't get it. I thought we've been getting along perfectly well. Why are you making everything so complicated?"

"I'm not," she said. "I'm keeping it simple. I'm not assuming that you plus me equals we. I wouldn't want to impose on your freedom."

"Is that your subtle way of accusing me of being selfish?" I asked her.

"Your words, not mine," she replied. "I confess, I may be a bit sensitive. Maybe I fear exclusion as much as you fear commitment. The least I can do about that is be honest with you, don't you think?"

I beat myself up about Polly's comment. I haven't given her much to count on, and she's been an amazingly good sport about it. She has the good sense to take care of herself. I admire that. She has the good sense to keep a distance that matches my uncertainty, but I'd feel more comfortable if she didn't have to use that self-protective strategy in order to be safe around me. It makes me feel like an arrogant prick. For the rest of the day I accused myself of not having learned one bit of anything over the summer, and then I confessed to Polly that I suspect I'm still an insufferable narcissist.

Polly didn't agree or disagree with my self-reproach. All she said was, "Rowland, that's heavy. Just take a deep breath."

"What does that mean?" I asked her. "You're not exactly humble-pie yourself, you know." I was thinking that maybe she is a good match for me if we're both arrogant. What do I know?

What I know for sure is that she is not like Andrea, because by now Andrea would have shattered a wine glass, stomped out of the house, or found exactly the place to put in the dagger. On my side, by now I'd be thinking about leaving for good. This was different.

"Here's the thing," Polly said. The sound of her voice broke into my thoughts. "I wonder if insufferable narcissists worry about being narcissists. The worry's a good sign."

That's when I kissed her. It was a soft kiss. I felt like a boy. It felt a little like the way I remembered Mom putting her head next to mine and humming when I couldn't sleep. It felt so different from all the times I've kissed a woman by devouring her lips, grasping at her with ardor, imitating the way it's done in the movies or on TV in order to prove I'm a man. It was a different longing I felt, an urge to press myself against her and say, "please don't go away." But I didn't say that. Instead I said, "You and me, Polly. We're a good team."

"I love you too," she said.

Toward the end of the evening during our last dinner at Mom's condo, I turned to Alethea and asked her, "What's going to happen to you next? What do you see in your future?"

"The sweet thing about age," said Alethea, "is that you no longer have to plan far ahead. Planning for a short while is enough. In the immediate future, Randolph and I are going to travel. We'll go first to England so he can show me where he grew up. I've always wanted to see Stonehenge and visit at least one good British tearoom for high tea, and then of course I would like to see Randolph's familiar places."

Alethea glanced at Randolph as if she were checking in about something, getting permission to continue with what she was about to say next. "There is still a burr under the saddle. When we are in London I want to go to the British Museum and see the Parthenon Marbles that good old Lord Elgin plundered from Greece. It annoys me that Randolph calls them The Lord Elgin Marbles and dares to suggest that the British have been their guardian and protector. The first time this came up we actually got huffy with each other."

"Why visit them if it'll cause a fight?" Jenna asked.

"We're going to see them. We're both too old to leave dreams for later, and we've both wanted to see them long before we got into this disagreement about them. We'll look at them together, maybe read up in advance so we know what we're seeing," Alethea nodded one of those slow determined nods.

"But what about the disagreement?" Polly wanted to know. This was her sort of topic. "The removal of antiquities is a big deal."

Randolph was listening. His eyebrows were raised in question marks. "Okay, I see the look," Polly said. "I'll grant that the neglect of antiquities is a big deal too, but not as big a deal as stealing them. Anyway, what I really want to know is how the two of you have resolved this conflict between you."

"We haven't," said Randolph. "Maybe standing in front of those marbles we'll discover how much room there is between the two of us for differences of opinion. Let's face it, I don't have the power to decide that the Marbles should stay put in London, and Alethea doesn't have the power to insist they be returned to Greece. The disagreement is pretty much theoretical for us. Okay, I admit, maybe also a little emotional. All the same, it would be sad if we got so caught up in the argument that we couldn't see the Marbles. People do that, you know. Their own heads get in the way of seeing things for what they are, and as a result they aren't able to see them together."

"I'll own the fact that I get more stirred up about this than Randolph does," Alethea admitted. "It's hard to be on the losing team. For now Randolph and I have agreed to refer to them as 'The Marbles.' His willingness to do that helps me. Honestly, I know he has good intentions."

"What will you do after England?" Polly asked.

"We'll go on to Greece and together find the cliff on which my father formed the vision he carried with him for the rest of his life. And of course we'll go to Athens and a few other places. We'll eat good food and hear some good music. We'll watch people dance, and maybe we'll dance with them. Who knows? After our visit to Greece we're thinking of going on a cruise that will take us east, always east."

"That's my idea," said Randolph. "I think at our age we should always travel toward the sunrise if we can. We'll keep traveling east until we end up where we started. Sounds good, doesn't it?"

"It sounds like an adventure. Did this just come up?" I asked.

"We've been talking about our next moves for some time now," said Alethea. "Randolph, you can speak for yourself," she looked over at him with a soft smile, "but I've been thinking that I need to spend my days doing more than shopping and housework for just myself. Growing old can be lonely."

"And I've been thinking along the same lines," said Randolph. "I don't spend my days doing shopping and housework, and my apartment is becoming disgraceful. You know those bad magazine pictures of lonely old men who cook a can of soup on a hot plate and never wash up after cooking? It could be me in that picture."

"So we began to talk together about what we would do if we had someone with whom to do it, and we both realized we'd like to make a trip back to our beginnings," said Alethea.

"What will you do when you get home?" asked Jenna.

"That's the next piece," said Alethea. "Randolph and I have known each other for decades. Neither of us has children. We're both alone now. There aren't many surprises after all those years, at least not after living in a circle of friends as frank as our friends have been. It might make most sense for us to team up together, face the unknown future side by side as long as we can. We enjoy each other's company, and we also know each other's worst traits. That helps. We know what we're bargaining for."

"Are you going to live together?" Jenna asked. "That sounds nice for both of you."

"We've agreed to give it try." Randolph gave the business-like answer.

"Will you sleep in the same bed?" I asked.

"C'mon Rowland," Jenna broke in. "That's not a fair question. Grow up! You're not fourteen anymore. You embarrass me." She gave me the look.

"It's okay, Rowland. You say things out loud that the rest of us think," said Alethea. "Your mother used to do that too. She would have asked that question. It's one of the things I loved about her.

Candor keeps the conversation on track. We all know that feeling when we're telling a story, and we look around and know that no one's listening because every one is off somewhere wondering about the missing detail. Your question is obvious."

"Thanks for understanding," I said. "Sorry if I was intrusive, but I agree with you that it's an obvious question. C'mon, Jenn, you were thinking the same thing. And you were too, Polly."

"So let me answer," said Alethea. She was blushing a little, but also, like Alethea always is, she was completely in control of herself. "Randolph uses one of those nighttime machines that wheezes a bit," she said. "On good nights it doesn't bother me at all, but sometimes it does keep me awake. And I get up for the bathroom quite a few times in the night. It worries me, especially toward morning that too many ups and downs on my part will rob Randolph of the beauty sleep he deserves. So we've decided to keep a rescue room to which either of us can go for a quiet place to finish up the night and get the rest we need. It will also be a guest room for visitors. That's important to me." Alethea glanced first at me and then at Polly.

"That's the practical side of the proposal for living together," said Randolph. "There is a brighter side. We both like to read ourselves to sleep at night. You have no idea how dear it is when we're reading side by side, and one of us finds a passage too good not to share. We read to each other for a little while, and then go back to our own books. It's very efficient. You actually get two books read at once. Then one of us suggests it's time to turn out the light. We kiss each other goodnight and saunter off to dreamland hand in hand. It's so much better than sleeping alone."

"I say 'yes' to all of that," said Alethea. "It's a good way to end the day, and very sweet for me is the fact that early in the morning Randolph sneaks off and brews the tea. When I wake up, he brings a tray with two good cups on saucers and a little dish of English tea biscuits by the side. We talk about the day ahead and ease into it slowly. Now what's not good about that?"

"I'm glad Alethea will have you," I said. "Remember, Randolph, she won't have me a few floors away to share the woes of the world with her."

Randolph nodded. "She'll miss you and your woes," he said. "I'll try to make it up to her by reading Hesiod at bedtime."

When Randolph finished speaking, I looked across the table at Polly. "So what think you of that, Ms. Polly Tropos?" I wanted to be sincere, hoping she'd catch my intention.

"I think it's lovely," said Polly. She held my gaze. She was saying it to me and not the whole table. "By the way, Rowland, do you know what was left in the jug after curious Pandora opened it up and unleashed all the miseries of humankind into the world?"

"No idea. That's not my field." I wasn't telling the truth. I was setting Polly up so she would have to give the answer. The old Rowland pattern, trying to get someone else to say things I don't want to say myself.

"Hmmm," said Polly. "Maybe we should read it together."

"That could make good nighttime reading," Randolph tossed in. He was interested as well to see if Polly would answer the question for me, and it impressed him that she had the good sense to leave it to teamwork and the future.

The evening went long. Thomas excused himself toward midnight, but the rest of us resisted drawing a good time to a close. Finally it was Alethea who said, "I think we all need some rest. Tomorrow's another day." That's exactly what my mother might have said.

I had asked Jenna to stay over with me in Mom's condo for my last night there. Polly would be staying with Alethea, and I'd stay over in a hotel before leaving for Minneapolis the following day. I didn't relish being alone when the moment came to close the door and turn the key in the lock the last time. It was painful to think that soon a young couple with an enormous TV screen and a very tiny dog might be living Mom's condo. And then it occurred to me that they could paint the walls orange, raise weed under grow lights, and never take out the garbage, but for me this space would always be home.

WHEN I ARRIVED TO pick up Polly before heading to Minneapolis, Randolph had a hearty English breakfast waiting for us. It was a happy and a sad breakfast. The end of a rich time together with

Alethea. The happy prospect of going home and moving on for Polly and me. Jenna had driven over to say "Goodbye" one more time. She had grown fond of Polly, and while she knew she would see me again, she wanted reassurance that she would see Polly too.

While we were at the table, the phone rang, and Randolph answered it. "Yes, they're still here," he said. "I'm sure she'd appreciate that, but you should come right away because they need to be on their way soon." When he hung up he said it was Thomas, who wanted to come over to see us off.

"Do stay in touch; it's important," Randolph said to me several times over. "We don't want to break the circle. It's been such a pleasure being together again."

"Are we a circle now?" I asked him.

"It does seem so," Randolph replied; "where two or three are gathered, that's the circle."

I hugged Alethea several times. I was sitting next to her at the table, and I leaned over to put an arm around her shoulders and give her a gentle squeeze. It occurred to me that I was collecting embraces to carry me over an absence.

Randolph and Alethea were clearing the dishes while Polly and I were gathering up our last items. Thomas arrived and Jenna greeted him at the door. "I'm so glad you came," she said. "Watching people leave is never easy for me."

Finally the inevitable moment came; the car was packed. I had already tucked my backpack behind the driver's seat. In it I'd stowed the flash drive onto which I'd scanned all of Mom's journals as well my own reflections during my time in Chicago. I didn't want to be burdened with a carton of papers, but when it came time to shred them, I couldn't bear to erase the words entirely.

The last hugs had been given. The last promises made. Polly and I were in the car with seatbelts in place. Randolph, Alethea, Jenna, and Thomas were lined up at the curb. Jenna had tears rolling down her cheeks. Thomas was standing behind her with a protective, fatherly arm around her shoulders. As we pulled away, I turned to Polly and said, "If I'm not mistaken, Randolph and Alethea are holding hands."

Twenty-six

THE FIRST THING I did when I returned to my office at the University was check the bottom drawer of the file cabinet to the right of my desk. That's where I'd stored my father's letterbox. It was a well-worn walnut box Dad always had in his office on a shelf. He'd given it to Will, but it got passed along to me because inlaid on the top were the initials RB. I'd never valued it much, except that it was a handsome old piece, and it had been a practical place to store a few items I kept for their sentimental value.

I passed my hand over the smooth surface of the box and considered why I'd chosen it as a holding place for my keepsakes. The alternative would have been a shoebox or the sturdy white box in which my last laptop computer was shipped. I liked the silver apple on the white surface of that well-made box, and I'd set it aside thinking it might be a good place to store something sometime. But when it came time to gather up the sentimental things I kept in my top dresser drawer or in the letter drawer of my desk, it was Dad's walnut box with his initials and mine for which I reached. I figured no one would throw out a good wooden box without looking at what was in it. I was planning for a future when I'll no longer be around.

I'd already put a few precious belongings into the letterbox, although "precious" is hard to define. Included were the fountain pen Dad gave me when I finished my degree, the first handmade birthday card I'd ever gotten from Meredith, the wedding ring I took off soon after I married Andrea, and a picture taken with Zach when we finished the first section of the Appalachian Trail and promised each other that before I was too old to hike we'd finish the rest. From my sister Jenna I'd gotten the locket with the picture of my grandmother that looks like Emily Dickinson and from the shelf in Mom's condo I'd taken that other picture I think might be of my grandfather with a cane pole and a straw hat. Those pictures are now in the box. There is a picture of Steven at age twelve. I'd carried it in my wallet for years. Once when I opened my wallet to lend Steven a few bucks, he noticed that I had his picture, and from that time on I couldn't bring myself to remove it. Only when Steven died did I take it from my wallet and tuck it away so I could decide later what to do with it.

In the letterbox there is a picture of Mom and her four children, all dressed in black, taken on the day of Dad's funeral. I keep Mom's rosary in the box too, the one she received from her mother on the day of her first communion. It has an aura. I mentioned to Polly once that I like to hold Mom's rosary in my hand. "Of course," she said. "Pay attention to that, Rowland. That rosary passed through your grandmother's hand, and your mother's, and no doubt a priest blessed it with a prayer before it was given to your mother at her first communion. There's a lot of spiritual energy in those beads. Decide to whom you'll give it some day."

"Meredith," I said, "that's who will have it, and I need to be sure to tell her why I've saved it for her. And I'm going to give Zach the paperweight that Estelle gave to Mom when Steven died, and Mom gave to Randolph after Estelle died. Randolph gave it to Alethea to give to me after Mom died. That's a lot of hands it's passed through. It's heavy with grief, but I think Zach is the kind who will be able to understand that someday."

On that day in my office at the University when I was sorting through the contents of the walnut box, from the zippered pocket of the fleece I was wearing I took out the flash drive with Mom's journals and reflections from my time in Chicago after evenings around the table. I tucked the flash drive and Mom's postcard from Cordoba into the walnut box. I also wrote a note and placed it on top of all the other things I'd collected there.

Dear Zach and Meredith,

The flash drive in this box has copies of Gramma Maggie's journals and some things I wrote during a very important time I spent in Chicago. When Gramma Maggie died she left her journals for me. Now I am in her shoes. In this box are many items that have special meaning for me, and I hope there will be an occasion when I can show them to you. As long as I am living I intend to take care of them myself. When I am gone I will be entrusting this box and the things in it to you. You can decide what to do with them. I trust you because I know how fortunate I am to have children like you. That is the way it is with every generation. We leave the past to you, and the future too. Looking back I wish I could have made the story better, but it is what it is.

Love,
Your Dad

Acknowledgments

As I write stories about older characters, I see memory with a certain slant. Perhaps it is a result of accumulating years, during which I have been adding to my own collection of memories. What ought I remember? What is best forgotten? What difference does it make?

There are many people who have helped me see my way into the stories I write. Writing a first novel is a brazen venture. Writing a second novel seems no less a risk. I will never forget how much their encouragement kept me going.

For over a decade I have enjoyed a Monday Night Writers Group. We meet, we read, we comment, and we encourage each other. The balance between candor and kindness in this group has made it a writer's sanctuary. Thank you to Edie, Barbara, Carol, Jane, Sylvia, Kristy, Sheryl, Hank, Beth, Katy, and Otto.

For fifteen years I have been discussing books in the PW Book Group, a circle of discerning readers. What a delight it has been. Our talks add dimensions to the solitary pleasures we each find in reading, and inevitably our gatherings also are occasions for sharing our own stories with each other. Thank you to Maryann, Sally, Helen, Barbara, Christiana, Corrie, Evonne, Therese, and Claudia.

My students earning college diplomas in the Calvin University program at the Richard A. Handlon Correctional Facility in Ionia, Michigan have been models of empowerment. They are living proof that the most remarkable personal stories are not predictable.

I thank them for what they have taught me about memory and hope. To my students: you know who you are.

Charlie and Shannon White at Adaptive Momentum designed my website at www.maryvandergoot.com. Before beginning their work, they read my books. Thanks so much for thinking deeply with me.

Several friends stepped up to read early drafts of *Broken Glass*, the first novel in this trilogy. Their encouragement kept me writing. Thanks to Barbara Carvill, Joan Plantinga, Rick Plantinga, Henry Baron, Yolanda Polet, Rubén Degollado, Roy Anker, and Julie Yonker. They and others have also read early drafts of *A Certain Slant*. Turning over a freshly penned manuscript to first readers is like leaving a baby with a sitter for the first time. It takes trust. Thanks to each of you for fulfilling that trust.

I am fortunate to have several friends who also write novels. They understand the challenges of the long haul, and they have been generous with encouragement. I am grateful to Todd Huizinga, Elizabeth Huergo, Cynthia Beach, and Jane Griffioen. They understand the challenges of putting down the work and then picking it up again. They also understand how first drafts and multiple revisions have a way of changing an author's mind. As you have said to me often, I now say to you: Keep writing!

Special thanks to my sister, Helen Westra. She was there the day I was born, read stories to me when I first discovered books, and celebrated life with me along the way. Recently she has offered her skills as a Professor of English to coach away some of my worst habits as a writer. Thanks for being my big sister.

My gratitude to James Vanden Bosch, master grammarian and linguist, who worked over my manuscript with a fine lead pencil in hand and was more gracious than I deserve with the comments he wrote in the margins.

To Ruth Stubbs, the tireless reader, who was so good at asking the right questions.

To Matt Wimer and the team at Wipf and Stock, thanks for seeing potential in my Maggie Barnes stories. With *A Certain Slant* we have two down and one to go, and you've been so good about keeping up the momentum.

To my family—Henry, Sara, Jana, Mike, Andrew, Peter, and Anna—I want to assure you once again that you are not in this novel. Having said that, I keep discovering how your stories and my own story are weaving together. For all that may be forgotten or confused, I hope you will always remember that I love you.

CPSIA information can be obtained
at www.ICGtesting.com
Printed in the USA
FSHW020153300421
80977FS